Dear Readers,

Roses, candy, and champagne are wonderful—but they're not the same without the Valentine of your dreams. This year, celebrate the quest for true love with four spectacular new romances from Bouquet!

Nothing's better than an unexpected—and unexpectedly perfect—romance. In talented Vanessa Grant's **Think About Love,** a businesswoman with an orphaned baby niece plans to cut a deal with the boss for some time off, until she discovers her boss has a deal of his own to offer—matrimony! In Sandra Madden's uproariously funny—and teasingly sexy—**Since You've Been Gone,** a young widow who's started over finds there's only one problem with her plans for the future when her "dead" husband walks in the front door!

Sometimes when one dream comes true, others take the hint. That's certainly true for the spunky heroine of Kathern Shaw's **Make-Believe Matrimony.** Winning the lottery has resulted in dozens of very determined suitors—and the live-in protection of one very attractive, very single cop. And in Linda Simmons's **Just the Way You Aren't,** an important commission at a famous hotel is sure to land a young artist the attention she needs to rev up her career—but attracting the attention of the hunky hotel project manager is much more appealing!

Enjoy!

Kate Duffy
Editorial Director

A BUSINESS DEAL . . .

"I don't know, Cal," Samantha said. "Cal, we just can't . . ."

She looked at the baby in his arms. He held Kippy as if he'd always held babies, but why was he here, holding her hand and the baby, slipping his way into their lives? Why wasn't she sending him away?

What if she did it? Married Cal. . . .

He made it sound logical. A vice presidency for her, and she could make her own hours . . . and Kippy could have a father.

She took the baby from Cal, hugging her closely and kissing her soft cheek before she laid her in the crib. As if Cal had exerted some magic spell, Kippy's eyes drooped and she sighed.

Cal rose from the sofa and she put out one hand, as if to hold him off. "A business deal, you said?"

"A business deal," he replied.

He bent his head and covered her lips with his.

She stood staring up at him, wanting to run, yet frozen. . . .

THINK ABOUT LOVE

Vanessa Grant

ZEBRA BOOKS
Kensington Publishing Corp.
http://www.zebrabooks.com

Thanks to Ann and Anne for the hearts,
Janice and Missy for baby calendars,
Grant for the open house and "that thing they do,"
and Janyne for family court

One

The call came on Samantha's direct line at thirteen minutes after three Wednesday afternoon. Cal, she assumed, because he'd been hovering restlessly all week. With a multimillion dollar contract just signed and fifty high-tech jobs to fill, Calin Tremaine was at his most restless.

She let the phone ring a second time, then a third as she finished answering an e-mail from the security company she'd hired for Friday night. Then she picked up the phone, ready for Cal's next question.

But the voice on the phone wasn't her boss's.

"Samantha?"

"Grandma Dorothy?" Samantha eyed the stack of unanswered messages on her desk. "How are you and the baby? Still terrorizing Gabriola Island?"

She expected her grandmother's breathy laughter, felt a shaft of unease when it didn't come. "I'm in Nanaimo, Samantha. I need you."

"Is it Kippy? An accident?" It was no use telling her heartbeat to slow, her breathing to quiet. Ever since the plane crash, she'd been too jumpy, too quick to assume the worst.

"No accident, sweetheart, but we need your help."

Marcy stuck her head in the door, mouthed Cal's name,

and pointed to the phone. Samantha held up one hand, fingers spread, indicating she'd be five minutes.

"Tell me," she urged her grandmother, her voice taking on the calm tones that had become habitual for her in times of stress. "Tell me what the problem is. If you need help with Kippy or money—" Money, she thought. Dorothy was probably short of money. Samantha kicked herself for not insisting she accept a monthly check to help with Kippy.

"Moonbeam, you have to come up here."

Moonbeam. It was years since Dorothy had called her that.

"I can be there at the end of next week. I'll take a long weekend and we can work out whatever—"

"Sam—Samantha . . ."

Dorothy was *crying!* "Grandma, what's wrong?"

"They say I'm not fit to look after Kippy."

"That's crazy. You're fitter than most forty-year-old women. Grandma, *who* . . . ?"

A hiccup that might have been a sob. "I was in overnight. I shouldn't have been in at all—it was just a little pain, but Diana insisted. You know Diana Foley?"

"Yes, of course I—*in?* What do you mean, *in?* In the hospital?"

"I told the doctor I mustn't be in more than overnight, but he insisted and Diana said it would be fine. Absolutely fine, that Kippy was no problem. Samantha, you must do something!"

"Grandma, I'll look after everything. Explain to me exactly what's happened. You're sick?" Dorothy had perfect health. At the age of sixty-nine, she walked three miles a day, pushing Kippy's baby carriage to the mailbox each day. "Why are you in the hospital?"

"It's nothing serious. It's Kippy we need to worry about."

"If Diana needs help with Kippy, I'll arrange for someone, and I'll come up this Friday night. We'll sort everything out." If necessary, if Dorothy really *was* sick, Samantha would bring Kippy back with her until her grandmother recovered.

"You have to come *now*, Samantha."

"I promise you, I'll look after everything. We talked about this last winter. If there's any problem, I can look after Kippy. We'll—"

"The social worker put Kippy in a foster home."

Samantha felt a lurch of nausea. "Kippy in foster care?" She remembered how frightened Sarah had been all those years ago, how Samantha had hidden her own fear and pretended confidence for her sister. How Dorothy had come and saved them both.

She found a pen in her hand. "I need the name of the social worker. And Diana's number. Have you called a lawyer yet?"

Dorothy gave her Diana's number. "The social worker is Brenda Simonson. I don't know her number. She'll be in Nanaimo, but I'm not sure which office. I called Dexter Ames, the lawyer we used to arrange Kippy's guardianship last winter."

Her mind seemed numb. She had to *think*. "I'll talk to Dexter, and I'll find the social worker."

"Samantha, what if they don't let Kippy come back?"

"Of course they will. We're Kippy's family."

"You're coming, aren't you?" demanded Dorothy as the door to Samantha's office opened again. She had one hand in the air to shoo Marcy away, but her assistant ignored the gesture and strode across the office to drop a message slip on Samantha's desk.

Meet me ASAP in the boardroom. Cal.

Her fingers crumpled the note.

"I'll do some phoning," she told Dorothy in a supercalm voice. "I'll find out exactly where we stand, get things in motion. Then I'll call you back. I'll look after this. What about *you?* This pain?"

"I'm *fine,*" snapped Dorothy in the voice Samantha remembered. "It's probably indigestion."

Marcy was waiting, motionless on the other side of the desk, while Samantha wrote down Dorothy's hospital-room phone number, then said good-bye, promising to call back as soon as possible.

"He wants to know how long," said Marcy as the receiver settled in its cradle.

"Fifteen minutes, and get me the phone number for Dexter Ames. He's a lawyer in Nanaimo."

"Where?"

"Nanaimo. British Columbia. Canada."

Fifteen minutes. It wasn't enough. If only this had happened on another day, another week, when she could rush to Nanaimo instead of acting at a distance. She had to find that social worker before her office closed for the day. She needed to talk to the lawyer, to Dorothy's doctor.

Exactly when did government workers quit for the day in Canada?

Diana Foley had the worker's phone number, but the woman wasn't at her desk. Samantha hit the intercom just as Marcy came through the door with Dexter Ames's phone number.

Only five minutes until she was due to meet Cal in his boardroom. "Get Ames on the line. Tell him it's about Dorothy Marshall."

She dialed her own phone, said, "Diana, it's Samantha Jones again. I haven't been able to get the social worker. Do you know anything else?"

"Hi, Sam." Diana sounded breathless, as if she'd run to the phone. "All I know is that there's going to be a hearing. I asked if they could put Kippy with me as a foster child until Dorothy's out of the hospital, but the worker said no. I'm so sorry, Samantha."

"Diana, I know you did your best. It's all right." Samantha saw that her telephone was flashing and hurriedly said good-bye.

Dexter Ames, and she was due in the boardroom in two minutes.

"I don't have the family court date yet," said Dexter. "I'll know more within the hour."

One minute late for her meeting with Cal and nothing was settled. Family court sounded bad and urgent. Please God it wouldn't be until next week. Tomorrow was Thursday. By Monday she just might be able to slip away, but it would be irresponsibility of the worst kind to walk out now, less than forty-eight hours before she was due to oversee a massive employee screening process at the recruitment open house.

She glanced at the pile of message slips on her desk, picked up her portable computer in its case, and walked out of her office. No time to check lipstick and hair. No time to think. She stopped at Marcy's desk, said, "I'm expecting a call from Dexter Ames. When he calls, put him through to the boardroom. And get hold of Del in development. Get a list of the volunteers he's enlisted for Friday."

If all went well Friday night, Tremaine's would be playing host to dozens of top e-commerce developers in a massive headhunting expedition. The developers who already worked for Tremaine Software were an essential element of the open house. They would greet the candidates, talk about their own experience with Tremaine's, and generally build enthusiasm to work in a rapidly expanding, forward-looking company rich in advancement opportunities.

The open house had been Samantha's idea. If it went well, she'd be one large step closer to a seat on Cal's board and a director's position in the company. Somehow, in the next few days, she needed to look after the welfare of Cal Tremaine's massive staffing needs, while rescuing her six-month-old niece from the clutches of the foster-home system.

Two

Cal Tremaine paced the boardroom. He disliked waiting, always had. He recognized his restlessness as one of the characteristics that had built Tremaine's into a company that could successfully bid on the Lloyd contract. But this week, he'd have been better off turning his back on things he couldn't control and leaving Samantha Jones to do what she did best.

He'd successfully landed the contract to bring Lloyd's into the world of electronic commerce, and next spring, once Lloyd's Web farm was finished, Tremaine's would take over external management of all Lloyd's information technology. The contract meant huge new racks of hardware in their New York server site, dozens of new employees, and a tight deadline.

He was itching to get to work, but nothing could happen until he had the men and women he needed, top developers who were probably even now working for the competition.

Tremaine's was reeling from the consequences of doubling in size overnight. New premises to house the new personnel, negotiations with bank managers, developers, and equipment suppliers. New human resources people to deal with the endless regulations and complications of being an employer. Without Samantha Jones, he'd be up to his knees in mud about now.

For the last year and a half, ever since he hired Sam from Mirimar Consulting, he'd been free to do the work he wanted, free to keep Tremaine's moving and growing. He loved the challenge of nailing a deal like Lloyd's from under IBM's e-commerce division, putting together a program design that could show the owners needs for information and e-commerce they hadn't imagined having. Loved the stimulation of seeing the project manifest from plan to reality.

But he hated the damned details of running a business. He'd never have started Tremaine's without Brent Martin as his partner to look after the admin. stuff—but Brent had walked out two years ago, leaving Cal in administrative chaos.

Desperate, he'd hired Mirimar Consulting, who had sent Samantha Jones, M.B.A. Cal had taken one look at Sam's shining brown hair and soft matching eyes, and he'd known she wasn't up to it any more than Brent had been.

Now he swung from the window and stared impatiently at the door Sam should have walked through three minutes ago. When he first met her, it had taken only five minutes to realize he was wrong about her.

"I'll need all your financials," she'd announced ten seconds after the introduction, "and access to personnel records, especially people who've quit in the last two years."

"Don't waste time on people who are gone. I need you to organize the future."

Her eyes had flashed with penetrating intelligence. "Programmers like freedom, not chaos. It's worth your while to know why the valuable ones left. I've made a list of the information I need. If you authorize me to have access, I'll look after everything."

She handed him a long list, then she relaxed in the chair, right here in this room, and for the first time he saw her smile. Why did Sam's smiles always seem to cover some secret he felt impelled to know?

"Tell me where you want your company to be five years from now, then give me two weeks to collect information. A week from this coming Friday we'll meet again. I'll make suggestions and you can decide whether my ideas make sense."

He'd quickly discovered it wasn't just Samantha Jones's ideas he needed. He needed the woman, her smile, her magic. Almost immediately, he'd felt the waters calm. Project leaders who'd been at odds for months seemed to have buried the hatchet, and Dee, Cal's assistant, stopped turning up at his desk with administrative emergencies several times a day.

When Sam gave Cal her recommendations, she offered to find a manager to put them into practice. Cal had a better solution. He wanted Sam full-time, with no divided loyalties. She liked her consulting job at Mirimar's, and he smiled now, remembering that it wasn't the outrageous salary that had won her over. It was the promise of a director's position and a seat on his board after two years if she did a good job.

When he bought Brent out, he'd vowed never to give up control of even the smallest part of Tremaine's to anyone again. But that was before Sam. The impulse to hire her away from Mirimar's was the best decision he'd ever made. Whenever he thought of the chaotic days before she came, he counted his blessings that, unlike many of his other employees, she seemed to have no private life. He just hoped to hell that she didn't do something stupid like decide to marry and have a couple of babies.

If he had any say in it, Samantha Jones's ticking clock would remain silent until they were both old directors of Tremaine's.

The clock had eaten another four minutes, and he fought the urge to pace through the new premises they'd just settled into, storm into Sam's office, and demand an explanation for her lateness. He'd been doing too much of that sort of thing lately. Frustrated because he had no choice but to wait until they ramped up their head count, he'd been looking over Sam's shoulder constantly. He shouldn't be demanding her presence in the boardroom for a review of Friday's strategy when in truth, he knew she would have the whole damned thing organized to perfection and would be busy as hell for the next two days keeping it that way.

He wondered suddenly if her lateness might be deliberate, a tactic to remind him of their agreement that he wouldn't interfere in her administrative realm, so long as she kept him informed in their weekly meetings.

No, he decided. Not Sam's style. They'd had a few territorial skirmishes, Sam's quiet firmness against his volatile impulsiveness. He doubted Sam had ever backed down from a battle, and he'd given her plenty of cause to balk by looking over her shoulder, interfering. But Sam was always direct. If she had a complaint, she'd tell him straight out.

When he finally heard her heels clicking outside the boardroom, he stepped across the carpet to open the door. She had one hand out, reaching for the handle, and he saw her freeze when the door opened.

"Did I startle you?"

She shrugged and slipped inside, but the smile didn't come. "Sorry I'm late."

She looked uncharacteristically harried. Why? He said, "I wanted to go over the procedures for screening the recruits Friday night, but if you're overloaded, we can do it tomorrow."

She stood in the middle of the boardroom floor, the expensive carpet she'd chosen all around her, her eyes troubled in a way he'd never seen before. Something was wrong, but what? There was always some crisis in the computer business, but Sam always handled the rough spots so calmly they seemed smooth.

This was different. She moved abruptly to one of the chairs at the side of the board table, and he thought her face wore the sort of look people had when they were about to say something unwelcome.

Something like: *Cal, I'm quitting.*

Panic boiled in his gut. Sam couldn't leave.

She opened her computer case and set her laptop on the table. "This is probably a good time to go over the screening procedure, just in case there's—this is a good time."

He frowned and prowled to the other side of the table. He didn't like the way she said *just in case,* as if she *had* come in here thinking of quitting.

Inactivity was making him paranoid. Sam wouldn't quit. She was an ambitious woman. Six more months would get her the seat on his board she'd held out for when he hired her.

"I've got the list of volunteers here," she said, turning her computer on. "All the project leaders are on it, except the two on vacation, and Tom Brennan. You left him in New York."

"He's working with Lloyd's IT personnel—such as they are—getting a handle on their network. Do you want me to bring him back?"

"We don't need him." Another of those smiles. "I've got a meeting scheduled with the volunteers today at five-fifteen. I sent you a memo about it?" He nodded and she said, "At the open house, when the recruits start coming in at three in the afternoon, Jason will take their resumes, prescreen them, and mark them as candidates or not, then introduce them to one of the volunteers. Accountants get someone from accounting; developers get a developer. Depending on the prescreening, the volunteer will either take the recruit to an interview or an information session about Tremaine's. The NFT's—not for

Tremaine's—will get the information film about the company, refreshments—"

"And be told to buzz off."

"Nicely," she said with another of those smiles. "The ones we interview will either be passed on up for a second interview or marked NFT, and sent to the information session."

"This better work. We need those developers yesterday."

"We've had good feedback, plenty of phone calls. We're hoping for five hundred people at the open house. It's going to be hectic, but it's innovative. Developers don't like working for stodgy companies, and this open house tells them that we're part of the new wave, not the old guard."

"You've done a good job, Sam." Had he told her that often enough? What exactly was it that motivated her? He didn't think it was power—she was too good at delegating. Money? Praise?

"I'm having fun," she said, hitting him with that smile again. He had the urge to move closer instead of pacing back to the window. For perhaps the thousandth time, he blocked the images her smile so often drew to his mind: Sam wearing something soft and clinging in place of that gray suit, her feet bare, her shining brown hair flowing free. How long was her hair? Shoulder length? What if. . . .

No! Samantha Jones was far too valuable to be risked in a temporary romance.

The ring of a telephone interrupted his fantasy.

"I told Dee not to put any calls through," he growled.

"I'm expecting a call." Sam walked rapidly to the telephone and picked it up. "Hi, Marcy. . . . Yes, put him through."

He frowned at the tension on Sam's face as she wedged the receiver between shoulder and chin and pulled her electronic organizer from her jacket pocket.

"Hello, Dexter." She frowned and juggled her stylus, organizer, and telephone. "Any way we can put it off? No, Friday's impossible. Can you— Yes, I agree. I—yes, I'll be there."

"Problems?" he asked when she'd cradled the receiver again.

"No," she said. She switched off her portable computer and slipped it into its case.

"Sam, hold on a minute."

She stood waiting for his words, eyes inscrutable, lips unsmiling. This was pure impulse, but he'd learned to trust his impulses.

"We signed a contract when you started working here. I assigned you a block of shares that would become vested in two years."

Her eyes met his, unblinking. "Provided you're satisfied with my work."

"I'm satisfied." Why the devil were they talking so formally? "I've been making things hard for you these last few weeks."

"You've been a nuisance, Cal, but I know you're itching to get started on this project. Once this recruitment is over, you'll get off my back."

"I think it's time to vest your shares, give you that seat on the board. I'll call the lawyer in the morning and set it up."

She looked stunned.

"This wasn't supposed to happen for another six months." She picked up her computer case, looking a hell of a lot less pleased than he would have expected.

"What the hell's going on, Sam?"

She shifted her grip on the computer. "We've got a meeting in about ten minutes. Can we talk afterward?"

"Yes," he agreed. "We'll talk afterward."

*　*　*

We'll talk afterward. Samantha shivered as she closed her office door.

She should have told Cal when she hung up from speaking to Dexter, but until that moment she'd thought she could rely on phone calls and the lawyer to keep everything under control up in Canada—at least until after the open house.

If Samantha didn't show up at the family court hearing, the court would give temporary custody to the Ministry of Children and Families. Kippy would be with strangers. Just a baby . . . she wouldn't understand; she'd be pining for Dorothy. Maybe Samantha wasn't Dorothy, with her easy, maternal ways, but at least she'd held her niece in her arms many times. Kippy would know her.

She needed to convince the judge that she was the obvious person to care for her niece until Dorothy got back home, that there was absolutely no need for a foster home.

She should have told Cal during their meeting in the boardroom, but first she needed to organize the details.

She pushed the intercom and called Marcy in.

"HR has all the handouts ready for the meeting," Marcy said.

"Thanks, Marcy. While I'm in the meeting, book me a flight to arrive in Nanaimo by two P.M. tomorrow. You'll probably have to route me through Vancouver, Canada."

With any luck, there'd be a jet flying to Vancouver about noon, with a connecting flight to Nanaimo on Vancouver Island. She probably couldn't get everything done in time to fly back home tomorrow evening. She'd have to rent a car, take a ferry to the mainland and drive home—probably with a baby in the car.

With any luck, she'd be back at work Friday morning.

She'd need day care for Kippy. Tomorrow morning she'd call the employment agency.

She was glad she'd told Cal to hold off on the board seat. Bad politics to accept, then irritate him with an un-

scheduled absence. After the meeting, when he'd seen
how completely everything was organized, she'd tell him
she needed half a day, just a few hours to straighten out
a personal matter across the border in Canada.

Maybe she wouldn't mention Canada. It made the journey sound bigger than it was. She'd have her cell phone
and computer with her, and she'd be back hours before
the open house to settle any crises.

She'd never before had a personal crisis that interfered
with her job at Tremaine's. She'd prided herself in being
the perfect businesswoman—reliable, available, and
driven to succeed. She'd seen other women distracted by
lovers, by marriage, by motherhood, and Sam knew she
didn't want any of that. Lovers and husbands, with their
potential for conflict and fighting, were the last thing she
needed.

After the lessons in married life she and Sarah had wit-
nessed as children, she'd been amazed when Sarah married. But Jonathan Morrison had been a good man,
considerate of Sarah, and Sarah had claimed to love him
madly.

Tragically, Samantha's sister and her new husband
weren't given the opportunity to test their marriage with
time. Last December, en route to Mexico a few weeks
after the birth of their first child, Sarah and Jonathan
lost their lives in an airline crash off the coast of California.

Samantha pushed away the familiar grief. She had a
meeting to orchestrate, then Cal to face. Tomorrow, she'd
convince a judge that she was a fit guardian for Kippy Morrison until Dorothy got out of the hospital. One way or
another, she was determined to manage both as Calin Tremaine's second-in-command and Kippy's substitute
mother, for as long as Dorothy needed her help.

* * *

By the time the meeting concluded, Samantha knew Cal was impressed. The employees were determined to make this open house a huge success.

"They love being in on exciting projects," she murmured as the room emptied. "Your projects."

She laughed when she realized he didn't know what to say to that. For a man determined to carry the world along with his own vision of the future, Cal was remarkably naïve about the power of his own charisma.

"Let's get something to eat," he said. "I need food."

And she needed to talk to him. During the meeting, Marcy had slipped her the bad news from the travel agent. No available flights. She would have to drive, although she had no right to take twenty-four hours for private business tomorrow. No choice, either.

"I just need a couple of minutes of your time, Cal. There's no need for a dinner meeting."

"Did you have lunch?"

"I'm not—"

"I'll meet you down at the parking lot."

Frustrating man, she decided, watching him walk through the meeting room's double doors. Over dinner it would be difficult to avoid explaining the reasons for her trip to Canada, almost impossible to keep the distance she needed between her private and professional lives.

She didn't want Cal thinking of her as someone with encumbrances, someone he couldn't count on because of a complex personal life.

She headed for her own office to pick up her purse, cell phone, and portable computer. Downstairs in the parking lot, the spring evening felt pleasantly warm. She breathed in the salt air from the harbor and remembered childhood days spent running on the grassy hill below Dorothy's house, sea smells carried on the wind, and Sarah laughing as they raced for the water.

Sarah, who would never laugh again.

Cal opened the passenger door of his low red sports car as she approached, and Samantha frowned. Better to take separate cars but awkward to tell him so. She'd never felt so awkward with Cal before. Until now their relations had always been strictly business.

This was business, too, and of course he wasn't going to be unreasonable about a personal emergency, but it could change the way he thought of her. Until now, she'd been careful never to let him down.

She wondered what her stepfather would say about this whole predicament, and she figured Wayne would probably tell her she should get comfortable with having weaknesses, that maintaining the image of superwoman was an impossible task.

Better not to make an issue of driving in Cal's car, she decided.

"Thanks," she said, slipping into the passenger seat. Leather and horsepower, the red Porsche suited its owner to a "T".

"I thought Eduardo's," Cal said as he started the engine.

Should she tell him before dinner or after? After, she decided. He'd have less time to work on getting details from her.

When the waiter seated them in a quiet corner of Eduardo's, she asked, "How's Tom doing in New York?"

The distraction worked, and they discussed Tom's struggles to make sense of Lloyd's outmoded computer network until the waiter delivered seafood salad to Samantha, and a medium-rare New York steak to Cal.

Cal cut a piece from his steak and said, "Once we've got the e-commerce teams in place, you should take some time off."

Now was the time to tell him she'd be taking tomorrow off, abandoning him in the crucial hours before Friday's event. It shouldn't be hard to say the words, but her throat felt dry. She realized she was hoping for a magic solution that would let her look after both Tremaine's and Kippy's needs without sacrificing either.

"What about you?" she asked stiffly. "Will you be taking time off?"

"Once the teams are in place and working, I might grab a week."

She speared a prawn with her fork, but her stomach protested at the thought of food. "Where would you go?"

"Maybe fishing. A week in the mountains."

Cal hadn't been fishing in more than a year. There'd been that one trip, two months after she started working for him. He and an old friend had flown into the mountains for a week with fishing rods and packs. He'd returned four days later, exploding with questions about events in his absence.

"No telephones in the mountains," she said wryly. "With this new project, you'd never last forty-eight hours."

"True," he admitted. "So if I do take time off, I'll probably visit the family. Lots of phones in San Francisco, no problem hooking my portable computer to a modem."

"Go to Hawaii or Tahiti. You'd still have phone lines, but also beaches and sunshine—and it's harder to hop a shuttle home."

If he did go to one of those island paradises, she wondered if he'd take a woman with him. She knew he dated. Dee, his personal assistant, had mentioned sending flowers to one woman, booking dinner for Cal and another. He was an obviously virile man, but she'd seen little evidence of his private life over the last eighteen months. If he had a steady girlfriend, Dee didn't know about it.

"What about you, Sam? Where will you go on your vacation?"

"I haven't decided." She would go to Gabriola Island, just a few miles from Nanaimo. She'd help Dorothy clean out the storeroom and hold Kippy, doing her small part to give her orphaned niece a home and a loving family.

When the waiter took away their plates—Samantha's almost untouched—Cal placed his elbows on the table and leaned toward.

"Sam, I offered you a seat on the board today. Your reaction was less than enthusiastic. What's wrong?"

She picked up her coffee and cradled the cup in her hands. "I—I don't think this week is the right time."

"Why?" His eyes were gray, too penetrating.

"I need tomorrow off. I'd put it off until next week if I could, but I have no choice. I don't want you calling the lawyer to vest my shares and set up the board meeting and feeling annoyed with me for taking off tomorrow at the same time."

She expected an immediate reaction, certainly questions. Not silence while he studied her for a few seconds, his eyes unreadable.

"The open house is Friday," he said. "Day after tomorrow."

"Everything's organized, delegated. I'll be in touch by cell phone to tie up any loose ends. I'll be back late tomorrow night, at work early Friday in time to put out any fires before the event starts at three."

He studied her as if he could see beyond the calmness of her voice. "Personal business?"

"Yes." His gaze was too intense and she said irritably, "The reason doesn't matter. Or is my private life open to your scrutiny as a requirement of my employment?" She flushed at the sound of her own words. "I'm sorry, that was nasty."

"And unprovoked?"

What on earth was wrong with her? She'd done battle with Cal many times before, had always held her own, but this time she felt crazily off balance. She'd overreacted, before he even asked the questions. She supposed it was because, for the first time, the subject was her own personal life.

"I'm sorry. You've never probed about my personal life."

"It hasn't been relevant to your job until now. What's so urgent, Sam?" His eyes told her he knew he had the upper hand.

"My grandmother is in the hospital."

Cal's eyes softened. "Seriously ill?"

"She says not. Cal, I wouldn't take off at a time like this if it weren't necessary."

"True." The frown lines radiating from the corners of his eyes told her he wasn't satisfied. "When do you leave?"

"Early tomorrow." Had she told him she was leaving town? "I'll be back late tomorrow night."

"Flying or driving?"

She put her cup down on its saucer, the sound of china on china ringing between them like a warning bell. "Does it matter how I travel?"

"Yes."

She'd shared her ambitions with Cal, her ideas and plans for Tremaine's, but not herself. She knew he regarded her as an efficient mystery, knew he didn't understand how she smoothed the chaotic waters around him, but he respected her. She liked it that way, the balance of power even between them, her own feet firmly on the ground, immune to the winds of Cal's forceful personality and volatile emotions,

Nine out of ten women in her position would be overwhelmed by Cal, probably in love with him. Samantha was the tenth; she'd seen enough of passion and volatility to know the dangers. She admired Cal, loved working for him, understood him well enough to make herself indispensable professionally. But she wasn't tempted by his gray eyes, his love of a challenge, his waving dark-blond hair. She certainly wasn't about to let herself slip into some kind of "personal friends" situation that gave him a handle on her own vulnerabilities.

"Is there some reason you need to keep your travel plans secret?"

"Is there some reason you need to know them?"

He looked as if he'd scented something intriguing and meant to explore it. "If I see news of an air crash on television tomorrow, shouldn't I know whether or not you were on the plane?"

An air crash. She swallowed hard, remembering endless hours after last December's air crash, watching CNN nonstop with Dorothy, keeping the phone lines clear because someone might call to tell them Sarah and Jonathan were alive and well.

"Sam?"

For heaven's sake, Samantha M. Jones, snap out of it!

"I'm driving."

He said nothing, just waited, until she added, "To Nanaimo."

"Canada? You'll be driving north to Vancouver, taking the ferry to Vancouver Island?"

"You know Nanaimo?"

"I can even spell it. I did a cycling tour about fifteen years ago. The Canadian Gulf Islands: Galiano, Salt Spring, and Gabriola."

"My grandmother lives on Gabriola Island," she said before she could filter the words. "I grew up there."

"I didn't know that." He leaned forward, curiosity in his eyes. "How did you go from being a Canadian kid to an American woman?"

"Dual citizenship. Look, I need to leave now. You've got my cell phone number. If there's anything you need tomorrow, just call."

"What time do you expect to arrive in Nanaimo?"

"Two-thirty in the afternoon." She put her napkin neatly on the table beside her plate, pushed her chair back.

"I'd better fly you in the chopper. We'll leave at noon.

The flight will be less than two hours, but we should allow some time for customs."

"No." She couldn't spend two hours in Cal's helicopter, two hours worrying about Kippy and Dorothy, with Cal right there, watching. "I don't need— You have other things to do."

"You know damned well there's nothing for me to do but wait for Friday."

Flustered, she shook her head and felt strands of hair coming loose. "I need my car when I get there."

"I'm sure a competent M.B.A. like Samantha Jones can manage to rent a car at the Nanaimo airport."

Trapped. He had her trapped. She was half standing, the urge to run pumping through her veins, and she realized suddenly just how out of proportion her response was. As if Cal were threatening her, instead of offering help.

"You're right." She forced her voice to calm appreciation. "I'll arrange a car rental. I'll see you tomorrow at noon." She stepped back, pushed her chair into the table, and even managed a smile as she picked up her portable computer and handbag. "Thank you for dinner. I'll take a taxi back to my car." She held up a hand to still his automatic protest. "I'd rather."

She could tell from the itching along her spine that he watched her walk out of the restaurant, that his eyes didn't leave her until she turned out of sight and reached for the door.

Three

Samantha expected the helicopter ride to be an agony of persistent questions from Cal, blended with her apprehension about flying.

She'd messed up yesterday, telling him she needed to go away. Somehow, she'd stirred his curiosity. Usually his curiosity focused on computer matters—on questioning executives about their needs, exploring new ways of making computers serve people, taking apart his new electronic organizer to examine the circuitry.

Cal's curiosity was the driving force behind Tremaine Software. She'd occasionally seen it trained on a person, had sat in airports with him, enjoying his speculations about passersby. She'd always been grateful that when he trained that curiosity on her, it was limited to questions like: Why did you decide on the open house? What makes you believe it's a better solution than the employment agency we've used before?

After last night's personal questions, she'd prepared herself for more, rehearsed her lines. *I prefer not to discuss my personal life. I appreciate the ride, Cal, but it doesn't give you the right to question me.*

She was ready for him, but the only question he asked was, "Did you get the car rental arranged?" as he checked her seat belt.

"Yes."

"Good." Then he walked around the helicopter before settling in the pilot's seat, and she took five careful, deep breaths, concentrating on relaxing her body to escape the tension that had accompanied any sort of flying since last December.

"All set?" he asked.

"Yes."

She wondered if she'd be in Nanaimo early enough to slip up to the hospital before she met the lawyer, early enough to see Dorothy for herself before she listened to whatever the social worker had to say. She needed to know if her grandmother was telling the truth about her minor medical problem. If it was *only* indigestion, why would Dorothy be hospitalized?

This morning she'd called June at the employment agency, and tonight after she and Dexter had regained custody of Kippy at this afternoon's family court session, she would drive Kippy back to Seattle in the rental car and get her settled with the temporary nanny. Then, tomorrow, she'd be able to focus on the open house, knowing Kippy was in expert hands.

Samantha jumped at the sound of Cal's voice. "What?"

He handed her a set of headphones. "Once I start the engine, the headphones will blank out some of the noise and let us talk without shouting."

"Thanks." She didn't want to talk, not today.

She watched as he flicked switches, wondering how these machines really worked, whether she'd feel panic when he swept them up into the air. She felt the urge to ask questions, nervous talk, and suppressed it. The engine began humming, and she saw the helicopter's blade slowly rotate.

A moment later the helicopter lifted, tilting forward and sweeping upward into the sky, sweeping panic into Samantha's throat. As they lifted over Seattle's harbor, the world straightened and they were flying level, out over the water.

It was all right, perfectly all right, she told herself, watching Cal's hands on the controls.

"How long have you had this helicopter?" she asked stiffly.

"Three years." He studied something out the side window, his voice oddly intimate through the headphones. "Brent and I used it for fishing trips in the mountains. Then Brent moved to California, and I bought his share."

He'd bought Brent's share of the business, too. The documents were filed under AGREEMENTS in the company minute book.

"You should have gone away this week, Cal. You could have had a few days fishing before the open house."

He flashed her a grin. "As you said last light, no telephone. How could I have harassed you all week, watching over your shoulder, with no telephone, no cell phone reception? Have you ever been up in a helicopter before?"

"No."

"Nervous?"

"Not now." She was surprised to find her words true.

Below, a sailboat leaned into the wind, crossing Puget Sound toward Port Townsend. She twisted her head, watching as Cal flew past the sailor. "What do we do about customs?"

"I've called ahead. A customs officer will meet us at the airport."

Had he checked entry procedures since he offered her the ride yesterday or had he always known? "Have you ever been fishing on Vancouver Island?"

"No. I haven't done much fishing at all lately."

And he probably wouldn't for some time, she thought, once he began the new project. She'd expected his curiosity to make this journey very difficult, but he seemed relaxed, and she felt her tension ease in response.

He gave her a sideways grin. "I'm pretty hyped about this new project. I doubt if I could sit waiting for fish to bite. You've been going flat out for quite a while yourself, getting us into the new premises. Great location, by the way. Several of the project leaders have mentioned that they appreciate looking out over the harbor instead of the rock-face view we had in the old place."

"Thanks." It was a bonus that Cal was so often appreciative of her efforts.

"Will you come up here when you take your vacation?" he asked.

"Probably."

"Is this where you came in December?"

"Yes."

"You didn't look all that rested when you came back after Christmas."

She turned away to stare at a small island passing by on their right. She didn't want to talk about December, about her vacation on Gabriola Island. She'd come back in shock from the plane crash that had taken her sister's and brother-in-law's lives, knowing Dorothy too was still grieving deeply. It was only after she'd made her first couple of monthly visits to Dorothy that she'd realized having Kippy was the best thing that could have happened to help them recover from Sarah's death.

Now the authorities were threatening to take Kippy from Dorothy. She mustn't let it happen, couldn't allow Sarah's child to stay in foster care.

She realized Cal was still waiting for an answer and said, "I brought along copies of some of the likely resumes that have come in this week for the development jobs. Do you want the details?"

"Give me a rundown," said Cal.

The closer Cal flew to Nanaimo, the more distracted Sam seemed to become. Why? Was she thinking about problems ahead that she needed to resolve? Exactly what problems?

She'd been damned secretive about this urgent personal journey. Until last night, he hadn't realized just how little he knew about Samantha Jones. They'd flown together several times, to San Francisco, New York, and once to London. They'd met frequently for planning sessions, working lunches and dinners. Twice, she'd attended major trade fairs with him, and several times she'd acted as his hostess for business dinners. Since Sam came to work for him, Cal had spent more time with her than with any of the women he'd dated. He knew she took her coffee black, preferred fish and chicken to beef, and would rather read a romance than watch a movie on long flights.

Twenty-four hours ago, if someone had asked him, he would have said he knew Samantha Jones very well indeed. Certainly, he knew that he could tell her he needed fifty more developers and support staff, with premises for them to work in, and she'd listen carefully, then say simply, "I'll look after it."

And she would. Despite the way he'd been hovering this week, he knew she'd do exactly what she'd promised. But yesterday he'd realized that he didn't know anything *personal* about her, nothing beyond her relationship with Tremaine Software. She had an M.B.A. from the University of Washington's business school, but he had no idea where she'd lived before attending there. He knew she was unmarried but didn't know if she had boyfriends, lovers, or even an ex-husband.

Hell, she could be living with a man and, if she didn't tell him, he'd never know.

If she was in a relationship, she probably *wouldn't* tell him. He didn't know where she spent those weekends she took away from Seattle. He didn't know where she lived, although he could probably find that out by looking in her personnel file on the computer.

The only personal details he knew about her were scraps gleaned yesterday evening. She had a sick grandmother, she'd grown up on Gabriola Island, and her parentage or birth circumstances were such that she'd managed to acquire dual American and Canadian citizenship.

By the time he brought her back to Seattle, he fully intended to know more. Tremaine's relied heavily on Sam, and he had a right to know exactly who she was.

When he brought the helicopter to a stop outside the hangar at Nanaimo's Cassidy Airport, Sam immediately scrambled out.

"Customs," said Cal, gesturing to the uniformed man approaching.

The formalities were brief, and within moments they were alone on the tarmac again. "In that door," Cal told her, gesturing toward the terminal. "I'll bring your bag to the car rental counter."

She snagged a tendril of hair that had blown free and tucked it behind her ear. "I'll carry it in. I appreciate the ride, Cal. I'll be back late tonight, in the office early tomorrow morning."

"I'll fly you back."

He saw her eyes widen, realized she didn't want him to hang around and decided immediately that he wasn't going anywhere.

"I'll find my own ride home," she said sharply.

He shook his head. "You'll want to be here for more than a couple hours. Stay overnight. If we take off at six tomorrow morning, we can be back in the office before nine."

The wind whipped around her, molding her jacket tightly against her breasts. She wrapped her arms around her midriff as if she were cold. "Cal—"

"Get inside, Sam. I'll bring your bag."

She hesitated, probably trying to think of a way to get rid of him; then she shrugged and turned toward the terminal.

He pulled her bag and his own out of the chopper before he locked it. Then he hurried into the terminal, keeping her bag with him while he reported in and closed his flight plan. By the time he was clear of the paperwork, she was just turning away from the car rental counter, computer bag slung over her shoulder and keys in her hand.

When she saw him, she held her hand out for her overnight bag.

"I'll carry it to the car. You can give me a ride into town."

He saw her drag in a deep breath. "Cal, I'm uncomfortable about this."

"Why? We've shared a car before."

"Yes, but . . . that's not. . . ." He was fascinated by her confusion. "I appreciate the ride—the flight—but you should leave. This is my private life, and you have no—I shouldn't have agreed to this in the first place."

He shook his head and held the door for her. She stepped quickly outside, her words lost to him in the sudden gust of wind.

"Windy and warm," he said, catching up a few steps down the concrete walk. "I can't help wondering why you're so prickly about this. I need you back in Seattle to look after the open house, and I know you're determined to be there. I'm trying to make the business of getting here and getting back as smooth as I can for you. Why is it a problem for you to take some help with transportation?"

She stopped behind a white Ford Escort, popped the trunk, and swung her computer in. He put her overnight bag in beside the computer, then watched as she stuffed her hands in the pockets of her suit jacket and tilted her head up to meet his eyes.

"You're hovering, looking for clues. I know my asking for time off makes you curious, but I won't let you treat me the way you treat a computer problem. You don't want

a ride into town, you want a chance to find out what I'm
doing here."

In her voice, he heard reflections of frustration. In her
eyes, he saw dark turbulence. He said, "If you told me
what's going on, I wouldn't have to probe."

They'd clashed horns before, but it had always been
business, and he'd never seen this hot, irritated look in
her eyes, this edge of nervousness. It made him wonder if
the coolness in her was soul-deep as he'd always believed,
or a mask.

"I'll let you off at the Coast Bastion Inn," she said
abruptly, "but I can't fly back at six tomorrow. I'll pick you
up at the Coast at six-thirty. If you need to know why the
delay, you can forget the whole thing. I've been working
eighteen hours a day for weeks and I deserve a few hours
off the leash."

He opened the back door and put his overnight bag in
the backseat, then slid into the passenger seat. Sam didn't
say anything at all as she started the car and reversed out
of the parking space. Before she flashed a glance at him,
they were on the highway, headed north to Nanaimo.

"You brought an overnight bag, Cal. Did you intend all
along to stay over?"

"I was a Boy Scout."

"Be prepared?"

"That's right."

He saw her gaze flick to the side view mirror. "I apologize if I've been a bit. . . ."

"Touchy?" he suggested.

"Yes." She glanced in the mirror again, then pulled out
to pass a transport truck. "I don't like mixing my personal
and business life."

"Why is that, Sam?"

Her lips parted on an answer, then snapped shut again.
Fascinating how her lips could be so soft and full, then in
a flash of irritation, could turn rigid and impregnable.

"It's just information, Sam."

She shrugged. "Knowledge is power. What will you do with yourself all day?"

"Perhaps I'll rent a car and explore Gabriola Island. I remember some spectacular cliffs there—what are they called? Those sandstone cliffs sculpted by the winter storms?"

"Malaspina Galleries. You'd better stick to Nanaimo. Visit the museum. You can find out about the old mining tunnels that run under the harbor from Newcastle Island."

"You'd rather I stayed away from Gabriola Island?"

"I don't care," she snapped.

He grinned. "You'd prefer that I go back to Seattle?"

"Yes." She was uneasy, almost twitching. It fascinated him.

"I'll have my cell phone," he said as she slowed for a speed-limit sign, "in case you need me."

When she stopped at the light ahead, she turned and met his eyes with her usual cool directness, the familiar Sam he'd assumed was the real woman, until yesterday.

"I won't need you," she said.

By the time she dropped Cal at the Coast Bastion Inn, Samantha's nerves were frazzled. She was half an hour early for the appointment with Dexter Ames, not enough time to drive up to the hospital and visit Dorothy. Besides, she needed to calm down.

Why had she ever agreed to Cal's offer to fly her to Nanaimo?

Because it seemed logical, of course, but she should have known better. Yet how could she, when his helicopter had given her the whole morning at work? She'd approved the final changes in the caterer's menu, then spent an hour with Jason in human resources working out final details on procedures for the screening of candidates at the open house. She'd even managed a fifteen-minute telephone meeting with a local television producer, with the result that the TV station had decided to put *Around Seattle*'s camera outside Tremaine's from three o'clock tomorrow afternoon. Great exposure, and who knew: The extra publicity might tempt some hot but dissatisfied developer from Microsoft to print off a copy of his resume and meander down to Tremaine's.

Once Cal offered his helicopter, there hadn't been any real choice, but she wished she hadn't agreed to let him fly her back tomorrow morning. Unless Dorothy got out of the hospital today, she'd have Kippy with her, and she wasn't willing to spend two hours locked in a helicopter with Cal while he fired off constant questions about the baby in her arms.

Somehow, between now and tomorrow morning, she had to come up with an excuse to get out of that ride in Cal's helicopter.

She wasn't sure exactly when she'd be able to pick up Kippy from the foster home—shortly after the hearing, she assumed. If so, she would take Kippy to the hospital to visit Dorothy, then head to Dorothy's house on Gabriola to pack enough baby clothes to last a week or ten days— however long it took for Dorothy to return home able to care for the baby. Dorothy must have some kind of virus, stomach problems, maybe ulcers. Whatever it was, Dorothy insisted it wasn't serious.

Samantha would straighten out the authorities, pick up Kippy, talk to the doctor, and head for one of the early ferries to Vancouver tomorrow morning. Hopefully, Kippy would sleep most of the journey, though she might be restless, upset by living with strangers, then being taken off to strange places by her Aunt Samantha.

Why couldn't the social workers use their energy seizing children who really needed to be removed from their

homes? Any fool could see that Dorothy had more moth-
ering skills in her baby finger than any ten foster mothers.

Cal would be angry when she called him tonight to can-
cel on tomorrow's helicopter ride. And he'd be curious.
Better, she thought, to have him angry with her ducking
out than to let him see Kippy. The last twenty-four hours
had proved that given enough information and enough
rope, Cal could end up running her life. The rest of the
world had to live with unsatisfied curiosity. Why should Cal
be different?

What about the nanny? Samantha parked the rental car
outside Dexter Ames's offices and yanked out her cell
phone. After a minute on hold, she was put through to
June.

"I have two good candidates," June told her. "A fifty-
year-old retired nurse who's an active grandmother, and a
twenty-four-year-old single mom with her own two-month-
old baby. They're both reliable, good references, both
looking for full-time work but willing to take something
temporary meanwhile. The single mom would be bringing
her own child with her."

Yet June had short-listed the girl along with the grandmother. "If you were hiring one of them yourself, June,
which would you pick?"

"The single mom. I saw her with her baby."

"I need her to start at eight tomorrow."

One more detail resolved.

She switched the cell phone off, locked the rental car,
and crossed the street to Dexter Ames's office. She thought
of Dorothy's house, empty, silent. What if her grandmother was much sicker than she'd said?

Samantha pulled open the door to the lawyer's office
and announced herself. She'd expected to wait but was
shown right in. Dexter greeted her with a handshake and
a frown.

"The Ministry of Children and Families took your niece

into custody Tuesday night on the recommendation of your grandmother's family doctor. He says Dorothy needs to go into a nursing home and isn't fit to care for a child. At today's hearing the Ministry will ask for an interim order of custody. Once they get that, they must return within forty-five days for the protection hearing. Unless something changes with your grandmother's condition, our only way to keep custody at the protection hearing is for you to apply for custody yourself with Dorothy's consent."

"Can we do that today?"

"No. Today the judge must either rule that Kippy be in the custody of the Ministry or returned to Dorothy."

"But she's in the hospital."

"I think we can get them to agree to your looking after Kippy on your grandmother's behalf, but it means you can't go home until we get the custody agreement through. With luck, you might be able to take Kippy to the States in a couple of weeks."

She couldn't walk out of her job for two weeks with no notice.

She couldn't leave Kippy with strangers.

"Yes," she said. "I'll stay."

An hour later, standing behind Dexter in front of the robed judge in family court, Samantha felt as if she were still in shock. At Easter she and Dorothy had walked together every evening, Dorothy pushing the baby carriage as often as Samantha. If Dorothy knew she had a health problem, she'd managed to hide the fact from Samantha.

Was Dorothy secretive? Samantha had never thought so, but as she listened to the social worker reading the doctor's report, it was obvious that Dorothy had sheltered her granddaughter from her health problems.

Congestive heart failure.

"Your honor," said Dexter. "Dorothy Marshall is in the hospital, but she's instructed me to advise you that she has appointed the child's aunt, Samantha Jones, to act as caregiver to the child while she's there. I have with me the child's aunt. We request that Katherine Morrison be returned to Dorothy Marshall's care, and that the protection hearing be scheduled as soon as possible."

The judge asked Samantha several questions, then the social worker murmured to the Ministry's lawyer, who protested, "Your honor, Ms. Jones is an American citizen who lives and works in Seattle. Does she intend to remove the infant from Canada?"

The judge said, "Ms. Jones, are you willing to accept a restriction against removing Katherine Morrison from this jurisdiction?"

"Yes, your honor."

After some discussion with the lawyers and the social worker, the judge said, "I'm going to order that the child be returned to the care of Dorothy Marshall under the supervision of the director, with the restriction that Ms. Jones is not permitted to remove the infant from this jurisdiction. We'll set a date for the protection hearing as soon as possible."

Dexter murmured, "You understand, Samantha, that you'll be getting supervisory visits from the Ministry of Children and Families? The social worker?"

"Yes."

"OK. I'll see Dorothy tomorrow at the hospital, talk to her about applying for a permanent transfer of custody under the Family Relations Act."

An hour later, Samantha stood outside the front door of a small, blue house with the social worker, Brenda Simonson. She'd just obtained Ms. Simonson's grudging permission to fly back to Seattle Friday for the open house, leaving Kippy in Diana Foley's care for the afternoon and evening. Now if Cal would agree to act as her chauffeur with the helicopter, she'd be able to attend the open house.

Cal wasn't going to like it when she told him she needed a two-week leave of absence, with no notice.

The social worker said, "I'll be visiting several times over the next few weeks. If Katherine isn't being cared for properly, I have the authority to remove her again."

"Of course I'll care for her properly. She's my niece."

The social worker glared at her. "This infant has already been subjected to enough traumatic change. I don't see the point of giving her to you. You're supposedly family, but you're taking off, leaving her within hours. How many trips do you plan to make to Seattle, Ms. Jones? Katherine doesn't need a caregiver too busy with her job to care about her orphaned niece."

"Look, Ms. Simonson, I—"

"Just don't forget: I'll be watching you."

Samantha's lips were parted to retort when a middle-aged woman wearing a soft blue tracksuit opened the door.

"Hi, Brenda." Her smile included Samantha as she said, "You're Katherine's aunt? I'll get her."

"We call her Kippy," said Samantha, stepping inside the house.

Seconds later she heard the cries of a baby. Kippy? She wasn't sure, and wondered if the social worker would criticize her for not being able to recognize her niece's cry. As the cry grew louder, closer, Samantha nervously wondered if Kippy would cry even louder when Samantha took her in her arms. Would the social worker make another negative note in her file about Samantha Jones?

Then she saw Kippy, the baby's familiar face creased in outrage as she struggled in the matronly foster mother's embrace.

Samantha held out her arms.

Kippy stopped in midhowl and held out her arms toward her aunt. Seconds later, the baby clinging tightly to her, Samantha fought away sudden tears. The dried tears on Kippy's face told their own story, as did the baby's clinging grip on Samantha. She'd been with strangers, lonely and miserable despite the obvious warmth and maternal urges of the foster mother.

Now, said her tight grip on Samantha's shirt, she was with someone of her own, and she wasn't letting go.

"I just realized." Samantha said unsteadily, "I don't have a car seat."

"Her infant seat came with her," said the foster mother. "I'll get it and her diaper bag."

Brenda hissed, "It's not enough that the child cares for you. You're a single woman with a high-powered career in Seattle. How much time are you going to have for a small child?"

"As much time as she needs," said Samantha, although she was filled with her own doubts about her ability to mother Kippy. What did she know about looking after a baby? What if she couldn't give Kippy the loving security Dorothy had given Samantha and Sarah?

Brenda doubted her. How much weight would the judge give to the social worker's testimony? Surely he wouldn't deny Samantha's claim to Kippy? She was Dorothy's choice, Kippy's aunt, a mature woman who earned an excellent salary and lived in a spacious apartment with a room available as a nursery. She'd never been in trouble with the law, wasn't promiscuous, and was Kippy's only relative other than Dorothy.

Samantha vowed she would win the social worker over before the protection hearing.

Outside, she shifted Kippy and opened the front passenger door.

"You can't put her in the front seat!" shrieked Brenda.

Samantha froze. "Why not?"

"The air bag! Don't you know anything about child safety? If you're in an accident and the air bag inflates, that child could be horribly injured, even killed."

"You're right. Thank you." She made herself smile at

Brenda and turned to the back door. She'd seen items on the news about air bags and children, hadn't really listened, she supposed, because it didn't seem to apply to her.

Kippy began to cry when Samantha put her into the car, was shrieking by the time Samantha climbed into the front seat and started the engine. Did she need a bottle? A new diaper?

Kippy gulped in the middle of her cry.

"We're going to visit Dorothy," Samantha told her.

Brenda was staring at her through the window. Samantha didn't know what to do: Drive away, or get out and pick up Kippy and try to soothe her under Brenda's watchful eyes.

"I'll change your diaper at the hospital," she promised Kippy, shoving the car into gear.

Two blocks from the hospital, the baby miraculously stopped crying, but when Samantha parked in the visitor's lot, Kippy immediately began fussing again and didn't stop until she'd been picked up. Walking to the hospital, Samantha realized Kippy had grown heavy enough to cause aching arms by the time she got inside.

Samantha had phoned earlier and got Dorothy's room number. Now she walked straight to the elevators, hoping no one would challenge her. Babies probably weren't allowed, but surely both Kippy and Dorothy needed this meeting, and Samantha needed it, too, both to reassure herself and to find out more about Dorothy's health.

Kippy started fussing again. Was she hungry? Two months ago at Easter she'd been living on bottles of baby formula and a couple of spoons of cereal at bedtime. Had that changed? Did Dorothy have formula in the house? There was none in the diaper bag.

When Kippy caught sight of Dorothy, she immediately began squirming in Samantha's arms, reaching for her great-grandmother.

Dorothy looked pale and haggard. She looked—well, she looked her age.

"You got her! Oh, darling, I knew you would!"

Samantha gave the baby into her grandmother's eager arms and sank into the chair beside the bed.

"Oh, Kippy, darling," crooned Dorothy. "Samantha, honey, thank you."

Samantha's arms were aching from the baby, and she hadn't yet pulled off the miracle Dorothy thought she'd already achieved—making Kippy safe and secure. Looking at her grandmother's pale, drawn face, she realized the doctor must be right. Dorothy was ill, very ill.

"Kippy's so glad to see you," said Samantha. She needed to question Dorothy, to know just what the medical situation was, how long she'd been sick, whether this nursing home the doctor talked about was what Dorothy herself wanted and needed.

"I'll never forgive that doctor," muttered Dorothy, still clinging to Kippy, although the baby was now struggling for freedom.

Samantha held out her arms and Dorothy surrendered Kippy. Her grandmother looked even paler now and seemed to be having trouble breathing. With the baby sitting on her lap, still squirming, Samantha said, "I'm worried about your health. If you're not happy with your doctor, I'll arrange for—"

"Not happy? I'm furious. What right had he to go behind my back and do that to Kippy?" Dorothy's breath came in short hard bursts as if the energy of her anger exhausted her.

"Grandma, he thinks you should go into a nursing home."

"He's delusional. A couple of days and I'll be fine. I overdid it a bit and had a few cramps, and he's ready to call the funeral home. I won't have it, Samantha!" She stopped to take a few breaths, said more quietly, "If you'll just look after Kippy for a few days, I'll be home and all this nonsense will be over."

Holding her niece in her arms, Samantha knew the judge wouldn't give custody of Kippy back to Dorothy, not after the medical report he'd seen today. A few cramps, Dorothy said, but the doctor called it congestive heart failure, and two days in the hospital had left her looking old and weak. Samantha couldn't imagine Dorothy confined to a nursing home, but what were the alternatives?

She needed to talk to Dorothy's doctor and talk to other doctors, too. She had an uneasy feeling that she might have to battle for custody of her grandmother as well as her niece.

"We'll work it out," she promised. "Dexter's coming up to the hospital to talk to you tomorrow morning. Right now, you and Kippy both need a rest. I'm taking her home to Gabriola, and I'll call you in the morning."

Wayne was right, Samantha thought as she walked out of the hospital carrying a struggling six-month baby in her arms. She wasn't superwoman. It was one thing to say, "I'll look after it," to the judge, the social worker, her grandmother, and Cal, but just how was she going to manage?

She'd promised Cal she'd look after his recruitment open house, but today she'd stood in court and promised the judge she'd stay in Canada for two weeks. She'd chosen Kippy over Cal Tremaine and his company.

Samantha knew what it was like to be a child ignored in the chaos of adults' lives. There was no way she'd let that happen to Kippy, even if it meant giving up the job she loved.

Four

I won't need you.

Cal couldn't have said why the memory of Sam saying those words bothered him so much. The idea of her *needing* anyone seemed laughable—she was the most capable woman he knew. Hell, the most capable *person*. It hadn't irritated him until now. After all, when a man hired someone to look after an administrative nightmare, he'd be crazy to resent her for competence.

Cal sure as hell wasn't crazy—at least, he never had been before. But here he was, on the eve of doubling the size of his company, which was enough to give a man ulcers, unable to stop thinking of the shadows in Sam's eyes, the evasiveness in her voice.

Had she always been evasive? If so, why hadn't he noticed?

What kind of problems would put a woman like Sam off balance? She'd been prickly this morning, and he'd sensed ragged emotions, disconcerting when he knew her as calm and perfectly controlled.

Two hours after she dropped him off, he called her cell phone only to be told by an annoying computerized voice that the caller he wished to reach was away from her phone. Hadn't she said she would have her cell phone and computer with her? What if he'd been calling with an urgent message? What if *he* needed her?

What the hell was up with Samantha Jones?

Why hadn't she told him where she was staying? She'd grown up on Gabriola Island—was she staying there? His memory of the island included a network of little gravel roads that could take hours to cruise. And she might not be there at all. She could be here in Nanaimo, in a hotel somewhere. He'd already checked the Coast Bastion to be sure she didn't have a reservation, but he would check the others too.

I've been working eighteen hours a day for weeks and I deserve a few hours off the leash.

He couldn't deny that, but damn it, every instinct he had told him that something was wrong. What if this personal emergency led to her quitting? Why had he let her get away with being so evasive? When an employee took time off for a family emergency, surely it was normal to explain the damned emergency?

Sam hadn't explained, not really. Her grandmother was sick, but she'd said it wasn't serious, hadn't she? And why couldn't she meet him tomorrow at six, but six-thirty was OK?

Because she would be sleeping on Gabriola Island, and she'd have to take a ferry to get to Nanaimo? He grabbed the phone book and one quick call gave him the information that the first morning ferry off Gabriola sailed at quarter to six. A twenty minute ride, then what? Ten minutes to unload the ferry? She wouldn't be able to be at the hotel at six, but six-thirty—

He found the Gabriola Island section of the phone book. Four listings for Jones. He could call them all, looking for Sam's parents or her grandmother, but was Sam's grandmother named Jones? For all he knew, Jones might not be Sam's birth name. What if she'd married, then divorced, but kept her husband's name?

The idea of Sam married bothered the hell out of him.

Damn the woman! Why couldn't she have stayed the way he knew her—cool, remote, and capable?

She would have filled out next-of-kin information on her personnel forms.

He might have hesitated if he'd had to ask Jason in human resources for the information. He didn't want company gossip going around about Cal asking for Sam's personal information, but personnel's records were on computer and he had the master password.

Five minutes after he formed the thought he'd connected his portable to the hotel's modem port and made a virtual private network connection to Tremaine's.

Samantha M. Jones's next of kin was listed as Dorothy Marshall, who lived at 1401 Crocker Road on Gabriola Island.

Kippy wouldn't stop screaming.

Samantha had bathed her, setting her on the antislip rubber mat in six inches of warm water in the big bathtub. Kippy hadn't been able to sit on her own at four months, but tonight she sat solidly in place, a rubber duck clenched in one fist as she splashed and emitted high, happy shrieks while Samantha soaped and rinsed her. Then she'd eaten the half jar of peaches Dorothy said she took with her cereal each night before bed, and guzzled her bottle.

The baby was obviously sleepy, her head drooping against Samantha's shoulder as she carried her to the little room at the back of the house. But as soon as Kippy's head touched the sheet, her tiny body scrunched up and she began screaming.

Samantha desperately needed a book on baby care. She should have bought one at the mall near the ferry terminal. Why hadn't she thought of it before she brought Kippy home?

She'd bathed Kippy, fed her, changed her diapers, held

her, and played with her on an average of one weekend a month. But she realized now that whenever Kippy cried, it was Dorothy she reached for. Samantha had no experience with calming baby hysterics. If it weren't for the fact that Kippy stopped screaming each time Samantha picked her up, she'd think the child was ill.

She carried Kippy to the kitchen table where she'd set up her portable computer and sat down with her. "Why don't we work together?" she murmured. "You just lie there and fall asleep, and I'll hook up my modem and check my e-mail."

Kippy squirmed and began crying. Samantha rubbed her back, talked to her, and even sang a half-remembered version of "Old MacDonald Had a Farm."

Kippy screamed.

"Honey, I don't know what to do for you."

She didn't want to worry Dorothy with a phone call to her hospital room, but perhaps Diane knew some magic cure for whatever was troubling Kippy.

When Samantha stood and walked to the telephone at the end of the kitchen counter, Kippy fell magically silent, only to begin whimpering again as Samantha dialed Diane's phone number.

"She may be teething," said Diane, "but it's more likely separation anxiety."

"Separation anxiety?" echoed Samantha.

"I noticed it the last couple of times Dorothy left her with me. It's normal, usually around the time babies start to notice the difference between people and realize that Mom—in this case, Dorothy—isn't always there. They go through a stage where they cling if they think Mom is going to go away and cry when she does."

"She's crying every time I put her down." Kippy was worried, anxious because Dorothy wasn't here. Samantha couldn't blame her. "What should I do?"

"Try walking her, or sitting in the rocking chair upstairs.

The motion will soothe her. If you're desperate, you could try putting her in the infant seat and taking her for a drive. That always used to put my babies to sleep."

Miraculously, Kippy had fallen silent again. Samantha turned her head and found the baby's head resting on her shoulder, eyes open and staring.

"Thanks, Diane. Right now she seems OK."

"That will probably change when you put her down. Good luck, Mom."

"Thanks. Diane, I have to go to Seattle tomorrow afternoon to tidy up some loose ends before I'm free." Brenda Simonson hadn't liked the fact of those loose ends, and the judge had given Brenda the power to take Kippy away again if she thought it necessary. "I'll be back late tomorrow night. Can you look after Kippy for me?"

"I'd love to. Anytime, Sam. I'm almost always home, and I enjoy Kippy. I wish mine were babies again."

Now she needed to talk to Cal.

Samantha hung up the phone. With Kippy's wide eyes staring at her, she knew there wasn't much sense trying to put her down in the crib again. She carried Kippy upstairs to the room she and Sarah had slept in through their teenage years, the room that had been her own mother's as a child.

After Samantha and Sarah had moved out, Sarah to marriage and Samantha to university, Dorothy had replaced the twin beds with a double, but otherwise left the room as it was. The bookshelves held a chaotic mixture of romances and kids adventure stories, with a couple of school textbooks mixed in. The contents of the closets were more up to date. Samantha and Sarah had sorted through the closet last summer and had given most of their old clothes away to the Goodwill.

Samantha put Kippy on the big bed. This time, instead of screaming, the baby squirmed a little, then shoved her thumb into her mouth and stared at Samantha as she stripped off her damp blouse and slacks.

"Next time, kid, I'll change before I bathe you," she promised, pulling the pins from her hair and finger combing it as the long mass tumbled over her shoulders.

Kippy gurgled, blinked, and reached for a strand of hair.

"Wait a minute," said Samantha, pulling out a pair of faded jeans and a loose sweatshirt. "You're wide awake, aren't you? Completely wide awake."

She stepped into the closet and grabbed a hanger for her suit.

Kippy started crying.

"You're telling me it *is* separation anxiety?" Her voice seemed to calm the baby, so she kept talking, saying, "I'm here, Kippy. Right here. I'm not going anywhere."

Kippy gulped and made a noise that might have been a gurgle.

How did Dorothy do this? Did she pace the floor with Kippy every night, soothing her anxieties? Or would Kippy settle down if Dorothy were in the house? This baby tending took a lot of energy. The doctor and social worker were right—a woman with congestive heart failure had enough to worry about without looking after a small baby.

How long would it take Samantha to learn the tricks of being a mother? And when would Kippy fall asleep, so Samantha could call Cal and give him the bad news?

Cal tried Sam's cell phone a couple of times throughout the afternoon, as well as the home number of Dorothy Marshall, Sam's next of kin.

At five-thirty, he had dinner in the hotel's dining room, hardly tasting the food. Afterward, in his room, he tried both numbers again. He wasn't sure what the hell he meant to say if she answered, but his anger had been building all day. He was certainly entitled to more of an explanation than she'd given him. He disliked being treated as the enemy, as someone she needed to keep secrets from.

They needed to clear the air.

He knew it would make more sense to wait until tomorrow, when she was committed to meeting him at six-thirty. Earlier, he'd decided that instead of taking her to the helicopter in the morning, he'd take her somewhere for breakfast and get some answers. He was pretty sure, though, that Sam wasn't going to tell him a damned thing more than she already had.

After a day spent cooling his heels in the small town of Nanaimo, he'd had his fill of coal mines, stunning harbor views, and waiting. To hell with phoning her. She'd obviously mastered the art of deflecting personal questions, and he wanted answers. He knew nothing about this woman he was planning to put on his board, except that she'd turned his company into a well-oiled machine and given him the chance to concentrate on what he did best.

He couldn't figure out why the hell it had never bothered him until now, but it damn well did. He needed to know what made her tick. He'd go to her island now, tonight. If he'd guessed wrong and she wasn't at Dorothy Marshall's house, he'd have wasted a bit of time, but so what? He'd already wasted the whole damned day.

He called a car rental company and impatiently waited for them to turn up with a car for him. Once he had the keys, he realized he didn't remember where the Gabriola Island ferry terminal was and had to ask at the desk. He got to the terminal about seven, only to be told the ferry had just left. The next sailing was at five minutes to eight.

In fact, the ferry finally sailed at eight-thirty, and he spent the twenty-minute harbor crossing standing on deck, staring at the long, low shape of Gabriola Island with the cool evening wind blowing through his hair. As the ferry approached Gabriola, the clouds shifted from white and gray to shades of red and pink. Water, islands, and flaming sky—a world away from Tremaine's hectic atmosphere.

When the ferry docked, he drove off and pulled into a parking spot in front of the pub. Inside, he asked for directions. Crocker Road was miles away, almost at the far end of the island. Light faded as he drove east on the two-lane pavement, trees crowded on both sides of the winding road. Ahead, he saw evergreen branches stretching to touch each other over the road, and when he entered this tunnel protected by overhanging branches, he seemed to have driven into another world. The cathedral of trees blocked the small amount of light left in the sky. He'd seen houses earlier, but now all sign of human habitation had disappeared, except for the road itself.

Ahead, something moved at the side of the road.

He braked and found himself staring at a deer—a doe, he realized. She stood at the edge of the road, staring at him. Something in her eyes reminded him of Samantha. Then, suddenly, she turned and fled into the trees.

He took a deep breath and drove on, deciding he'd been right to follow his instincts and take the trip to Gabriola. Here on the island, it would be more difficult for Sam to hide behind her cool mask. He hadn't suspected it was a mask until yesterday, but if this island was the place she'd come from, the part of Sam that he got to see was only the tip of the iceberg.

Perhaps a mile later, he drove out of the tunnel of overhanging trees. A farm on his left . . . another on his right. Power lines overhead. He spotted the turn and followed his instructions, turning right, then right again a mile later, onto gravel road. Population density about one house every quarter mile, he decided. Less, if you counted the farms and the unpopulated tunnel of trees.

Most of the light had left the sky by the time he turned onto Crocker Road. Nine-thirty. According to his mother's rigid etiquette, he'd arrived too late for a social call.

Someone had put the house number on a tree at the road. He couldn't see the house, but the drive began just to the right of the tree, leading uphill through tall evergreens. He turned into the shadowy drive, easing the rental car over humps and bumps. Someone should bring in machinery, gravel, asphalt, to make this long drive less of a hazard.

He was halfway up the slope, wondering if there really *was* a house, when he spotted a log home nestled under evergreen trees. He wasn't sure what he would have done if the lights had been out—probably knocked on the door anyway. He didn't know exactly why it felt so imperative to confront Sam *now*, tonight, but it did.

He pulled up behind the white Ford Escort with the rental company sticker on the bumper. At least he'd got the right place. Beside the house, he could see a battered old Honda, telling him she wasn't alone here.

He got out of the car, slammed the door behind him. No one appeared to investigate the noise. Those thick log walls probably masked the sound. He crossed the open grassy area in front of the house and stepped onto the veranda, touched a comfortable-looking wicker chair that could have been older than he was. The varnished wooden door was set in a frame with a tall, narrow window to its right. He could see an oak dining table through the window, a portable computer open on the table—Sam's.

No sign of life, neither Sam nor the Honda's owner.

Standing on the log cabin's veranda, he couldn't imagine Sam in this setting. She was a city creature, a businesswoman from her immaculate low shoes to her smoothly disciplined hair. She didn't belong here.

Was she inside with her grandmother?

Who really lived in this cabin and what the hell was Sam doing here? What was so important that she'd leave Seattle on the eve of a major event she'd planned, to come to this tame wilderness, to commune with deer and stare out at magnificent sunsets over tall, green trees?

He hammered on the door.

No answer. He waited a minute, knocked again, then prowled the veranda. If she were inside with her grandmother, surely she'd get up and answer.

So it wasn't her grandmother. A lover, and with the dining room and what he could see of the living room empty, they could be in the back of the house. In a bedroom.

He shoved his jacket aside and jammed his hands into his pockets. Maybe he didn't know Sam beyond the business world, but he was damned sure she wouldn't walk out on the open house preparations to go off and tangle the sheets with a lover.

He heard the sound and spun in time to see the door open. He closed the distance with two long strides, froze when he realized it wasn't Sam at the door.

The woman had a baby held against her chest, and had long, shining, rich brown hair streaming over the shoulder opposite the baby. It must be almost to her waist, the hair . . . and her eyes. . . .

He stepped back instead of forward. Sam's eyes, her mouth. She was barefoot, for crying out loud, and—how had she managed to hide all that hair?

"Cal." Her voice was flat, not Sam's voice at all, but this *was* Sam. "You'd better come in."

She didn't step back to let him through the door, and he couldn't seem to stop staring. "You've got a baby."

She shifted the baby in her arms. "I suppose I have."

He didn't know what the hell to say. The baby wasn't more than a few months old. How the hell could she have a baby? He would have noticed that, wouldn't he? Maybe he hadn't known about the hair, hadn't realized her bare feet would look so—well, sexy. Hadn't known she even owned a pair of jeans. But he sure as hell would have noticed if she'd been pregnant.

"How old is he?"

"She." Sam hugged the baby tighter. "Six months old."
She seemed to realize she was blocking the door then and
stepped back. "Close the door behind you, please."

She walked away from him, swaying with the weight of
the baby, all long, lean legs and a waterfall of tempting
hair. In bed, that hair would—

Cal closed the door with a bit too much force, then
cleared his throat. Six months. Maybe he was unobservant,
but not that damned unobservant!

"It's not your baby." He couldn't remember when he'd
been more taken aback than by the sight of his cool second-
in-command holding a baby, her hair down to her waist and
her feet naked.

She turned to face him, still holding the baby, who
seemed to be soundly asleep.

"It's not your baby," he repeated.

"Genetically, that's true." She sounded like Sam now,
except there wasn't a trace of a smile. "I tried to call you."

"I'm here. You can tell me whatever it is in person." He
felt his jaw flex with tension, said, "That child in your arms
doesn't look like your grandmother to me."

She just stared at him, until he said, "You told me you
had to look after some business for your grandmother."
Watching her hold the baby was unnerving him, or maybe
it was her hair, the odd look in her eyes. "Shouldn't the
baby be in bed?"

"I'll try putting her to bed again," Sam said. "Make
yourself comfortable in the living room."

She disappeared and he almost called out for her to
watch her step, because she'd strung the modem wire from
her computer across the archway into the kitchen, where
he presumed it was plugged into a wall. But she stepped
gracefully over the wire and disappeared into a hallway to
the right of the kitchen.

He prowled into the living room, studied an aging, overstuffed sofa and chair, a big window looking out on a shadowy stand of cedar trees, a set of split log stairs leading up into a loft. She'd grown up on Gabriola Island. Here, in this house? Or was this someone else's house? It said Dorothy Marshall in her employment records, listing this address. But Cal hadn't checked the phone book to see if Dorothy Marshall really lived here. This house could belong to someone else. The baby's father, perhaps? Or Sam's parents?

Just whose baby was Sam putting to bed? Where was the owner of the Honda he'd seen outside? And what the hell had happened to the Sam he relied on every day?

He heard Sam returning, turned his back to the window, and watched. When she saw him, she reached one hand up and swept her hair back over her shoulder, as if seeing him made her aware that she didn't have her hair up.

"I think she's really asleep this time," she said, and after a few seconds he realized she was talking about the baby.

"I've never seen your hair down before."

"It's not businesslike."

He said harshly, "The computer industry has a pretty loose dress code."

She shrugged and that half smile appeared. "People tell me I look about sixteen with my hair down. It's hard to get people to take you seriously when you look like a teenager."

She looked all woman, and as she moved he suddenly realized that she wasn't wearing a bra. The sweatshirt was thick, loose, but when she moved he saw the motion of her breasts.

He jammed his hands in his pockets again. The last time he'd felt so uncomfortable in a woman's presence he'd been fifteen.

"It's time for an explanation," he said harshly.

"Do you want coffee? A soft drink? I don't think Dorothy keeps alcohol in the house, so the choices are limited."

"Who's Dorothy?"

"My grandmother."

"So there is a grandmother. I'll have coffee."

When she brought the coffee into the living room, he was staring at Dorothy's collection of pictures and certificates in the stairwell leading up to the loft. He pointed at a picture of a young girl sitting on a tall horse. "Is this you?"

"My mother. She was fifteen there." The picture had been taken less than a year before her mother met an American draft dodger on Drumbeg Beach, fell in love, and ran away with him only weeks later.

"You look very much alike."

"Looks can be deceptive."

He shot her a penetrating glance, then moved to the next frame, a document certifying that Moonbeam Jones had successfully completed the beginner's swimming class.

"Who's Moonbeam Jones?" he asked as he took the steaming mug from her hand.

Samantha had been expecting Cal to question her about the baby, about her reason for being here, about almost anything but her mother and Moonbeam. No one had called her Moonbeam in so many years, except her mother of course, and her grandmother who sometimes slipped.

She took her own coffee mug and settled on the big armchair before she answered. At this point, keeping her private life to herself was the least of her worries.

"My mother had me at the end of the sixties—hippies, flower children. She named me Moonbeam and my sister Star. I had swimming lessons here, one summer when I visited." The first time Dorothy rescued Samantha and Susan from foster care, at the ages of ten and eight.

"Samantha M. Jones. That's what the *m* stands for?"

"Yes. Cal, there's something I need to tell you."

He stood there at the bottom of the stairs, cup in one hand, staring at her. Waiting.

"Would you please sit down? You're making me nervous."

It took him a minute to decide, long enough for her to realize that something had put him in a temper. What she had to tell him wasn't going to improve his mood.

She waited until he was settled on the sofa, until he'd taken a sip of the coffee she'd fixed. She wanted to wait longer, but putting it off wasn't going to change anything.

"I can't go back to Seattle tomorrow morning. I can go in the afternoon, for the open house, if you can give me a ride with the chopper." She sucked in a deep breath, realized there wasn't any good way to do this. "I'll have to leave before the open house is over. I have to be back to Nanaimo before the last Gabriola Island ferry sails at ten fifty-five. I know it's bad timing, but I need two weeks off."

She heard Cal set his cup on the end table, realized she was staring at the floor instead of him, and forced herself to meet his eyes.

"What the hell is going on?" he demanded. His eyes looked furious, hot, and she had difficulty holding his gaze.

Some hair had fallen forward over her face. She pushed it back with her free hand and muttered, "I should have put my hair up."

"You should explain."

She cradled her cup in both hands and managed to take in a big breath without it being obvious. She was a businesswoman. She'd better stop sounding like an airhead.

"The baby is my sister's daughter. My grandmother's been looking after her, but Dorothy's in the hospital now. I know it's bad timing, but I'll keep control of everything from here, by phone and e-mail."

"This doesn't make sense," growled Cal, pushing himself to his feet and pacing to the window. "Where's your sister? Why can't she look after her own child?"

"She and her husband died in an air crash last December."

"Last December?" He was glaring at her. "Five months ago?"

"Yes." She swallowed. "Two days before Christmas."

He shoved a hand through his hair, freeing the curls he must have brushed into submission before he came. "You came back from your holidays last Christmas, and I remember asking you if you'd enjoyed yourself, and you said it was good to be back. Nothing more. Your sister died, and you came back to work as if nothing happened?"

With the exception of crying last Christmas with Dorothy, Samantha hadn't cried in front of anyone since she was ten years old. Tears were threatening now, and she was afraid to speak because she mustn't cry in front of Cal.

"Why didn't you tell me?" Cal demanded.

"I didn't tell anyone. I couldn't talk about it without crying, so I . . . I just didn't."

He raked his hand through his hair again, then picked up his mug and took a big swallow. "So—so, this baby? You're looking after her while your grandmother's sick?"

"Maybe permanently. My grandmother is going into a nursing home."

He took long seconds to consider that, then demanded, "Is there some reason you can't look after her in Seattle?"

"It depends on the judge. But right now, no."

"The *judge?*"

"I'm applying for custody, but right now I can't take Kippy out of the country. The judge gave permission for me to look after her, but I'm being . . . supervised. I have to stay here."

He looked as if he wanted to pace. She wished he'd leave.

"Supervised?" he demanded. "By whom?"

"The Ministry of Children and Families. A social worker. They've applied for custody; there's another hearing in two weeks. I need to stay until it's settled, until I have custody, and I have to prove I'm a good mother for Kippy. I'm sorry, Cal, but it's probably best if I resign."

Oh, God! Why had she said that? She didn't want to resign at all. She'd find a way to keep things together without that. Dorothy said she didn't have serious health problems, that the doctor was wrong, and Cal might want her at Tremaine's enough to get over this involuntary absence.

Right now he was glaring at her so angrily she had to fight her impulse to cringe back into the chair. Then he walked past her, to the front door, opened it, and stepped through.

Confused, she followed him. Was he going to drive away without a word?

She found him on the veranda, staring at the grassy slope below the house. Bewildered, she watched as he jumped lightly down to the ground and walked away from the house, away from the car he'd brought. She needed to take back her words. She wasn't resigning. No way.

He came back a moment later.

"I assume you have a baby-sitter lined up for tomorrow afternoon?"

"Yes. Diane, a neighbor."

"I'll pick you up here at twelve-thirty."

"You don't need to. I can drive into town."

"There's room here for me to land the chopper." He jumped back up onto the veranda, and she backed two steps away from him before she stopped herself. "Twelve-thirty," he said. "You'll be ready?"

"Yes."

Then she watched him drive away, wondering what was going to happen tomorrow. He was upset, she knew that, but tomorrow she'd reassure him and she'd take back that suggestion about a resignation.

She'd intended to tell him on the phone, using her business voice. Instead she'd worn jeans and a sweatshirt, her hair hanging around her face like a child's. As she turned to go back into the house, she stubbed her toe on the old wicker chair.

And bare feet! She hadn't even had her shoes on.

Five

Cal parked the rental car in the lot across from the hotel and locked it.

Because he knew he'd go nuts pacing the anonymous hotel room, he headed downhill and found himself exploring a deserted waterfront mall sporting a closed cappuccino bar, art gallery, and souvenir shop.

He finally emerged on a concrete walk bordered by grassy slopes and strode north along the curve of the harbor. He couldn't see another soul, although he heard the muted sound of vehicles up on Front Street where he'd parked the car.

Sam. . . .

He couldn't get over the memory of Sam, barefoot and rumpled, holding a baby in her arms. Sam walking into the living room of that log cabin, her breasts moving seductively under an oversize sweatshirt.

It didn't matter what she looked like with a baby in her arms. The point was that his second-in-command was talking about quitting. Somehow, between yesterday and today, his administrative genius, the person he relied on above all others, had transformed into a barefoot woman with a baby in her arms.

He couldn't afford to lose her. Sam had spoiled him, and after a year without administrative hassles, he shuddered at the thought of going back to how it had been before Samantha Jones—Samantha *Moonbeam* Jones— saved him from bureaucratic psychosis.

He certainly wasn't going to accept her resignation. From what she said, it wouldn't be more than a couple of weeks before she could return to Seattle. Meanwhile, he'd show his face in the admin offices more than usual, and she'd delegate and organize via phone—Sam was, after all, an expert at organizing, at hiring the kind of people one *could* delegate to. One way or another, they'd get through the next fourteen days until Sam returned. She'd come back to Seattle with the kid, who would go into day care. Then Sam's world—and Cal's—would go back to normal.

Which didn't explain why Cal was prowling a cement pathway through manicured grass on the edge of Nanaimo's harbor, staring at the lights across the water, worried instead of wondering what the hell those lights *were*. Not Gabriola Island, which lay at the other end of Nanaimo Harbor. Maybe Newcastle Island, which the museum exhibit labeled a historic coal mining site. If that was Newcastle, there would be an old tunnel running under the harbor, joining it to Nanaimo. Built to carry coal from Newcastle.

Which, at the moment, he couldn't care less about.

The trouble was, Sam wasn't Sam anymore. She'd turned into a woman with a baby and a potentially complicated private life, either of which could be relied on to cause problems in the future. Being a single parent had to be a massive task at the best of times. When he thought of the chaos he and his sister had created in their parents' lives as children, he didn't figure Sam was in for much fun with this solitary baby-tending business. Even with day care, she'd be exhausted in a matter of weeks if she tried to keep up her previous pace.

Did she have a man in her life? A woman who hadn't mentioned losing her sister over the Christmas vacation certainly wasn't going to fill her boss in on her love life.

If she did have a love life, it stood to reason that now she was a family woman, she'd be thinking about marriage, a father for the baby. She wouldn't want the child growing up fatherless.

A girl like Sam—smart, sensible, and sexy—all she'd have to do to obtain a husband was to let some suitable guy know she was in the market.

And if looking after Kippy weren't enough to wear her out and make her decide she wanted a job that was less demanding, then having a husband—and, probably, a baby of her own pretty soon—would do it. That tiny, sleeping baby was just the first step toward disaster for Cal. In the end, she'd leave him.

Cal wasn't going to wait for Sam to get to the point of leaving him. He would come up with an offer she couldn't refuse, one that would keep her exactly where he wanted her—at Tremaine's.

By three o'clock Friday afternoon, the lineup outside Tremaine's extended east along the block as far as the television camera could see. Then the doors opened and candidates began pouring off the elevators into the reception area.

Three hours later, Samantha returned to the television monitor in the reception area and found candidates still lined up beyond the camera's view. She collared Jason, the human resources manager.

"We're not going to be able to process all these people."

"I know, but we can't go any faster. I've told Wendy to start taking them coffee."

"Good idea. And send one of the volunteers out asking for developers. If we don't get to everyone, we don't want to miss any developers."

"Samantha, with all this publicity, we've got about twenty

good developer candidates already lined up for interviews next week in addition to those we screened today."

"Good," said Cal's voice behind her. "But check the lineup for developers."

Samantha turned to face Cal. All day she'd been jumpy around him. Nerves, not knowing what was going to happen with her job. This morning she'd talked to Dorothy's doctor, who spoke about congestive heart failure and Dorothy's symptoms—chest pain, palpitations, erratic pulse, shortness of breath, weakness, and fatigue.

The idea of Dorothy living in a nursing home upset Samantha horribly. Although Dorothy still insisted she wasn't seriously ill, this morning she'd agreed that Dexter should file for a custody transfer to ensure Kippy's safety.

Her grandmother would hate leaving the house she'd lived in ever since James, Samantha's late grandfather, brought her to Gabriola as a bride. Was there some way Dorothy could come to Seattle, live with Samantha and Kippy? Would she need nursing care? Samantha wasn't sure her own medical insurance would cover Dorothy's care, but she earned good money.

This morning, as Cal checked her seat belt in the helicopter, he'd said, "You're not leaving Tremaine's. We'll talk about details later."

Details. The way he'd said it made her uneasy. After last night, he was seeing her as one of those women who couldn't be relied on, whose home life perpetually interfered with work. If Cal believed she couldn't give one hundred percent to her job, he wouldn't want her in charge. And if she had to work under someone who'd been appointed to her old position, she'd rather leave.

She was a single parent now—or would be, officially, once the judge agreed. All day she'd been trying to make herself believe that she could handle both her job at Tremaine's and a young baby. And Dorothy, who would need specialists, second opinions, treatment. It was all going to take time, too much time.

Now, with the muted roar of dozens of voices in conversation filling Tremaine's reception area, she acknowledged the truth. She worked long hours, exciting hours doing a job she loved. But how much time would that leave for Kippy?

Samantha's mother had sacrificed her daughters' welfare to her own obsessive needs for romantic love again and again. Samantha wasn't tempted by the lure of love and romance, but wasn't she doing almost the same thing as her mother, trying to keep her exciting job, her position, prestige, and power—all at Kippy's expense, and Dorothy's?

Until yesterday, she'd been a businesswoman with her future clearly mapped out. That future hadn't included children or a family, because she wasn't going to take on anything she couldn't make a success of and she'd *never* neglect a child. Her passion for her work meant she might not make an adequate wife and mother, might not be able to give enough.

The obvious answer was to avoid motherhood and marriage, but that decision had been taken out of her hands. Now she *was* a mother, and she vowed to be a good one.

She should have been with Kippy today. Brenda Simonson was right. The baby needed stability, needed to know Samantha was going to be there for her.

Samantha was needed at the open house, too. It would have been irresponsible of her to duck it, but the fact was, she'd chosen Tremaine's needs over Kippy's today. It mustn't happen again. Dorothy had never let Samantha or her sister down, and Samantha wasn't going to let Kippy down either.

She had to choose—Tremaine's or Kippy—and when she put it that way, there was no choice at all.

"We're leaving in forty minutes," Cal said.

"Okay," she said in the most businesslike tone she could manage. "I've got a few things to see to first."

She loved working for Cal, loved the constant challenge, the excitement, loved knowing she made a big difference to the company. But she couldn't sacrifice Kippy's welfare to her own selfish desires. She'd go back to consulting, where she had more control of her hours. She'd take only a few clients, work part-time.

Later she'd tell Cal; then she'd work with him—mostly from Gabriola—to find her own replacement. Monday, she'd phone Tim Mirimar and tell him she needed a month to get her life organized, but then she'd be available for a half-time load of consulting jobs.

Meanwhile, she had responsibilities at Tremaine's, and she'd find a way to fulfill them without sacrificing Kippy.

Forty minutes after Cal spoke to her in the reception area, she'd talked to Jason to arrange a telephone meeting Monday morning and talked to Marcy to tell her she'd be out of the office for a while. She managed five minutes with the head of development, two with the technical pre-sales director to arrange for his monthly report to be delivered in a conference call Tuesday. She'd also managed a brief conversation with Cal's assistant, Dee, to arrange daily telephone meetings. She would have liked time to go to her apartment and pack a few things as well, but she had casual clothes on Gabriola Island, and with her computer and cell phone she'd get by.

She had to be back on Gabriola tonight, for Kippy.

In the helicopter, Cal handed her a set of headphones, but she waited until he was airborne and flying over open water before she spoke.

"We need to talk about my job."

"When we get to the island," he said.

"I have to pick up Kippy as soon as we get back. She's likely to be cranky. Now's the best time to talk."

"I can wait."

What did that mean? He could wait to talk another time? Or he could wait until she got the baby settled? Ever since she'd told Cal she needed to go to Nanaimo for personal reasons, he'd been acting differently and she'd been off balance. She didn't want to have a business conversation with him with Kippy liable to start crying at any minute. On the other hand, she could see from the set look on Cal's face that he wasn't going to discuss business here in the helicopter. Actually, looking at his face made her want to put the whole thing off for a week or two, because she'd never seen him quite so grim.

It didn't matter. She had no choice but to leave, and although she'd naturally wanted a glowing reference, she had enough consulting credits that she didn't need it.

She'd miss him. The knowledge popped into her mind uninvited. She'd become accustomed to their frequent conversations about Tremaine's, to the way an idea would set fire to his eyes and her own pulse seemed to quicken with his excitement.

She studied the mass of Vancouver Island looming ahead, evergreen mountains and low hills. The smaller islands were indistinguishable from this angle. The whole thing looked like one massive land mass filling the horizon. She couldn't pick out Gabriola Island from the others.

When they landed, she'd tell him. . . .

When the helicopter settled gently onto the grass in front of Dorothy's house, Samantha saw Cal's hands move on the controls. Then the blur of the chopper's rotor resolved into a single blade, sweeping circles ever more slowly.

Samantha unclipped her seat belt and Cal turned his head, his hands still on the controls. There wouldn't be a better time.

"Cal, I'm leaving Tremaine's."

His eyes narrowed. Irritation? Impatience? Anger? Perhaps all three. She told herself not to *read* him, that he wasn't going to like her announcement, but he'd have no choice but to accept it. Better to get it over quickly, while he still had daylight to fly to Nanaimo.

"We'll talk later," he said grimly.

"It has to be now." Her heart pounded hard, as if she were at the wheel of her car in a skid on black ice. "I've done a good job for you, Cal, but now everything's changed. I can't give Tremaine's the same commitment, the same amount of time I have been until now. Kippy has to come first. I'll help you find a replacement, sit in on the interviews, advise you. I'm going back to Mirimar Consulting, part-time."

Cal was glowering at the line of cedar trees that edged up against the back of the house. Tight lips, rigid jaw.

"I'll finish the consulting job for Tremaine's," she said, trying for lightness now, telling her pulse to quiet. Employees quit all the time, and leaving might make an unpleasant scene, but it wasn't fatal for either the employee or the boss. "Originally, you hired me to organize Tremaine's administration. The end of the contract should have been my finding an administrative manager for you. I'll do that now."

"No," he said coldly.

She swallowed. "All right. I—then I'll get someone in, another consultant. Tim Mirimar or—"

"Samantha, shut up." He threw the door open on his side of the helicopter, swung out of his seat, and slammed the door behind him, jerking her body as if he'd slapped her.

She grabbed her computer case and scrambled out of the helicopter. He was striding toward Dorothy's house. She ran, caught up with him five paces from the veranda.

"Cal, there's nothing to discuss! Cal! Listen to me!"

He stopped and swung to face her. "What?"

"You don't have time for this! It's going to be dark soon!" She was shouting at him, screaming. She gulped and swallowed panic, forced her voice to calmness. "If you don't take off soon, you'll be stuck here overnight."

The fury in his eyes drained so fast it left her disoriented.

"I can handle that," he said quietly, in the sort of voice one probably used to calm hysterical babies. "Where do you want to talk?"

"I've already talked. I needed to tell you I'm leaving, and I've done that. Now I have to go next door and get Kippy. I have a child to look after. I don't have time for business tonight."

He studied her with those gray eyes.

"Look, Cal, I appreciate how helpful you've been with the helicopter, how understanding." Had he been understanding? She wasn't sure. "Why don't we have a phone conference tomorrow morning? Let's say about ten-thirty?"

"No."

"But—"

"Sam, you're a fantastic manager. None better. But you're not managing me." He took her arm and she jerked, but he held on. "Go into the house, put away your computer case; then we'll go over and pick up the baby."

He was moving her toward the house, and she stopped, pulling against his grip, finally pulling her arm free.

"Cal, I want to be alone. I need you to leave." She was proud of the reasonable tone of her own voice, especially considering the ragged state of her breathing, as if she'd been running uphill.

"I'm not leaving."

"I'll call the police."

"No, you won't. You've said your bit, Sam. Now it's my turn, but it's crazy to discuss anything as serious as this when you've got a baby waiting for you, when you haven't had supper. I'm starving. Aren't you?"

"No."

"Of course you are. Why don't you give me the computer and your keys? I'll go in the house and start cooking something for us to eat. You go get the baby—unless you want me to come with you? If she's heavy, I can carry her. How far is it?"

"Just next door." He wasn't going to give up. She knew that light in his eye, and he wasn't going to leave her alone, not until he'd had his say. He held out his hand and she gave him the computer case. "The house key's in my wallet, in the front pocket of the case."

She didn't want him making himself at home in Dorothy's kitchen, making it more difficult for her to keep the distance appropriate between employee and boss—ex-employee and ex-boss. But if he didn't cook, he'd have nothing to do. He'd probably pace, watching her as she looked after Kippy. Observing, making her nervous.

"There's chicken in the fridge," she said. "And fish in the freezer." Then she turned and walked away, along the path joining Dorothy's property to Diane's.

Cal put Sam's computer case on the old oak desk beside the front door, rubbed his shoes on the welcome mat, and headed for the kitchen.

He needed to handle her very carefully, he decided as he stared at the contents of the refrigerator. Sam was a woman who planned everything, and she'd already made her plan, one that didn't include Tremaine's.

White wine, an almost full bottle in the door. Would she sit with him after they ate, a glass of wine in her hand, her eyes soft and unguarded? Unlikely, he decided as he pulled a package of chicken breasts out of the fridge, then turned on the electric grill beside the coffeepot.

Potatoes in the pantry. He scrubbed them, pricked holes in them with a fork, set the microwave for six minutes to give them a head start. Then he pulled some spices out of the rack on the windowsill and shook a variety of herbs onto the chicken before he put two breasts on the grill. Both Cal and his sister had learned to cook by the time they were ten, and he went about making dinner without much thought.

For years, his sister had been laying traps for him, invitations to dinners where he'd find himself sitting across from a variety of her friends and acquaintances. Adrienne had been persistent, tossing a variety of women in his path. He'd dated a few, but there'd never been enough spark, enough fire to stop him canceling a date and saying goodbye when the latest project heated up.

And despite Adrienne's matchmaking urges—strange in a woman who declared she'd probably never marry—and his mother's campaign for a grandchild, he'd never considered marriage with any of those women.

He found a can of asparagus tips in the pantry, slipped them into a bowl ready for the microwave when the potatoes finished. A week ago, he would have said that he couldn't imagine proposing to any woman. But neither had he imagined Sam would announce she was leaving.

Whatever it took, he needed to keep her at Tremaine's, to keep her with *him*.

It was ninety percent business, of course it was. If any one of those women he'd dated had been as talented as Sam, he might have thought about marriage.

Pull the other one, Calin Tremaine. You've been fighting fantasies of tangling up the sheets with her for eighteen months. Now she's leaving, and if it were just business, you'd give her the consulting contract, get her to find her own replacement, and get on with business.

He didn't want a replacement. He wanted Sam. He trusted her, and damn it, he wanted to know that when he felt discouraged or worried, he could walk into her office, interrupt her with some unnecessary question, and soak up whatever it was about her that always made him feel no mountain was too high, no challenge too great.

With Sam at his side, he could do anything.

The microwave dinged and he pulled the potatoes out, slipped them into the oven. He heard a footstep outside on the veranda and hurried to open the door for her. Samantha Jones might not know it yet, but she wasn't going anywhere.

"Come in," he said softly, and for just a second he saw awareness flash in her eyes, and he fought the urge to yank her into his arms. Then, suddenly, she was the cool, contained Sam he'd come to expect.

He closed the door behind her, kept his voice low so as not to disturb the baby whose head was nestled against her breast. "She's sleeping. Where's her bed?"

"In the back." She pointed with a gesture of her head, avoiding his eyes. "I can—"

"I'll get the bedroom door," he murmured, his own heart hammering so loudly that he was amazed she couldn't hear it as he walked with her through the arch and down the hall into the back of the house.

In the bedroom, he pulled back the small blanket in the crib. She bent and gently placed the baby on the mattress. Cal lowered the blanket over the baby, and Sam's hand adjusted the edge over the infant's small shoulder, her face open and so tender he had to fight an overwhelming urge to take her into his arms and show her another kind of tenderness.

"She's out for the count," he murmured.

"She hardly slept at all last night."

He took Sam's hand, felt a jolt of something pass through her body, but she didn't pull away until he'd led her back to the kitchen.

"Dinner will be ready in ten minutes," he said.

When she pulled her hand away, she got to the far side of the kitchen before she stopped, standing under the archway to the living room. If it weren't for the fact that she was rubbing her hand, the one he'd held, he might have been fooled by the coolness in her eyes.

"Thank you," she said, remote voice matching her eyes. "If you'll go sit in the living room, I'll make coffee."

He ignored her attempt to take over the kitchen and opened the fridge. "I think we've both had more than enough coffee at the open house. I'll pour us some wine." He pulled out the bottle of white wine, opened a cupboard, found a massive selection of teas. Herbal teas, black teas, varieties he'd never imagined existed.

He closed the door, opened another. Plates, bowls.

"Here," she said, opening the next cupboard and taking out two thin-stemmed glasses.

He poured the wine, concentrating on the level of the liquid in the glasses, aware of the soft sound of her breathing, the scent of her shampoo . . . almonds. He corked the wine, followed her into the living room. She didn't stop walking until she got to the window, then turned, placing her back to the view.

Careful, he thought, be very careful. She would run in an instant if she knew the thoughts in his mind. "You said you'd help find your own replacement?"

She nodded, her eyes meeting his. "Yes, of course I will, Cal."

He wanted to shake her, to shout that she knew damned well she couldn't go out and find someone to replace all she'd become to him. He forced the anger down. It would weaken his position. He thought of the Lloyd deal, of meeting with Jake Lloyd in New York knowing that other firms, bigger firms had tried to get a contract and failed. Yet Cal had felt confident, certain he could demonstrate the benefits, using Jake's own paranoia to make his case.

A piece of cake compared with guaranteeing Samantha didn't leave.

"So . . ." He made his voice thoughtful, saw her eyes narrow and wondered if she could see through to his anger. "What sort of person are we looking for? Where will we find this person?"

"You'll need more than one person." She was more comfortable now, talking business. He saw her body relax as she spoke, and she lifted the wineglass to her lips, sipping unconsciously. "My job has grown into a collection of different jobs—some finance, some human resources, some planning, a little marketing. Eighteen months ago, you needed one person to look after the top level of all those functions, but now it's different. Human resources is shaping up very nicely with Jason Prendall in charge, but with your projected rate of growth over the next year or so, you're going to need an experienced negotiator in finance."

"Stacey," he suggested, knowing their accountant was no negotiator, wondering why he'd never understood that Sam's quiet enthusiasm showed only the tip of her own passionate fires. On some level, he realized, he'd known and had responded with fantasies of another kind of passion.

She was saying, ". . . not going to be able to move up to more responsibilities. You need a CFO, someone from one of the big companies, experienced in negotiations. We brought in Oscar to help out with the Lloyd contract, but you're going to need someone of your own."

How could he have been so stupid as not to know how much he wanted her? Why had it taken the threat of her leaving?

"You need to start searching for that CFO now, and for someone to head up the technical sales force, an expert in the kind of technical presales research you do yourself. You won't be able to handle it all now, so you need someone you can trust. Your job's going to change, Cal. You'll need to spend more time liaising with these new people or look at someone as vice president."

"Vice president?"

"For the moment, you should hire someone to replace me, someone you can groom for vice president. You'll need to be sure. Compatibility's a big issue."

"I know who I want."

She frowned. "We can start—"

"You're my vice president."

"Cal, I told you. I can't."

He crossed the carpet and took the wineglass from her hand. He set it and his own glass on the windowsill before he took her shoulders in his hands. He felt her jerk in surprise, and his gaze got caught in her startled wide eyes, her parted lips.

"Cal . . ."

He heard the panic in her voice. Her eyes looked exactly like those of the deer he'd seen last night. He said quietly, "Vice president, Sam. You make your own hours, oversee the search for the executives we're going to need, delegate. If you need more people, hire them. You're not leaving."

The light from the lamp behind the sofa caught in her eyes, showing golden flecks in the deep brown. "Cal, there are other people, very talented people who could do my job standing on one leg."

"No, there aren't." He took her hand because he needed to feel her pulse beating under his fingers. "Before you came, Tremaine's was growing fast, the details spinning out of control. No one but you could have persuaded me to give up control. After Barry defected, I swore I'd never trust anyone with that much control again. Then you came. Without you, Sam, I'd still be trying to do it all, working on an ulcer and a heart attack. You taught me to delegate, taught me to trust you."

She wouldn't meet his eyes. "You've still got a bit to learn about delegating," she said in a husky voice.

"I need you, Sam. I'll do whatever I have to, to make it worth your while. I need to know you won't change your mind, decide to quit again in six months time."

He felt her hand stiffen but didn't release it.

"Kippy has to come first."

"All right." He knew he was gambling, but he wasn't going to let her walk away. "You're going to be Kippy's mother," he said slowly, "but she'll have no father. Is that what you want for her, to grow up without a father?"

She jerked her hand free, then crammed both hands in the pockets of her suit jacket. "Lots of well-adjusted kids live in single-parent families."

"It doesn't matter that she has no father?"

"Of course it matters!" Her eyes were suddenly hot, militant, her body transformed in a heartbeat, and he fought his own response to the heat. Last night, walking the beach, he'd told himself this was business, but he'd known it was a lie. He wanted her, in every way.

He turned away and paced to the varnished dining room table. "You could give her a father," he said.

"I'm not going to get married just to give Kippy a father! What do you think I am?" She was breathing heavily again, hadn't gotten her coolness back in place.

He wondered how long it would have taken him to discover Sam's passionate side if she hadn't threatened to leave, wondered why it was so damned arousing to find so much heat under such a calm surface.

It took a lot to keep the desire out of his voice.

"I think you're a woman who would never let her orphaned niece down. I think you're one hell of a gifted executive. You have a magic way of getting people, business, everything sorted out, and neither Kippy nor I can afford to lose you. Have you thought what will happen if this social worker decides that Kippy would be better off without you?"

Her eyes widened in shock. "That's not going to happen. She disapproves of me right now, but I'll win her over. Even if I don't, she's got no cause. I'll get permanent custody of Kippy."

"You might have a better chance if you were married."

"Dorothy's a widow. She didn't have a problem getting custody last winter."

"When your sister died?"

"Yes." She blinked tears back. "I'll get custody, and I'm not getting married just to give Kippy a father."

"What if there were other reasons?"

"What reasons?"

"Marry me." He saw her shock and knew he'd better talk fast, before she got her breath back and threw him out. "You'd get a stable, conventional family to present to the court, a father for Kippy."

"That's insane." He heard her swallow. "I don't need—why would you—"

"Because I'd get you as vice president, completely committed to Tremaine's. I'll settle a block of shares on you—twice what we agreed on previously."

"This is a business deal?"

"Yes," he said and told himself it wasn't completely a lie.

Six

A business deal.

"You're crazy, Cal."

In the kitchen, a bell rang.

"That's the chicken," he said. "Why don't you change into something more comfortable while I get the food on the table."

Something more comfortable. Her face flushed. He didn't mean that, of course he didn't. "What kind of business deal? It's crazy, Cal. You can't be serious."

"Crazy?" His eyes had that light in them, like those mornings when he stormed into her office, interrupting her routine to tell her about a new idea, a new way to make computers dance to his vision. "Sam, this is probably the best business decision I've made since the day I hired you."

She had to make him see sense. "Cal, I don't think we should—"

"We'll work out the details after supper. When you go home after work, do you usually eat dinner in your suit?"

"No, I—"

"Then change now. We'll eat; then we'll work out the details."

"And will I get to finish my sentences?" she snapped.

He laughed, a low, warm rumble. "Change first," he

said and turned his back and walked into Dorothy's kitchen.

Cal, dishing up dinner in her grandmother's house. The world had gone mad, but wearing a business suit wasn't doing anything to keep control of this conversation, so she may as well be comfortable.

She hadn't realized how hungry she was until ten minutes later when she sat down to the smells of fried chicken, baked potato, and tender asparagus tips.

"How did you do this? There wasn't time for baked potato."

"I cheated. Six minutes in the microwave, fifteen in the oven."

"Oh."

She didn't know this man. She'd eaten with him many times before: business dinners in fine restaurants, clients entertained at his home with caterers providing the food, tepid meals in airplanes, and many pizzas eaten while working late in the board room on market plans, expansion requirements. Even one memorable dinner eaten long after midnight, during an endless night in which they examined travel schedules, expense claims, and computer-log entries to discover which employee was giving company secrets to the competition.

"You can cook," she said.

He placed a baked potato on her plate, added a chicken breast. "My mother taught both my sister and me. She's a doctor—my parents both are. Mom was always determined we'd eat properly, even if she wasn't there to cook. Once she'd taught us, we all took turns."

She cut into the potato, saw that he'd found sour cream and chives. She wasn't certain what to do with a Cal who made dinner, who suggested a business deal that required marriage.

"You have a sister?"

"Adrienne. She's three years younger, a doctor as well—

an obstetrician. She's always trying to find a woman I'll fall for, marry."

"I didn't know you were looking for a wife."

"I wasn't."

She concentrated on the potato, the sour cream. Then she cut into the chicken, a small piece because she wasn't sure she could eat anything. How could she, with Cal's suggestion of marriage between them?

"I guess I should ask if there's someone else," said Cal.

She swallowed a mouthful of chicken without chewing. "No."

"Marrying me wouldn't be stepping on someone else's territory?"

She put her fork down. "I have no intention of marrying, ever," she said abruptly. "I thought we were going to eat before we talked about this?"

He smiled, actually *smiled.* "OK, so tell me about your family. I know almost nothing about you. I wish I'd known you lost your sister last Christmas. You should have said something, Samantha."

She didn't know what to say. Why was he calling her *Samantha?* He never called her that, always *Sam.* Sarah was the only other person who had always called her Sam.

"Tell me about your family," he urged quietly.

"I'm not going to marry you. It's crazy."

"I'll tell you about mine, then."

He picked up her fork, handed it to her. Mechanically, she began eating as he told her about his sister, Adrienne, who had nursed wounded birds and stray animals as a child, who'd gone to college intending to become a vet, until a pregnant friend asked her to be her labor coach.

Samantha had never placed family around Cal in her mind, and doing so now, seeing him with his sister who loved babies and wanted to marry off her brother, made him somehow much too real, much too potent.

"She's not married?"

"No, and she claims she never will be, unless she can find a man like our father, who isn't threatened by a strong woman."

A man like Cal, she thought, remembering the times they'd argued about what was best for Tremaine's. As a consultant, she'd learned to be very careful opposing a client's conviction about what was good for his business. When the clients were men, they too often resented being given advice by a woman. With Cal, she'd gradually relaxed as she'd come to realize that although he would argue hotly when he disagreed with her recommendations, if she could give him good reasons, he would accept her ideas with none of the aggressive male insecurity she'd learned to expect.

"My parents are a hard act to follow," Cal said as he carved his potato into pieces and began eating. "They've worked together since before they married. Partners in work and in life." He chewed a large mouthful of potato, swallowed, then said, "You and I are good partners. We have been from the beginning."

There were a thousand things she could have said. Business partners didn't necessarily make life partners. She wasn't the sort of person who should ever marry. She didn't want to marry anyone, not Cal, not. . . .

Would they share the cooking, take turns as his parents had? Would Kippy learn to cook early and take her own turn? His family didn't sound conventional, but what did she know of conventional families? Would he play with Kippy, the way she'd seen other men play with babies in the park? Would he hold her high and send her into delighted squeals?

A business deal, but he'd gone with her when she put Kippy to bed, had covered her tenderly, as if he really cared about this small baby whose world had suddenly turned upside down.

She couldn't marry Cal. The idea was preposterous. She

had to think about Kippy, had to forget about Tremaine's, and Calin Tremaine. When she picked up Kippy at Diane's, the baby had clung to her tightly again, then had fallen asleep in her arms as if she were only now secure enough to sleep. Diane said she'd been awake all day, hadn't napped. Pining for Dorothy?

She pushed her plate away. "Cal, this would never work. You can't marry someone just because you don't want them to quit a job."

He carved a piece of chicken, chewed it, swallowed, then pushed his own plate aside. "Not them, Samantha. *You.* I don't want to lose you. Why are you determined never to marry?"

"I'd make a mess of it."

"You wouldn't. I can't imagine you making a mess of anything you set out to do."

"I stick to what I do well."

Mercifully, Kippy began crying at that moment. Samantha excused herself and hurried back into the baby's room. When she picked the baby up, Kippy twisted against her and wailed. She carried the baby out to the dining room. Time for Cal to leave, and she wasn't going to be diverted with talk of marriage.

"There's one motel on the island. You can take my rental car. I'll give you directions." Kippy wailed even louder as she spoke and thrashed about in her arms.

Cal stood and reached out to touch the baby's face. Samantha's lips parted to protest, but somehow the words didn't come. He slipped the tip of his smallest finger between the baby's gums and suddenly, Kippy stopped crying and began sucking on his finger.

"She's—she's hungry," Samantha stammered. Cal was too close, far too close, and although he was staring at the baby right now, any second he'd look up. She wasn't sure what he'd see then, but she knew she couldn't let him hold her gaze when her heart was pounding like this.

"Not hungry," he said. "She's teething. She needs something to chew on. Why don't you give her to me, while you go see if she's got a teething ring."

"A teething ring?"

"Yeah. They're usually plastic, or maybe rubber, sometimes shaped like a pretzel. Or there might be some teething biscuits." He took the baby out of her arms and cradled her in the curve of his arm. Kippy still had Cal's finger clamped between her gums, and she accepted the change of arms without protest.

Teething ring . . . or biscuits. Samantha walked into the pantry, feeling oddly unsteady. She found a package of biscuits evidently intended for babies, judging by the picture on the box.

"Will this do?" she asked, returning to hold the biscuit out to Cal.

He took it in one hand, brushed it against the baby's cheek. Kippy turned toward the teasing touch and began gumming the biscuit enthusiastically.

"You have your finger back," Samantha said awkwardly.

"Yes." And he had one hand free. He used it to brush a wisp of hair back from her face.

"Cal. . . ."

"I won't let you down, Samantha. I won't let Kippy down."

"It's not that exactly."

He took her hand and led her to the sofa, still holding Kippy in one arm. He sat, drawing her down beside him. "You said the social worker doesn't approve of you?"

"Because I left today, for the open house. I shouldn't have gone, but I had to—" She spread her hands. "That's when I realized I couldn't do a proper job for you and give Kippy what she needs. I had to choose."

Cal didn't comment but asked, "When do you see the social worker next?"

"Tuesday morning. She does care about Kippy, but she's

got the idea I'm a big-city businesswoman who can't be trusted with a child."

"She'll change her mind. How long does it take to get married in British Columbia."

"I don't know. Cal, I can't—"

"We'll find out Monday morning. Tuesday I'll meet the social worker with you. We'll win her over."

"Cal!" She softened her voice for the baby in his arms. He held Kippy as if he'd always held babies, but why was he here, holding her hand and the baby, slipping his way into their lives? Why wasn't she sending him away? "How did you learn about babies?"

"My aunt and uncle had four kids, all ten to fifteen years younger than me. My cousins were around the house a lot. Adrienne and I did our share of feeding and changing diapers. If we change Kippy's diaper now, I think she might go back to sleep."

"I'll do it." She took the baby from him and went into the back—fled into the back.

What if she did it? Married Cal.

He made it sound so logical. A vice presidency for her, and she could make her own hours, look after Tremaine's welfare in her own way. He would interfere, she knew he would, but she'd never minded his interference. She could hold her own, and she enjoyed the stimulation of his challenges.

Enjoyed Cal.

I won't let you down . . . won't let Kippy down.

If she'd learned anything in the last eighteen months, it was that Calin Tremaine could be relied on. She could have it all: the seat on Cal's board, the work she loved on her own terms, and time to care for Kippy.

Kippy could have a father from the beginning, a permanent, forever father.

Samantha thought of Wayne, who had come on the scene too late to be a real father to her, who'd played such an important part in her life and Sarah's. Of her grand-father, who had died three years before she and Sarah came to live with Dorothy permanently. Of her own father, a man she couldn't remember.

The baby gurgled and yanked her legs out of Samantha's grip as she began to change her. "You're getting a new diaper," she murmured, stripping off the old one and cleaning Kippy's bottom with a baby wipe. "But what about a daddy? What should I do, Kippers? Should I get you a daddy?"

Kippy gurgled and shoved her thumb in her eye.

Samantha fastened the new diaper and lifted her. "Are you really going to go to sleep? You'll be leaving me to deal with him all alone."

Kippy yawned hugely.

"OK," she whispered, hugging the baby closely and kissing her soft cheek before she laid her in the crib. This time, as if Cal had exerted some magic spell from the living room, Kippy's eyes drooped and she sighed.

Samantha switched off the light and slowly walked back to the living room. Cal was sitting where she'd left him. She'd expected him to be on his feet, pacing, but he was . . . simply waiting.

She stopped in the big log archway that divided kitchen from dining and living rooms and spoke. "A business deal, you said?"

He rose from the sofa and she put out one hand, as if to hold him off.

"A business deal," he agreed.

"We'll need a prenuptial agreement."

"I'll call Max, get him started on it." He crossed the room, took her hands in his. "Don't worry, Samantha. Everything will work out." He lifted their joined hands and used one to tilt her chin up. "We are friends, aren't we?"

She was frightened, run-for-your-life scared. "If we weren't friends, I wouldn't agree to this."

"We'll go see your grandmother tomorrow, tell her the news."

She shook her head slowly. "I can't tell her I'm getting married as part of a business deal."

He bent his head and covered her lips with his. The shock made the words jam up in her throat, then drain away.

"She wants to know you'll be happy," he said in a low, hypnotic voice. "And you will be."

He emptied her mind with his lips, his words, and she stood staring up at him, wanting to run, yet frozen. Frozen by what she'd just agreed to do—surely that was why? She hadn't realized how difficult it would be, how her certainty would drain away because everything had changed, because Cal wasn't a man on the other side of the desk anymore, because she wasn't safe behind a suit and a job title.

His lips had tasted clean, strong, overwhelming.

"Did you sleep at all last night, Sam? Where's your bedroom?"

"Upstairs," she squeaked. "We can't—I don't—"

"I'll sleep on the sofa. If the baby wakes, I'll look after her."

"I'll see to her. Last night I slept in Dorothy's room, beside Kippy's, so I could hear."

"Go upstairs. I know what I'm getting in a vice president for Tremaine's, but you don't know what you're getting in a father for Kippy. Consider this a trial, to check me out."

"If she cries, if she wants me. . . ."

"I'll wake you." He touched her cheek, a soft brush against her skin like the one he'd given Kippy earlier. She wondered what would happen if she turned her head, captured his finger between her lips as Kippy had.

"Dishes," she said. "I'll just clean up."

"I'll look after it. It's eleven, and your eyes are drooping. Get some sleep. You've got a busy day tomorrow."

She was pretty sure it was a bad idea to just turn around

and walk upstairs, to obey him as if he ruled her in some way deeper than the relationship of boss and employee.

She didn't know what else to do.

She'd just agreed to marry a man, to trade her services as vice president for his services as father to her orphaned niece. A business deal.

"I'll see you tomorrow, then."

"You could smile," he said, his own lips a straight line.

"No, I can't. I'm not sure about this."

"Tomorrow."

She nodded and turned away, feeling there was something she should do or say, self-conscious as she walked to the stairs and climbed them. He watched her, she knew he did.

At the top of the stairs, when she was out of his sight, she said, "Good night, Cal."

"Good night, Samantha."

She went to the room she'd slept in as a teenager, closed the door tightly, and pulled off jeans and blouse. In the middle drawer of the big old dresser she'd shared with Sarah, she found a T-shirt advertising Nanaimo's dirt-racing track. Sarah had borrowed the shirt from her date one day at the beach, and she'd somehow never returned it.

Pulled over Samantha's head, it stretched to midthigh.

How could she sleep? Impossible!

If she did marry Cal, where would she live? Where would she sleep? He'd kissed her, and she'd felt the warmth of his lips right down to her toes. She hadn't had a lover in a long time.

They'd made a business deal, but if she married Cal, his kiss told her there would be a physical aspect to their marriage.

She laughed, though even to herself it sounded more like panic than laughter. *A physical aspect.* She sounded like a virginal innocent, but it had been a long time since Howard. A long time since she'd been a young, immature girl in love for the first time. Thankfully, she'd been strong enough to break it off when she realized how completely Howard wanted to control her life.

This time, with Cal, was different. It wasn't about love or sex, but eventually, he was bound to expect . . . she'd need to be prepared for it to happen.

Friends. Partners. So long as she kept her head, so long as she didn't let herself lose control, it could work. She'd have to be very careful, though, because Cal was the sort of man who could take over. She'd held her own as his employee. She'd have to do the same as his wife.

Partner was a better word, one that gave her a feeling of control. As his wife, she'd be a partner. She'd do a good, efficient job, and the one thing she would *not* do was to let herself need him, to call on him for help, to cling. She'd keep her head and her sanity, and if they became lovers as well as husband and wife—well, then, they'd be lovers in friendship, not in lust and overwhelming passion.

Cal had been tender tonight, with the baby, with her. If they loved, it would be tenderness and friendship, controlled, not dangerous.

Smiling at last, she fell asleep.

The next day, Saturday, Cal flew back to Seattle, returning Monday morning to go to Nanaimo with Samantha to get a marriage license. She knew they needed the license but felt uncomfortably like an accessory to Cal's impulses, especially when he took the keys from her and slid behind the wheel of her rental car.

Why didn't she protest? Her name on the rental contract, her right to drive. She knew it was crazy to be bothered by something so minor, also knew that if she felt this ridiculous resentment over the issue of who drove the car, she should say something, assert herself.

At the BC Access government building, Cal locked the car and unstrapped Kippy's carrier from the backseat.

"I can carry her," said Samantha.

"She's heavy." He lifted the carrier out of the car, locked the car, and took Samantha's arm as they approached the building.

Inside, after standing in a brief lineup, they filled out forms and learned there was no waiting period before they could marry. When the clerk named the fee, Cal shifted Kippy's carrier to his other hand to reach for his wallet.

"I'll get this," said Samantha, pulling out her own wallet. The clerk gave her a receipt and a list of marriage commissioners who could perform the ceremony.

Outside the door, Cal stopped her with one hand. "What's wrong?"

"Nothing."

"That's bullshit," he said impatiently. "You yanked out your money as if we were in a quickdraw contest."

"All right." She stared at Kippy, who slept on as if this conversation weren't happening. "Ever since I said I'd marry you, your attitude to me has changed. You've changed."

Someone pushed the door open behind them, and they both moved to step out of the way: Cal to the left of the doorway, Samantha to the right. A woman towing a three- or four-year-old boy hurried between them and down the stairs.

"I haven't changed," he said.

The doors opened again. A man, wearing a business suit and a heavy frown.

"Let's talk in the car, Sam." He reached his hand to her shoulder, to guide her.

She stepped back, out of reach.

"I'm driving," she said, heading down the stairs, not looking back to see his reaction. At the car, she stopped, realizing she didn't have the keys.

"I need the keys."

He set Kippy's carrier on the hood of the car and pulled keys out of his pocket. "Sam, if you wanted to drive when we left the house, why didn't you say so?"

She took the keys and opened the car, slid in behind the wheel. She watched him pick up the baby carrier, but refused to turn around to see him strap Kippy into the backseat. She felt ridiculous. He was right. She should have said something about the car if it mattered. It shouldn't have mattered. In a few short hours, this marriage agreement had done something to her, something destructive. She'd lost something, and she knew that although Cal had mysteriously changed, so had she—and not for the better.

He opened the passenger door and belted himself in. "Head for the hospital, Sam."

She put the keys in the ignition, started the engine, and gripped the wheel with both hands. "The hospital?" she echoed.

"Yes."

"Why?"

She *felt* him turn his head to stare at her, didn't let herself look.

"I want to meet Dorothy."

"Cal—" She blew out a lungful of air. "Cal, this isn't going to work. This agreement, this—this marriage. I thought—ever since I agreed, you've started *steering* me around, telling me what to do, taking things from me."

His eyes were dark, filled with some emotion she couldn't decipher, his voice cold. "What have I taken from you? Car keys?"

"Yes, the keys. The baby, insisting you carry her because she's *heavy*, as if I'm incapable. You took away my right to decide when I'm tired, when I go to bed, sending me off to bed like a child Friday night. Now you're deciding when I'm going to tell my grandmother, and *how*. Did I try to tell you what to say to your family, when to say it?"

"For Christ's sake, Sam—"

Behind them, Kippy whimpered.

Cal ran a rough hand through his hair, then growled in a low voice, "Sam, you're on edge. It's been a tough week and—"

"Damn you! Don't minimize me, treat me like some stupid bimbo who doesn't know what she feels, what she wants."

Kippy's whimper turned into a wail. Samantha felt like wailing along with her.

"I'll get her," she said, reaching for her seat belt.

"I'll look after it," said Cal. He had the door open and was easing Kippy out of her baby carrier before Samantha finished unfastening her seat belt.

"That's exactly what I mean," she protested when he sat down in the front seat with Kippy in his arms. Her voice rising, she said, "Ever since I said I would marry you, you're acting as if you can just . . . just take over for me. As if I'm not capable of caring for my own niece, as if I need you to do the littlest thing."

Kippy seemed content in Cal's arms, had curled up and tucked her head into the curve of his neck. Samantha felt as if she'd been walking out in the ocean and suddenly the ground dropped away from under her feet, leaving only churning swirls of water.

"You don't want my help with the baby?"

"No, Cal. No, I don't."

He gently shifted the baby. "You'd better take her, then."

She accepted the warm weight of her niece, and as the transfer was made, Kippy stretched her neck and began to cry.

"Cal—"

"I think I'll walk."

And he was gone. The door opened, then closed, and

his long, lean body became only an image in the side mirror, walking toward Albert Street.

"Cal!"

Kippy responded with a wail.

She couldn't go after him, running, clutching a crying baby.

She rocked Kippy in the small space behind the steering wheel, felt her own shouted words echoing back at her. No wonder Kippy had woken, crying. She'd been shouting at Cal—had done entirely too much shouting the last few days. She *never* lost her cool, but she was losing it all over the place now. She'd been ranting at Cal, listing his faults in a tirade, just as if. . . .

Just as if she were her own mother. No wonder he'd walked out.

Kippy wailed louder, and Samantha pushed the car door open and began walking the baby along the sidewalk outside the BC Access building. "I'm sorry, Kippers. Settle down and I promise I won't do any more shouting."

The words had just boiled out of her, as if she had no control at all. She had to get control, keep control.

"The shortest engagement on record," she murmured to Kippy, whose cries had turned to snuffles. "Are you ready to go shopping?"

Kippy didn't answer but consented to be fastened and belted into the backseat of the car. When Samantha slid into the driver's seat, her niece was watching her soberly.

"We're going to the bookstore to find a book about babies," Samantha told her. "Dorothy didn't need one, I guess, but I do. Then we'll go to the hospital, stop in the washroom while I comb my hair, maybe put some lipstick on. By then I figure I'll have stopped looking like a woman who's just been screaming at a man."

How could she have lost control like that?

She started the car, drove to Albert Street, and turned downhill, the direction Cal had turned as he walked away.

No sign of him, which was a relief because she didn't know what to say to him—and a worry because it wasn't over They'd have to talk again. He'd find his way to Gabriola Island, she supposed. He'd have to return for his helicopter. Then they'd talk, say good-bye, because this obviously wasn't going to work. A business deal, he'd said, but she'd been deluded to think she could weave Cal into her personal life and have it work with the same ease their business transactions did.

"My fault," she told Kippy, pulling into a parking space at the mall. She lifted the baby's carrier out of the backseat and headed for the entrance nearest the bookstore. The carrier was heavy—Kippy was heavy—and Samantha's arm was aching by the time she'd reached the bookstore's entrance.

How on earth did all those young mothers manage to go shopping with a baby? Did they have biceps the size of Arnold Schwarzenegger's?

Carrying the baby was one of the things she'd ranted at Cal for. *She's heavy,* he'd said, and she'd listed it as some kind of takeover aggression, offering to carry the baby for her. Well, she'd have to apologize, even if the thought did heat her face with humiliation. He'd be relieved to see the back of her after this morning. He'd thought he was asking a rational woman to consider a partnership; instead, he'd got a hysterical fool.

She'd warned him she wouldn't be any good at marriage.

She bought *Baby's First Year,* and *The New Parent's Guide to Baby and Child Care.* Both books fit into the carrier beside Kippy, making it even heavier. In the corridor, she spotted a baby shop and stepped inside. The clerk, a twentysomething woman with a very tiny baby beside her in a bassinet, looked up inquiringly.

"Do you have any of those packs you can carry a baby in?"

Ten minutes later she'd exchanged a swipe of her credit card for a green corduroy snuggly that allowed her to lace Kippy into position nestled against her chest.

"When she's older, you can carry her on your back. Let me show you how to change it around."

Samantha walked out of the baby store feeling in control for the first time that day with Kippy nestled against her chest, her head drooping as if she were going to take another nap. The weight was comfortably distributed across Samantha's shoulders and back, leaving her hands free.

"Just a matter of finding the right tools for the job," she told the drowsy baby. "I'll get the hang of this baby-care business yet."

At the car, she unstrapped her niece and fastened her in the carrier with the seat belt in the backseat. As she drove out of the mall parking lot, her eyes flickered to the Gabriola ferry terminal across the road. Had Cal come here, to wait for her at the ferry? He must know she'd eventually return to the ferry on her way home.

But why would he wait for her after the way she'd treated him? If he'd started ranting at her like that, what would she have done? She didn't know, couldn't imagine him losing his temper. He was volatile, passionate about his work and his projects, but she'd never seen him out of control. When she first began working for him, she'd been nervous, recognizing his volatile nature, but it wasn't long before she realized Cal Tremaine was far too well wired to lose his temper.

She was the one who had lost it.

She swallowed a thick lump in her throat, blinked hard against the unwelcome pressure of tears. *Samantha Moonbeam Jones, pull yourself together. Snap out of it!*

She took a wrong turn somewhere around Dufferin Crescent, found herself back on Townsite and had to backtrack, following the hospital signs this time. OK. She needed to master this baby stuff first; then she'd be ready to take on the rest of her life. It was just as well she'd have a couple of weeks on Gabriola Island, just her and Kippy, waiting for the custody hearing.

She parked in the hospital parking lot, released Kippy, who hadn't gone to sleep in the moving car this time but seemed unusually quiet. She managed to get the baby pack on by herself, and Kippy snuggled against her as if she'd been waiting for the chance.

"This pack was a good idea, wasn't it, sweetheart?"

Kippy closed her eyes. Was she hungry yet? She would need lunch soon, the bottle in the diaper bag. So many details. Samantha got a parking permit from a machine at the edge of the lot, walked back to the car, and put it on the dash. Then she picked up the diaper bag and headed for the hospital building.

Cal was inside, standing beside the elevators. Samantha stopped in front of him.

"I'm sorry," she said soberly. "I don't know what got into me."

"I wasn't trying to take over," he said. He didn't smile. The elevator doors opened. Cal cupped his hand around her shoulder and led her two steps away from the elevators.

"You were taking over," she said. "Maybe it was some sort of guy thing, but I didn't know how to deal with it."

"We're going to be a family. The three imperatives of primitive man—protect, provide, procreate."

She felt heat flush her face, inappropriate laughter welling up at the same time. "You were trying to protect me, look after me?" And *procreate*?

"Guilty." He touched Kippy's head, brushed the baby hair with gentle fingers, almost touching Samantha's shoulder. Kippy smiled without opening her eyes.

"This pack thing you're carrying her in was a good idea. She's smiling. Do you think she's got gas?"

"You're the one who's used to babies, but no, I think she's smiling for you. What are we going to do, Cal?"

"Get married. Share the driving. Argue sometimes."

"You walked away." She hadn't admitted to herself how much that hurt.

"Stuck in a car with the baby crying, there was no way we could talk about anything. And I got angry. I didn't want to say something I'd regret." He ran his hand roughly through his hair. "The only thing I could think of to do was to kiss you. I figured that would be a mistake."

She felt like a grounded fish, her mouth parted in shock. She'd been *whining* instead of acting like the independent, assertive woman he knew, and he wanted *to kiss her?*

"Why would you kiss me?"

"Come on, Sam, you've got to know I find you attractive."

She wanted to deny it, but she'd felt it often enough, had pushed the awareness away. Last night she had wondered what it would be like to make love with him, and she hadn't needed to ask herself if he would want to.

"We haven't talked about it," she said slowly.

Her words drew a half smile to his lips, and he said gently, "I didn't think we needed a clause in our contract."

She felt herself stiffen. "Why not?"

"When it happens, it will be because we both want it. There wouldn't be any pleasure in it otherwise."

She knew she was blushing again, wished she could tame the red in her face as well as the tone of her voice.

"Fair enough," she said, then added, "if it happens."

"We've got to stop having important conversations in public places with a baby who's going to interrupt us at any moment. Let's go up. You can introduce me to your grandmother and tell her the news. We can talk later, in private."

I'll decide when to tell Dorothy. The words, fast and sharp, flew into her mind, but speaking them would have made her feel like a petulant teenager.

Cal wanted her sexually.

She wished she'd left her hair down, wished she could tilt her head forward the way Sarah used to do and have it slide over her face, hiding her expression.

"Let's go," she said.

A minefield, a bloody minefield, and Cal seemed to set off land mines wherever he stepped. He realized she was only comfortable with this marriage as a business proposition, but somehow the knowledge that she was going to marry him, that she'd be *his wife*, was acting on the primitive centers of his brain.

He'd started treating her differently, touching her, wanting to carry things for her, wanting to see emotion flash in her eyes, wanting her lips to curve . . . for him.

Wanting to make love with her, to touch her in secret places and hear her moan, see her eyes glaze with the storm of her own passion as she lost control and screamed his name.

Damn!

Last night, it had seemed so straightforward. The knowledge that he mustn't let Sam walk away, the flash of recognition, *knowing* that Calin Tremaine and Samantha Jones were meant to be together. Partners in life.

More than partners.

It was a damned good thing Sam didn't realize this marriage proposal was the impulse of a desperate moment. She'd only accepted because he'd pitched it as a business deal.

Risking everything for a hunch was more or less habit with Cal Tremaine. He'd been maybe thirteen when he felt the excitement hit for the first time. His friend Eddie had bought a couple of gerbils, got them breeding with plans to make a fortune selling the offspring back to the pet store.

Eddie's gerbils had escaped their cages, resulting in his friend's mother screaming loud enough to be heard next door at the Tremaine house. But Cal figured he knew exactly what Eddie had done wrong.

So, at the age of thirteen, in impulse and conviction, he'd taken his entire fortune—$110, given by his grandparents and intended for his higher education—and had founded a tiny empire on gerbils, selling the offspring to a pet store distributor, making his father proud, his mother vaguely worried, and his sister, Adrienne, fascinated.

He'd given up on gerbils two years later, replacing them with lab rats, in high demand by medical laboratories. He raised the rats in partnership with Adrienne. To the astonishment of both their parents, his share of the rats paid for the first two years of college, by which time he had turned the rats over to Adrienne. He didn't need them. He was selling his brain, writing computer programs for royalties from a games distributor.

Decisions made on instinct, on *feeling*, had always paid off for Cal. Until now, though, the only one at risk had been Cal himself. This time, he was risking Samantha as much as himself, on nothing but a feeling. What if it didn't work? What if *they* didn't work? Did he have the right to make an impulsive life decision for someone else?

As the elevator doors opened on the third floor, Cal placed his hand on the small of Sam's back.

Touching her again.

He slid the diaper bag from her shoulder. "I'll take that," he said, figuring they'd argue about it later.

Seven

"Married?" Dorothy Marshall's sharp eyes studied Cal, taking his measure. "You're planning to marry my granddaughter?"

"That's right." He stepped forward and held out his hand. She had the look of his Aunt Jemma, who had always known when he was hiding some boyish sin. "I'm very pleased to meet you, Mrs. Marshall."

Dorothy turned away from him, talked to Samantha as if Cal weren't there, "Why are you marrying him, child?"

Cal saw an expression on Samantha's face that reminded him of Aunt Jemma's inquisitions, hauling the truth from a ten-year-old boy who'd just fed the last of the Sunday roast to a dog named Jenson. He could have told Sam that lying to women like Dorothy and his aunt Jemma was a waste of time.

"Grandma, we've made a business arrangement," said Sam. It seemed she'd also realized there was no point lying to her grandmother.

"Business?" echoed Dorothy with a cutting look at Cal.

Sam said, "The social worker doesn't approve of me, and Kippy's protection hearing comes up in two weeks. If we've got the custody transfer underway by then and if the social worker believes I'm a good guardian for Kippy, Dexter says the ministry will drop the application for custody. So, Cal needs me for his company, and with the social worker complaining that I'm not a proper guardian for Kippy, the baby could use two parents at the custody hearing."

He wasn't sure what Jemma would say if she were thirty years older and her granddaughter made an announcement like that. Dorothy said nothing for a full minute, and Sam proved her strength of character by standing motionless under scrutiny, holding her grandmother's gaze.

"Give me the baby," ordered Dorothy finally.

Samantha shrugged out of the harness and handed her drowsy niece to Dorothy, who cradled the child in one arm, staring down at her soberly.

Sam said, "I'll look after her, Grandma."

"Until they let me out of this place," said Dorothy. "We're doing the paperwork to keep Kippy out of foster care, but this is temporary."

He could see that Sam didn't know what to say, but finally she said, "I want you to think about coming to Seattle. If you stayed with me, we'd be together, both looking after Kippy."

Dorothy stared at Cal.

"We'd like you to come," he said. "It would make Sam happy."

Dorothy shook her head. "Kippy needs her diaper changed. Take her, Samantha, and leave us. I want to talk to him."

Him.

When Sam had disappeared into the washroom with Kippy and the diaper bag, Dorothy demanded quietly, "Why are you marrying my granddaughter?"

"Sam explained it. I hope you'll consider moving to Seattle."

"I don't like the city."

"I live outside the city, on Lake Washington." He made his voice deliberately mild. They weren't exchanging any smiles, but Cal couldn't help admiring the elderly woman.

She obviously cared deeply about both Sam and Kippy. She looked fragile, tired, although not as weak as he would have expected from Sam's descriptions of her illness. "It's a big house. There's lots of room. There's a guest cottage. Visit us, see what you think."

Us. Sam would be living in that house with him. Sam sitting across a breakfast table, meeting his eyes with her direct gaze, her slow smile stopping his heart.

"They want me in a nursing home." She hitched herself up in the bed. "This crazy doctor thinks I shouldn't be living alone. That I need *care.*"

"There must be other options. Home-care workers. Private nurses. You should be with your family."

"You've got money, talking about home-care nurses."

"Enough."

"Exactly how much is Sam worth to your business?"

"A lot." He pulled a chair up and sat down. If she was going to put him through an inquisition, he may as well answer questions in comfort.

"Enough for marriage and taking on an old woman?" She picked up a plastic container of water and sipped through the straw. "You ever been married before, boy?"

He grinned. "My name's Cal—Calin—not *boy.* And no, I've never married."

"Why not?" She wasn't willing to smile back at him, not yet.

"No time." She glared at him, and he added, "No one mattered enough."

"How much does Samantha matter? How long until the divorce?"

"I'm not planning on a divorce," he said quietly. "Sam told you the truth; she's marrying me as part of a business deal. My company needs her. If I don't do something, she'll leave to take a part-time job, to make time for Kippy. This way, she doesn't have to leave, and marriage will help at the custody hearing."

"Samantha is Kippy's aunt. She doesn't need you to keep Kippy. I've just signed papers to transfer guardianship to her. Last winter, if Sam and I had applied for joint custody of Kippy, we'd never have had this problem. But I do have rights under law where Kippy's concerned, and so does my granddaughter. The judge can't deny that."

"It will go more smoothly this way."

She studied him, less critically now, although Cal didn't fool himself that he'd won her over completely.

"You didn't answer my question. Why are you marrying my granddaughter? Don't give me any nonsense about needing her in your business. You didn't need to marry her to get her to stay. That girl loves her job."

"She loves Kippy more."

Dorothy stared at him with Aunt Jemma's eyes.

"I don't want to lose her."

"You're in love with her."

He thought of Sam's head bent over the baby's sleeping face . . . her eyes startled, wide, as she looked up at him . . . her smile growing from some secret place inside, drawing him in . . . her eyes and her mind meeting his . . . Sam at his side . . . always.

"I guess I am," he said, the words echoing in his mind.

"You're doing it backward, boy. You're supposed to court your woman before you marry her. If you hurt Samantha, you'll answer to me."

By the time Samantha fell into bed Monday night, she was exhausted from the effort of trying to keep her life under control.

First, there was the wedding.

"I'd like my parents and sister to attend the ceremony," Cal had announced as they drove through Gabriola's forest tunnel on the way home. He had the wheel again, and it bothered Samantha that she hadn't made an issue of it when he slid into the driver's seat back in the hospital parking lot.

"We'll have the ceremony Saturday," he said. "I get back from New York Friday afternoon, and we want to be married before the custody hearing. Will you arrange the minister?"

"Marriage commissioner," she said. Sunlight flashed through the canopy of overhead branches. Saturday made sense as a wedding day, although she would have preferred it to be quiet, just the two of them, maybe Dorothy and Diane as witnesses—if Dorothy could leave the hospital.

"I'd rather not use a marriage commissioner," said Cal. "That suits the kind of marriage where the bride and groom have already planned the divorce, before the vows are exchanged."

She turned her head, stared at his hands, relaxed and confident on the wheel. Cal driving the car, driving her, driving Kippy, who had again fallen asleep with the motion of the car. She remembered reading a book on the meaning of dreams. In dreamland, the person driving the car was in control of your life.

"We have planned the divorce, Cal." She didn't like the nervous sound in her voice. "Eighteen years, we said. That'll be in the prenuptial. We'd be telling lies if we exchanged vows in a church ceremony. I won't do it."

Cal was silent . . . angry?

When the car emerged from the tunnel into full sunlight, he said, "All right. We'll do it your way. What about your family? Your parents? Can they come? I don't even know where your parents live."

"My mother's in Europe. She won't be able to come." She felt the web becoming even more complicated. His family would be there, and she knew Wayne would be hurt if she didn't invite him. "I should invite my mother's ex-husband. He's in Birch Bay."

He threw her a glance she couldn't interpret. "I'll head

back to Seattle this afternoon, check on the personnel situation. Is there anything I can do for you there? Do you need anything from home?"

She realized that saying no was a habit, that she'd have to find a way to be comfortable with his offers of help. This was the deal: her eighteen-year-commitment to Tremaine's in exchange for his . . . his *services* as husband and father.

"I'll make a list a list of things I need from my apartment. Thanks, Cal."

As husband.

Cal wanted more than her services as his second-in-command. He'd made that clear today. *When it happens, it will be because we both want it.*

She'd managed to avoid thinking about Cal Tremaine that way for eighteen months, but she'd be lying if she pretended she didn't find him attractive.

One day, perhaps a few months after the wedding. . . .

She could handle it. *She could.* She'd been with Cal long enough to know that although he tended to grab the reins, she had the strength to oppose him when necessary, to keep control of her job.

Of her life . . . of herself.

At the house, he lifted Kippy's carrier from the car. She followed him to the house, the diaper bag over her shoulder. In Seattle, she'd have to work out a routine for Kippy and herself. She wondered how many of Tremaine's employees had small children.

"What do you think about starting a day care?" she asked his back.

He stepped up onto the porch and swung to face her, Kippy's carrier in one hand, his brows lifted in a question.

"How many of your employees have small children? It wouldn't take many to justify a company day care. It would be a terrific perk for the employees. They'd pay day-care fees, of course, just as they would with a regular day care."

She stepped up beside him. "But the convenience—parents could stop in to check on their kids at lunch, coffee. Even nursing moms could keep nursing if the baby was in our day care."

His smile lifted something dark and worried that she'd been carrying all day. "This sounds like a done deal," he said.

"I'll need to see if there are enough children to justify it, what it will cost."

He reached out with his free hand and pulled her toward him.

"Get the numbers," he said, and he bent his head and covered her lips with his.

His hand spread over her back, holding her as he slowly explored her mouth. She told herself the dizziness was exhaustion, not being used to dealing with a baby, with hospitals, with marriage plans . . . with Cal's mouth on hers.

Slow, so slow. She told herself it was a light kiss, a nonthreatening symbol of their new partnership. Then his lips softened, lingered, and brushed the curves of her mouth, soothing her tangled nerves. His tongue traced the seam of her lips, slowly, lightly, and her mouth parted as she sank into sensation.

She breathed in the warm scent of his skin, felt her lips soften, clinging, accepting. Then he shifted and she sank deeper, her head tilting back, a tendril of panic crawling along her veins.

Something happened. Her lips, his tongue, sliding along the seam, opening her. She found the warm heat of his mouth, her tongue sliding over his, his mouth taking hers in a deep, slow fire that licked lazily through her body with growing power, then flared, drawing a moan from somewhere deep inside.

His hand tangled in her hair and he pulled her even closer, her breasts crushed against his chest, his mouth hungry, plundering, not enough . . . thirst, her pulse throbbing, breath tearing, fingers weaving through his hair, pulling his mouth closer, arching her body against his. Drowning. . . .

She gave up something, somehow drew him deeper into her, his mouth and hers clinging desperately, almost fighting now . . . now. . . .

He tore his mouth away, stared down at her with eyes blazing, searching.

"Sam?"

She felt a shudder run through her. Then, as if from a long distance away, she heard a baby whimper.

"Cal, I. . . ."

The baby's whimper became a choked-off cry.

Kippy, in the carrier Cal still held in one hand. His other arm holding her against him, her breasts crushed against his chest, someone's heart beating in hard, rough rhythm. Her hands tangled in his hair, trying to draw his head back, his mouth back to hers. A weight on her left arm—the diaper bag. It had slid off her shoulder and hung from her arm, bumping against Cal's shoulder.

She dropped her hands, tried to step back. Kippy's cry became a scream.

"Later," he said, his voice hoarse. "We'll come back to this later."

He released her and she crouched down to unstrap the baby from the carrier with trembling hands.

"Do you want lunch before you leave?" Her voice was pitched too high.

"Maybe some sandwiches." His voice sounded almost like the Cal she was used to. "I'll take them with me. What time's the social worker coming tomorrow?"

Samantha had the baby in her arms now, her breath almost normal again. Her breasts still ached, but she held Kippy tighter, as if to deny the sensation.

"She'll be coming at one. I've got some conference calls

set up tomorrow morning. Can you bring the Lloyd contract when you come back? I'm working on the pro formas for the bank, for the ASP stage. I want to check a few things."

"Yeah." For a second she thought he intended to touch her again, but he stepped to the door with her keys in his hand.

"When I come back," he said, "I'll have another of those."

"Another?" Why didn't he unlock the door? She needed to get inside, to start making sandwiches or—something, anything. "Another what?"

"Kiss." Then he did step closer and her breath dried up. "I won't bother with the sandwiches. Keep me a kiss, though, for when I get back." He brushed her lips, stretching over the shape of the baby to reach her.

Kippy started to complain as Cal's lips touched Samantha's.

"I'll be thinking about this," he growled.

Then he was gone, striding toward the helicopter on her lawn as Kippy started wailing, her mouth against Samantha's ear, her face scrunched up in distress.

"It's all right, baby," Samantha said mechanically. "Everything's all right."

A business deal, but the business part of it seemed to be slipping away, and she couldn't let that happen. Before they became lovers as well as man and wife, she needed to be ready. She needed to get used to the marriage, to being his partner in a new way. Then, when she had that under control . . . then. . . .

She'd better not stand here, watching him take off as if she were a pioneer wife watching her husband go off to the war, fearing he'd never return. This was *Cal,* and she was Samantha, a practical businesswoman with a firm vision of the future.

All right, so her vision had changed overnight. She'd acquired a baby, would add a husband in only a few days. But whatever that was, whatever she'd become, kissing him, it was only a kiss. They were going to marry, and Cal had kissed her. She was a woman, and he was a very attractive, virile man. The kiss had been . . . pleasant.

No wonder she felt off balance, though, considering the way she'd been behaving all day, shouting in the car at Cal, insisting she intended to pretend to Dorothy that this marriage was a love match, then telling her grandmother the stark truth.

Hormones, she decided. Some crazy fluctuation in her brain chemicals, brought on by stress, by worry about Dorothy, about Kippy, about fifty things unfinished at Tremaine's.

Stress. The pounding heart, shortness of breath. Probably the first signs of high blood pressure. She'd make a doctor's appointment when she got back to Seattle, ask for a thorough checkup. Meanwhile, she had a wedding to arrange, a baby to tend to, two books on baby care to read, and Tremaine's to look after by remote control.

She needed to organize, prioritize.

When the helicopter's rotors faded to silence, she mixed pabulum and stirred in two spoonfuls of pureed peaches. Then she strapped Kippy in the old high chair. Kippy showed her enjoyment of the exercise by grabbing the spoon, shoving it against her mouth, and gurgling, her laughing eyes watching Samantha. Ten minutes later, Kippy, Samantha, and the high chair wore a splattered layer of peaches and cereal, but perhaps half the mixture had found its home inside Kippy.

A bath, Samantha decided, and she took both Kippy and herself into the warm water. Afterward, the baby lay on the floor waving a pink, noisy rattle in one clenched fist. Samantha fired up her computer, collected her e-mail, and dashed off a series of responses involving everything from the additional leasehold improvements planned for the new premises, to personnel's question about a brilliant young developer who wanted some crucial clauses in the contract altered before he would sign.

She forwarded the protesting genius to Cal, with notes on options, then fired off a query to Jason in human resources, asking for the number of Tremaine employees with young children. The answer came back in twenty minutes, just as Kippy was beginning to grunt and twist her body into a pretzel.

Samantha changed the baby's diaper, cuddled her and sang a half remembered nursery song, then mixed a bottle of formula and settled Kippy in the crib. Amazingly, the baby fell directly asleep.

While she napped, Samantha called three marriage commissioners from the list before she found one who agreed that yes, she was available to perform a wedding Saturday afternoon. Samantha made an appointment for herself and Cal to meet with her the next afternoon at four, by which time Brenda the social worker would surely be gone.

Then she called Wayne, who demanded to know why he hadn't met this guy if Sam was involved enough to be talking marriage. Yes, of course he'd be at the wedding, along with his wife, Nora.

"Have you told your mother, Samantha?"

"I'm not sure where she is. Europe, I think." The last Samantha heard, Jessica was living with a psychiatrist she'd married two years ago, but going on the odds, her mother would have ditched the psychiatrist by now. After the wedding, Samantha would send a note to the address on Jessica's last Christmas card.

Once, Wayne had been the husband of the moment. Unlike the others, Wayne had remained a part of Samantha and Sarah's life afterward.

She got human resources busy preparing a questionnaire for the staff, asking about interest in a company day care. Then she delegated Marcy to check out day-care regulations.

By the time Tremaine's closed, Kippy had woken and Samantha felt as if she'd spent the whole day delegating duties she was paid to look after herself. Her e-mail in-basket was empty, though, and everything had been dealt with.

Cal had sent her several e-mails by the end of the day. She was relieved to be dealing with him on business matters, where she knew her ground. He also sent her the Lloyd contract by attachment, which made her realize she needed a printer, not just her portable.

He'd bring one, he said in his last e-mail of the day, then added: *Do you need the newspaper stopped at your apartment, the mail picked up, any plants watered?*

No, thanks, she replied and phoned the newspaper's circulation department herself after looking the phone number up on the Internet. Then she phoned her next-door neighbor but got no answer, so had to e-mail Cal back and say that yes, she did need her plants watered and thank you.

She was saying thank you far too often. If this marriage was to work at all, their contributions must be equal. She'd accomplished maybe ten hours work for Tremaine's in the last five days, while Cal had been flying back and forth to Gabriola, visiting her grandmother in the hospital, traipsing around after wedding certificates, checking her apartment, and planning another trip tomorrow to back her up with the social worker. Meanwhile, he'd been managing conferences with the project leaders while the new developers went through their six-day orientation.

Wednesday he needed to fly to New York to meet with Lloyd again, and he wouldn't be back to Seattle until Friday night. It seemed to her that while she was doing half a job, he was working double-time and doing personal favors for her besides.

Saturday they'd be married. A business deal and she'd better attend to business.

She spent Monday evening alternating between walking Kippy, who had begun crying again about five minutes after Samantha laid her in bed, and making notes on their rights and obligations under the Lloyd contract.

Monday night she walked Kippy until four in the morning when the baby fell into a deep sleep and Samantha fell into bed. Tuesday morning she had telephone conferences, business, while Kippy twisted and managed to move five feet across the living room floor without doing anything that could be described as crawling.

Samantha checked her e-mail after the phone conferences, found a message from Marcy about day-care regulations, a list of the new employees, and a draft of the questionnaire about day care. She scanned the employee list, approved the questionnaire with two minor changes, then opened an e-mail from Tremaine's lawyer.

The first draft of the prenuptial agreement.

It made no sense, but irritation drove her as she noted several items that needed to be changed. When did a lawyer ever write up a contract that didn't need changes, adjustments?

Eighteen years. She'd been the one to insist that the time be written into the contract—eighteen years, because she wasn't going to subject Kippy to a here-today-gone-tomorrow father. Better to have none at all.

She and Cal would live under the same roof for eighteen years, providing a home for Kippy. She'd be Tremaine's vice president, overseeing administrative, human resources and financial functions. She sent her notes back to the lawyer, with a copy to Cal who was probably already in the helicopter, on his way to Gabriola.

Eighteen years. By rights, she should be terrified.

At eleven, the sun came out from behind a cloud to throw the trees into brilliant green lushness. Samantha finished her last telephone call and lugged her computer outside, then carried Kippy and a blanket out to the veranda. Kippy played contentedly, making grabbing motions at the trees, which were far out of reach.

Watching her, Samantha felt a wave of unexpected tenderness. Such a small life, so precious. She put the computer aside and leaned back in the big old wicker chair Dorothy had sat in so often as she watched Samantha and Sarah playing out on the grass.

What had it been like for Dorothy, she wondered, saddled with Samantha and Sarah at the ages of 13 and 11? She couldn't have been anticipating being thrown into a motherhood role again. She'd been busy with her pottery, seemingly content in her solitary life.

If Dorothy had resented the sudden responsibility, she'd never complained.

Samantha wasn't going to complain either, and she wouldn't let herself resent the way her life had been turned upside down. She had an exciting career, a position of control in a fast-growing high-tech company, working with a man she admired and liked. As husband and wife, they would find a way to carve out their territories, to work together, just as they had at Tremaine's.

Kippy twisted, arching her back. Then she seemed to hesitate, almost off balance. As Samantha started to stand and reach for her, Kippy suddenly rolled over, ending on her belly with fists on the veranda and her head lifted high. As Samantha watched, the baby rose onto her knees, then seemed to dive forward, her face landing on Sam's bare foot.

When Samantha scooped her up, Kippy grinned and gurgled.

"Aren't you a smart one. When did you learn to do that?"

Kippy gurgled again, then began to chatter incomprehensibly.

Samantha laughed and hugged her close, then buried her face in the baby's tummy and hummed, making Kippy laugh gleefully and pump her legs.

"We're going to try to talk Dorothy into coming with us," she decided, sharing her thoughts with the baby as they formed. "We'll use Cal's money for a nurse, and we'll get her the best doctors. That way you'll have Dorothy back, but you're saddled with me too, now. You OK with that, Kippers?"

The baby pushed her feet into Samantha's thighs, as if launching herself from the floor in one of those baby jumpers.

"Would you like a jumper?"

Kippy laughed, then twisted and tried to dive off Samantha's lap. Samantha caught her close, gasping, laughing. When their laughter faded, she could hear gravel crunching. A car.

A red sports car. Cal.

She wrapped her arms more closely around Kippy and took a steadying breath. She was perfectly sane today, rational. When Cal stopped the car and stepped out, she saw he still had a cell phone in his hand, and she smiled.

"Lousy cell phone reception up here."

"Yeah," agreed Cal, frowning. "I lost him when I turned off Peterson." He put the cell phone on the table beside her.

"Hello," she said.

His hand caught in her hair and she held her breath as he brushed the flyaway strands back from her face.

"You're wearing your hair down." He caught a handful of it and lifted it in his hand. "It's incredibly soft. You should see the way the sunlight shines through it."

It wasn't blood pressure or brain chemicals. Maybe hormones, but not the PMS sort. She needed to look away from him, to break the spell holding her gaze in his, bringing his lips closer.

She eased away. "I thought you'd come by helicopter."

"I wanted to bring your car, but your keys weren't on the ring you gave me, so I brought mine. You can use it, turn in the rental car."

Like everything else he did, it seemed so reasonable, but she felt uneasy. "I doubt I can get the baby seat in the back of that thing."

"Thing?" His breath heated her cheek as he chuckled. "That's a Porsche. Treat it with respect."

"Right." She had her breath back now, almost.

The baby stretched out arms to Cal and readily abandoned Samantha.

Sex, she thought. It was raw sex, and she was off balance because she hadn't clued in, hadn't realized she was this susceptible.

"I think we can manage the car seat in the back," said Cal, "though it will be awkward for you to lift her in and out with no back doors." He smiled at her, and she saw in his eyes that the kiss he'd been about to give her wasn't evaded, only delayed. "I thought I'd take your rental back to Seattle tonight, turn it in at the airport when I fly to New York tomorrow. When I'm not here, you can put the car seat in the front. I'll bring your car next time."

"We can't put Kippy in the front seat. Air bags."

"Damn . . . you're right, I remember seeing that on the news."

"I didn't think of it either. The social worker told me when she caught me trying to belt the carrier into the front seat."

"I guess we've got some catching up to do. It's been a while since I baby-sat my cousins. I don't think anyone had air bags in those days." He turned to the sound of another car on the drive. "The social worker? Isn't she early?"

"Probably hoping to catch me off guard." Samantha wished for the baby to hold. "Don't tell her it's a business deal between us."

Cal bent to give her a swift kiss. "There," he said softly when he moved away from her. "You don't look at all like a businesswoman. What the hell is her name?"

"Brenda Simonson."

"It's going to be fine," he promised; then he turned, holding Kippy in his arms, walking toward the woman who climbed out of the government-issue midsize car.

"Ms. Simonson. Hello." He held the baby in one arm, his other hand out for a formal handshake, his voice warm and confident. "I'm Cal Tremaine, Samantha's fiancé."

"Hello, Ms. Simonson." Samantha stood to greet the social worker. "Would you like coffee or lemonade?"

"Lemonade," said Brenda stiffly, not looking at Samantha. "You're Samantha's *fiancé?* Nobody mentioned this in court."

"Sam came up here in a hurry when she discovered her grandmother was in the hospital, Kippy in foster care. We didn't have time to talk it over before she left, but when she realized Dorothy wouldn't be able to carry on as Kippy's primary caregiver, we decided it was time to marry—now, rather than later." His smile was natural, open. "Sam and I have been seeing each other for a long time."

Samantha escaped into the house, afraid of what might show on her face if she stood listening to Cal persuade Brenda that they were a match made in heaven, without ever telling a lie.

Would they have to do this in court, before the judge?

If a pastor married them, they would have had to do it in the ceremony, before God. Thank heavens she'd talked Cal out of that.

Samantha managed to maneuver her way through the rest of the week without dropping any balls. By phone and e-mail, she handled the developer, who suddenly realized he'd made a major mistake in his estimate on the leasehold improvements; the lawyer, who'd sent her the now revised prenuptial; and Marcy, who'd misplaced the specifications Cal had given her for the new computer server installations.

"Ask Dee to run a new copy," said Samantha.

"You're marrying the boss!" Marcy shouted Wednesday afternoon when they spoke. "You didn't tell me!"

Cal must have had made an announcement at Tremaine's, and she didn't know whether to be annoyed that he'd taken the decision out of her hands or relieved she didn't have to figure out how to tell everyone.

"I knew it," said Marcy. "I always knew you two were meant for each other."

Obviously, he hadn't told his staff that it was a business deal. She felt relieved, then disturbed. Of course they weren't going to go around announcing that this was strictly business, but who got the true version and who didn't?

Cal had led Brenda Simonson to believe they were a loving couple, but they'd told Dorothy the truth. What had he told his parents? She'd better find out before she met them. And what was she going to tell Wayne, who phoned from Birch Bay to say he and Nora would arrive Friday evening by car?

"Come to the house," Samantha said. "You can sleep in Dorothy's room." She said it before she realized that Cal would then be left with nowhere to sleep, because she'd planned to put him in Dorothy's room.

Brenda Simonson made two more visits. Samantha had spent the last two evenings reading child-care books, so was able to give intelligent answers to the questions she assumed were designed to test her competence to care for a small child.

As far as Samantha could tell, Brenda had come to accept Samantha as Kippy's caregiver. Because of Cal and the marriage, or because Samantha had proven her worth?

Thursday night, Cal phoned from New York. "I'll be back tomorrow night. I'm meeting Adrienne and my parents at Seatac; they're arriving from San Francisco just after my flight gets in. I'll fly them up in the chopper. Can you get the four of us rooms on the island Friday night?"

"I'll book you into a bed-and-breakfast."

So Cal wouldn't be sleeping at the house Friday, and she wouldn't have to worry about how to allocate bedrooms. He'd stay with his own family. He'd wanted tradition, which seemed so odd in a man as modern as Cal. Tradition said the bride shouldn't see the groom before the wedding on the wedding day.

"I'm picking Dorothy up Saturday morning," said Samantha. "She's got a day pass out of the hospital to come to the wedding, on condition that she spends the day resting, sitting."

"Actually, Sam. . . ." She heard the sound of voices in the background over the phone; then Cal said, "Just a minute."

She held the receiver and watched Kippy, who had managed to twist her way from the middle of the living room carpet to the kitchen entrance. From the tone in Cal's voice, she knew he'd done something without consulting her, and she told herself to be very calm. By nature, Cal tended to take over anything in his line of sight, but she knew how to hold her own with him. She'd had enough practice this last year and a half.

She could hear his voice through the telephone, talking to someone else, words not quite decipherable. It would be like this in Cal's house, she thought. Kippy playing on the floor, Cal on the phone telling her when he'd be home, calling from business meetings in New York and Miami. She'd taken these calls in the office, but here, with the baby gurgling and chattering gibberish a few feet away, herself in jeans and bare feet, the telephone suddenly seemed intimate, a family connection.

"Sam?"

"I'm here. I've arranged caterers after the ceremony, just sandwiches and so forth, and a cake because Dorothy insisted. The weather forecast looks OK, so we'll probably be able to have it outside. Otherwise, it'll be crowded inside." She didn't have a dress. It was a small, informal wedding, but she could hardly wear her jeans or her business suit. Tomorrow, Friday, she'd have to go shopping after her visit to Dorothy.

"This is turning into a lot of work for you, Sam. Get someone in to help."

"I've got it under control. I don't need help."

"If you do, get it."

The silence hung between them for long seconds.

"Did you get the prenuptial?" he asked.

"The courier brought it this morning."

"Is there anything we need to change?"

We need to slow down, she thought. This was happening much too fast.

She said, "Everything's as we agreed."

"Good. Look, Adrienne—my sister—is going to call Dorothy's doctor tomorrow morning. Mom and Dad need to fly back Saturday night, but Adrienne's staying for the weekend. She figures she can get Dorothy sprung into her care for the weekend. I told you she's a doctor, didn't I? Adrienne can pick Dorothy up Friday night from the hospital. She can share a room with Dorothy at the B&B Friday night, then stay at Dorothy's with her after the wedding. Dorothy can spend the weekend with Kippy."

He hadn't asked her, and if he had, she would have objected because it was too much to ask of a stranger, a woman named Adrienne who Samantha had never met. But Dorothy would be so grateful to have two days with Kippy and maybe Samantha would be able to use the time to persuade her grandmother to let them arrange her move to Seattle.

"Cal, I—thank your sister for me. Dorothy misses Kippy so much."

"I will. Take care of yourself."

"I will," she agreed and listened to the click as he hung up.

She reached for the baby, blinked away tears. Cal's week was even more hectic than hers, yet he'd taken the time to think about Dorothy. And his sister, who didn't even know Samantha's grandmother, was giving up a weekend for her.

"It's going to be a weird wedding, Kippers," she murmured to the baby. "Can you imagine? The bride and groom spent the weekend with her grandmother, his sister, and a beautiful baby named Kippy."

A marriage, a baby, caterers, relatives, chaos. There'd be no chance for the awkwardness of being alone with Cal, wearing the ring she hadn't seen yet, but knew would fit because Cal had e-mailed her two days ago demanding to know her ring size.

She changed Kippy's diaper, called a nearby bed-and-breakfast to make arrangements for three rooms Friday night—one for Cal's parents, one for Dorothy and Cal's sister, and one for Cal.

Cal wouldn't sleep at the B&B *Saturday* night, once they were man and wife. He'd be at Dorothy's house with Samantha—and with Dorothy, Adrienne, and Kippy. Wayne and Nora would be gone by then, but there weren't enough bedrooms. Dorothy would sleep in her own room, and Adrienne could sleep in the cot in Kippy's room, or if necessary, she could move the cot to Dorothy's room. But that left only one room—Samantha's.

Saturday night, she and Cal would have to share a room. *Come on, Sam, you've got to know I find you attractive.*

She hugged Kippy closer, but the baby struggled, reaching out as if to grasp the floor. They'd talked about it, and she'd responded more than she wanted to when he'd kissed her. She could hardly pretend she wasn't attracted to him.

But she wasn't ready. She needed time to become comfortable with the intimacy of living together, to get her balance solid, to make sure she had both feet on the ground, that she wouldn't be swept away, lose control . . . lose herself. If he were just a little less . . . less sexy, less tempting, less strong-willed, she thought wildly, it would be easier.

She wasn't ready. She had to tell him, because maybe he thought . . . expected. . . .

When it happens, it will be because we both want it.

She clung to the memory of those words. Cal had never lied to her, and she mustn't lie to him. If it weren't for those words, for the understanding that lovemaking wasn't going to be a part of the deal until they were both ready, she simply couldn't marry him. It would be like climbing a mountain without safety gear, trusting someone else to save her if she fell off a cliff.

Samantha had a simple formula for her life, based on the promise she'd made to herself long ago. At thirteen, she'd promised herself that from now on, nobody but Samantha would *ever* have control of her life.

Partnership she could do, but she wasn't about to let Cal Tremaine take over.

Eight

By this time tomorrow, Samantha would be his wife. *His.*

"She'd better be good enough for you," Adrienne declared militantly when he met her at Seatac airport.

"She is. You'll see." He felt the sensation of pleasure he hadn't yet become accustomed to. Whenever he thought of Sam, of *marriage,* spending a life together, being a family with her, he couldn't believe it had taken Dorothy's illness and Kippy's need to make him realize this was his woman, the one he hadn't even known he'd been waiting for. He hadn't known how deeply he wanted, needed a family of his own.

Love must have been there all along, lying in wait for him. He'd been too blind, too taken up with computers and e-commerce and networks to realize how necessary Samantha Jones had become to him.

He'd never been in love before. It wasn't that he didn't believe in it. He'd spent his childhood watching his parents, and there'd never been any doubt of their love for each other, but he'd never felt that kind of connection with a woman himself—until now.

Samantha Moonbeam Jones. He wondered at the whimsy that had led her parents to gift her with such a name. She didn't talk about her parents, though he knew they must have divorced because it was her stepfather who would be coming to the wedding. But they must have loved each other once, must have stared down at her as a new-born baby and given her the name Moonbeam with love.

Sam lit his life as the moon did. Softly, not glaringly like sunlight, but quietly, with the calm strength of . . . of love. Except she didn't love him.

Not yet, but he had to believe it was there, under the quiet surface. He smiled at that, because Sam hadn't been all that quiet this last week. There had been a few flashes of volatility, and now he found himself looking for the fire, the heat, hidden behind her quiet brown eyes.

Fire and quiet strength, a forever kind of woman.

You're supposed to court your woman before you marry her.

Dorothy was right, but Sam would have left Tremaine's if he hadn't stopped her. Once gone, with the walls of calm remoteness she wore around herself, Cal wasn't sure she would have let him near enough to court, to find the fire.

He figured the walls were cracking. Awareness in her eyes, passion in her kiss.

He got worried on the helicopter, with his parents and Adrienne questioning him through the headphones. His mother, Katherine, wanted to know how long they'd been dating; his father wanted to be sure Samantha wasn't a bimbo, which made Cal laugh aloud. Adrienne demanded to know where Samantha came from, why the wedding was so sudden.

"Is she pregnant?" she demanded.

He shot her a warning look. "Addie, if you put her through the third degree, I'll throw you off the island. You're here to help us celebrate a very special day, not give Sam a hard time."

"I wouldn't," said Adrienne, subsiding. "It's you I'm questioning, not her."

"Stop it, children," said Katherine, and Adrienne exchanged a wry look with Cal.

"Tell me more about the baby," demanded Katherine. "Kippy. Is it a nickname?"

"She was christened Katherine," he said, smiling back at his mother.

"Katherine," she echoed, looking pleased. "It's about time you gave me a grandchild."

He was pretty sure his family would behave, but he'd have to keep an eye on Adrienne, just in case she got an urge to take Sam aside for a sisterly grilling—the way Dorothy had taken Cal aside. He'd better watch for his mother, too. She wasn't saying much, but she might want to ask Sam a few questions, to reassure herself that her son was in good hands.

Loving families could be a pain.

At Nanaimo, he picked up the roomy BMW he'd arranged to rent, then drove to the hospital where Adrienne walked up to a head nurse and announced that she was Dr. Tremaine, and she'd come to collect Dorothy Marshall. His parents, two more doctors waiting in the wings in case Adrienne needed medical reinforcements, stood to one side and talked quietly. About him, Cal figured.

Dorothy and Katherine took to each other on sight and spent the ride to the ferry terminal comparing notes about Cal and Samantha. He hoped Dorothy wasn't going to tell his mother that Sam wasn't marrying him for love, decided there was no point worrying about things he couldn't control.

Adrienne, sitting beside him in the front seat, shot him a sympathetic look.

"Didn't know what you were letting yourself in for, did you, brother?"

He glanced in the rearview mirror, caught his father's amused glance, saw his mother and Dorothy still talking intensely. "No, I guess I wasn't ready for this. I don't know if Sam is either."

"There's a resort a few miles north of Nanaimo. Haida Sunset. Very nice, according to one of Dad's partners who stayed there for his second honeymoon. Dad's booked you

in Saturday and Sunday night. I'm the baby-sitting service—and Dorothy, of course, will be my advisor."

He pulled up to the ferry ticket booth and reached for
his wallet. Two days with Samantha alone. No baby, no
family, just the two of them. Time for courting, after the
wedding.

"Thanks, Addie. That's the best present you could give
us. Samantha wouldn't be willing to leave Kippy overnight
with anyone but Dorothy at this stage, and Dorothy
couldn't be here if it weren't for you."

"It was supposed to be a surprise. Dad's going to do
kind of a formal presentation after the wedding, but I figured you'd want to know, in case you and Samantha had
other plans."

"No." It wasn't that sort of marriage. Not yet.

They pulled into the ferry lineup behind a gray Honda
with Washington plates.

"Wayne and Nora!" exclaimed Dorothy. "We're on the
same ferry!"

Samantha's stepfather emerged from the Honda, a lean,
wiry man somewhere in his fifties. He studied Cal with the
same suspicion Dorothy had on that first day, while
Wayne's wife, Nora, immediately gave him an enthusiastic
hug and welcomed him to the family.

All these people descending on Sam, who had sounded
uneasy the last time Cal spoke to her. Had he made a
mistake, insisting on a family wedding? Maybe Sam's instincts had been right, a very private service with only the
witnesses required by law.

In secret. That's what had made him balk. He wasn't
going to marry Samantha Moonbeam Jones in secret,
damn it! They would exchange vows in broad daylight,
with the people who loved them as witness.

As he turned into Dorothy's drive behind Wayne's
Honda, he heard Adrienne ask a question, in response to

which Dorothy assured his sister she felt fine, no shortness of breath, and no pain.

Good.

He got out of the car in time to see Wayne envelop Samantha in a big hug she returned enthusiastically. She'd worn shoes today and had substituted tailored pants for the jeans, a sleeveless gold silk blouse for the sweatshirt. She'd dressed up, and he could see the unease in her eyes as she stepped away from Wayne to face the crew tumbling out of his rental car.

"My turn," he said, stepping past Wayne to pull her into his arms.

He'd dreamed of her, the soft gasp on her lips, the wide questions in her eyes. She'd put her hair up today, donning her smooth Samantha mask for his family—or for him.

He settled his mouth over her parted lips. God, he'd missed the feel of her, the sound of her breath. Her lips moved under his and he captured her upper lip, tugged softly and slid into her mouth as she breathed a soft moan and opened to him.

He settled deeper into the kiss, felt the fire run through his veins and through hers. Slid his hand up the narrow curve of her back and settled her against him, welcoming the restless twisting of her body as she came alive and hungry.

He pulled the combs out of her hair and tangled his fingers in it. His body hardened against the soft crush of hers. He felt a shudder go through her and braced himself for the ride as her arms wrapped tightly around him.

The world was spinning when he finally pulled his lips from hers. He saw her swallow, needed to taste her throat, but knew that if he did, he was lost.

"You OK?"

"I don't know." She breathed the words.

He released her and captured her hands, tangling fingers with hers. "Don't worry," he said softly; then he turned her, holding her in his arms as he introduced her to his family.

Samantha spent most of Friday evening in shock, trying to recover from that kiss. They'd be married tomorrow. There were details to be looked after, but all she could think of was the hot pulse throbbing at the pit of her stomach.

There'd be no waiting, no getting her balance, no cool friendship leading slowly to physical intimacy. She'd felt him, hard and demanding, thrusting against her belly . . . had felt her own pulse, wild and thundering, demanding she fling herself off the edge, trust herself to wild heat and lust.

Surely it was better to feel desire, because she could hardly expect Cal to commit to eighteen years of celibacy, and she would hate him to go to another woman while he was married to her. Any woman would hate it.

She remembered the screaming battles from her childhood with a shudder. She wasn't her mother. They couldn't be more different. Jessica might have thrown herself off cliffs regularly, taking her children with her, but Samantha Jones had control of her own life and nobody was taking it from her—not Jessica, not Cal. Nobody.

With Howard, she'd never felt that pulsing hunger, that feeling of losing control, of herself slipping away. She had to remember that this was about sex, not about life. Just physical sensations. Afterward, once they'd made love. . . .

Better to get it over with, she decided. Then sexual intimacy would be just another aspect of their partnership.

The house pulsed with life, with people. Wayne and Nora, looking pleased, as if this marriage had been their idea. Dorothy, thoughtful but smiling. Cal's parents and his sister, Adrienne, three vibrant people filled with the energy she'd always loved feeling from Cal himself. It was the thing that made working for him so exciting, so rewarding. That and the fact that in his own interfering way, he let her have control, let her do her job exactly as she wanted.

Kippy, gurgling and laughing, enjoying being handed from one set of arms to another, then suddenly making shy and crying for familiar arms.

Dorothy put her to bed under Adrienne's watchful eye.

"We'd better go," said Katherine, Cal's mother. She gave Samantha a light kiss on her cheek. "You need some quiet time after this mob. We'll look after Cal tomorrow morning, keep him away until it's time for the wedding." She smiled, affection in her eyes and her voice, though she knew almost nothing about Sam, only that her son was marrying her.

"Thank you," Samantha said, an unexpected wave of sadness threatening tears.

"No," said her husband's deep voice. So much like's Cal's voice, with a little more gravel. "You're the one who should be thanked. Welcome to the family, Samantha."

Cal caught her hand and drew her outside with them while Adrienne helped Dorothy to the car.

Cal's hand clasped hers, and she felt her body droop with lethargy. She wasn't ready for another kiss. Not yet.

"We haven't signed the prenuptial," she said.

"You're right." He frowned. "We can't do it tomorrow morning. My mother is determined the groom won't see the bride before the ceremony. Could we slip inside now and get Wayne to witness our signatures?"

She couldn't tell Wayne, who was so obviously pleased for her, that this was a business deal. "Can we get the commissioner to witness it, after the ceremony? When we're doing the paperwork, and she's giving us the marriage certificate."

"It wouldn't be a *pre*nuptial agreement, then, would it?" He touched her mouth to silence her as her lips parted.

"We'll sign it whenever you want, Sam. I trust you. The question is, do you trust me?"

Did she trust him? Certainly she trusted him to sign it if he said he would, but he seemed to be asking so much more.

"After the ceremony," she said. "We'll sign then."

"A skilled evasion," he murmured. His hand slid into her hair and she felt her head tilt back, her lips tingling, parting.

His mouth was just a breath away from hers when she pulled back.

"Sam, I want to kiss you." He brushed her lips with his thumb, and they had no choice but to part for him. "Earlier, I thought you wanted it, too."

"Your parents," she breathed. "Your sister. My grandmother."

"They're in the car. No one's going to be surprised if we spend a minute alone here, in the shadows."

He drew her arms around his neck and she gave her lips. The gentleness burned away as their mouths met. She felt herself swept into his heat, his hand hard on her back, her breasts throbbing against his chest, his tongue teaching her the sultry headiness of their mouths pleasuring each other.

The curls of his hair sprang tightly around her fingers as she pulled his head down. Closer and she kissed him back, her mouth hungry, needy, unable to get enough.

"God, Sam. . . ." He groaned and his hand covered her breast.

She heard herself whimper; then she sagged as his thumb brushed over her throbbing nipple. He staggered, cursed softly, pulled her into him, and dove deeper into her mouth, to her very center.

Someone honked a horn.

She clung when Cal's mouth slowly drew back from hers.

She could feel his breath, hard and ragged, against her face. She heard someone laugh.

"Come on, Calin, time to go!" Adrienne, his sister, calling from the car.

Samantha couldn't seem to let him go. He was staring down at her, too dark here in the shadows beside the veranda to read his expression, but she felt his pulse, beating with hers. His hand . . . his hand on her breast, aching sweetness. She couldn't talk, covered it with hers.

Cal turned his hand and threaded his fingers through hers, then lifted her hand to his lips. His laugh was harsh. "What the hell have we been doing this last eighteen months? Why haven't we done this before?"

"Cal, I'm not ready for this."

He took her hand. Darkness. "You're exhausted. You'll feel better after the wedding."

Then he was gone.

She listened to the car driving away. When it was gone, she heard silence, then the sounds of frogs, a nighttime chorus. She closed her eyes and slowly felt the peace of the island seep over her.

Only a few minutes ago, she'd been wrapped around Cal, burning in his arms, hidden from Dorothy and his family by shadows, but only a few feet away. And for a moment, she'd needed his touch more than life itself.

The frogs fell suddenly silent. She heard the door open, turned and saw Wayne step outside.

"Nora's tucked up on the sofa with a romance she's been wanting to read. I brought you a glass of wine, Samantha."

She took the glass from his hand, stepped up onto the veranda, and sank into the big wicker chair, glad of the shadows. Wayne leaned against the rail.

She held the wineglass in her hands, thought about the question for long seconds, then asked, "Why did you marry my mother, Wayne? Don't answer if—"

"It's time we talked about her," he said mildly. "It was a long time ago. There's no pain left. Sadness, a sense of failure, but not pain."

She put her glass down in the little table where she'd been using her computer all week. *"You* didn't fail."

"She was entrancing, fascinating. I married her for lust, of course, but also, she needed me. I guess I thought it was love, but Jessica doesn't do love. Jessica's like a comet—blazing, exciting, until the instant she burns out."

Samantha said, "I don't know anything about marriage, how to do it."

"You've got her fire. I used to see it in your eyes sometimes when you were a kid, before you became so damned controlled. When you told me you were getting married, I worried that you might try to do marriage from a distance, in complete control, the opposite of the way your mother did."

"Control is important." She felt the sensation again, Cal's mouth in hers, her own hunger. She would never forget now.

"Love is important, too," said Wayne. "I saw him kiss you when he arrived."

"Do you know how many times I watched her fall in love? Seven husbands now, isn't it? Not to mention the men in between. In the end, they all go sour."

"In the end she always leaves. What are you afraid of, Samantha? The only part of your mother in you is the energy, the fire, but in you it's solid, enduring. When Kippy needed you, when Dorothy called you last week, you came right away." He leaned forward. "That's love, Sam. Falling in love is the fire, and it's splendid, but it's nothing without the other—without loving. You've taken on this child now, you've made a promise to little Kippy in your heart, and if the going gets tough, if that promise means you have to rearrange your own life, it doesn't change the promise, does it?"

"No, it doesn't. You did the same for us, Wayne. You had no real obligation, but you looked out for Sarah and me, fought for us when we needed it."

"Jessica's promises were like water. She would promise whatever was necessary to get what she wanted, but when she was called for payment she ran every time. Love is only partly about passion and lust. The rest of it is character and commitment. You have both, and so does your man."

She couldn't tell him there was no love, couldn't say anything at all. But he was right even so. The heat and madness she'd felt in Cal's arms, still throbbing in her belly, wasn't the point. Marriage, any marriage, was about keeping promises, and both she and Cal would keep theirs.

Sex aside, this was a business partnership. They were two strong-willed people forging an alliance for mutual benefit. Once all these people went away, life would get back to normal, a new normal with Kippy woven into the fabric of Samantha's life and Cal back at work on the Lloyd project. They would probably have sex, but not that often. They would both be far too busy.

Samantha Moonbeam Jones and Calin Antony Tremaine were married in midafternoon on the sun-bathed lawn of the home Dorothy Marshall had lived in with Samantha's grandfather.

Samantha's hand trembled as Cal slid the plain gold band onto her finger. Trembled still as she placed the matching ring on his. Two gold bands. Two hands. Her family watching, and Cal's. She would not let this be a mistake.

She trembled as his lips covered hers, afraid she might overreact the way she had the last two times.

"Breathe," he murmured, his hand against her cheek. "And kiss me."

She lifted her arms to his shoulders, joined her lips with

his, felt his hand at her waist, firm, protecting her. His lips were gentle, almost soothing, and she felt herself relax.

He kissed her again, very softly. "If we can crack Lloyd together, we can do this."

Someone took a picture, and she felt Cal's hand on her shoulder. Steadying her. Then he led her to the table where the commissioner was waiting with documents to be signed. She hadn't seen Cal give the two copies of the prenuptial agreement to the commissioner, but there they were, and she signed her name with a steady hand.

Then she stood with Cal and heard the commissioner say, "Ladies and gentlemen, I present to you, Mr. and Mrs. Tremaine."

Someone started the music again, a CD playing on the stereo Nora had pulled out onto the veranda earlier. Then Samantha was walking with Cal toward these people who were their family, surrounded by old evergreens.

Cal stood at her side, his hand resting on the waist of her simple white sheath dress. Then Wayne was hugging her, saying, "I love you, honey. You're going to be fine."

Nora kissed her cheek and whispered, "He's a major hunk. Enjoy him."

Samantha flushed hotly and found herself being hugged by Katherine, being held against her generous curves. "You're absolutely glowing. Welcome to the family, dear."

Glowing? She felt a wreck.

"It's lovely to have a small wedding," said Adrienne, hugging her tightly. "So much nicer than those two-hundred-people deals where the bride and groom are crippled with stage fright."

Samantha laughed; it was that or sink into a ridiculous pool of nerves. It was done now, whether it had been wise or not. She drew in a deep breath and turned to find herself enveloped in Dorothy's arms

"You be happy, do you hear, Moonbeam? You're a good child, you always were. Don't be afraid to fall in love."

"Grandma. . . ."

Dorothy stepped back. "Now go off and have your honeymoon."

Honeymoon?

At her side, Cal murmured, "Are you going to call yourself Mrs. Tremaine?"

"I don't know. I haven't even thought of it."

"Been busy?"

"A bit." When he smiled, she felt her tension ease. This was Cal. She'd worked with him for eighteen months. She'd argued with him, supported him, struggled with him to make Tremaine's the best they could make it.

They'd been good partners, were still.

Cal was nervous. He didn't figure he should be, not after the way Sam had responded to him last night when he held her in his arms, but reason aside, as they drove north on Vancouver Island, Cal found himself worrying about the resort, about the night.

A breathless, mad kiss, the woman who was now his wife moaning in his arms. His blood flamed as he remembered the softness of her breast, the hard bud of her nipple under his thumb, the heat of her mouth.

He thought of the resort somewhere ahead of them. Cabins by the water, privacy amid the luxury of nature. His father had booked the resort, and he wasn't likely to have booked twin beds or separate rooms.

As much as he ached to hold Samantha naked in his bed, he wanted this marriage to work even more. He'd promised her nothing would happen until they both wanted it, and he had no right to assume that last night indicated consent. Not when she'd been trembling when he kissed her after the ceremony, her eyes wide with nerves or terror.

She'd looked stunned when his father presented them

with the gift certificate to Haida Sunset. She couldn't be afraid of him. He didn't believe she was really afraid of anyone, except perhaps the social worker and judge who held the power of Kippy's future. He'd soothed that fear, he thought. Brenda had told them she was recommending they be given custody, and Cal had already briefed Dexter and his own lawyer to work on adoption proceedings to make it permanent.

When they went to court next week, Kippy's future should be secured.

Theirs—Cal and Samantha's—was going to be trickier. Despite the fact that she was obviously attracted to him, Sam hadn't answered last night when he'd asked her if she trusted him. They'd worked together smoothly for months, but he was beginning to realize that the trust they'd developed between them at Tremaine's wasn't automatically going to translate into their marriage.

He'd have to earn her trust, and rushing her into a double bed was not the way to do it. Marriage and the prenuptial—*postnuptial*—agreement aside, a man had no right to assume that two incredible kisses constituted consent to sex. And he didn't.

But when they walked into the room at Haida Sunset and found the inevitable double bed, it was going to look like he'd assumed just that.

When Cal unlocked the door to the small cabin, Samantha walked in ahead of him. She heard him set their suitcases on the floor.

She stopped three steps inside the door, facing a king-size bed with a floor-length maroon spread. Cal's family had given them this weekend, and of course the room had only one bed.

Big, very big. Room for two people to sleep without touching.

"The bed wasn't my idea," Cal said.

She needed to turn around, face him, say something. Last night he had kissed her, touched her, and she'd felt flames. Now. . . .

What would they do? Undress together or one at a time? Here, or in the bathroom? When? Would the room be filled with early evening light?

Dark would be easier.

"Samantha?"

Coward, staring at the bed, afraid to face him. Thirty-one years old; too old for these jitters. She forced herself to turn, to meet his gaze. The gray of his eyes seemed darker, inscrutable.

"I told you that when we make love, it will be because we both want it. I meant that."

"What do *you* want, Cal?"

"I want you—when it's time."

She felt a wave of sensation, heat flooding her face.

He dragged one hand through his hair. "What I don't want is to put pressure on you. I wish to hell we hadn't ended up staring at this damned bed when we've hardly had five minutes alone with each other."

If he touched her . . . if he lowered his mouth to hers as he had last night. . . .

"Not tonight," she said, a whisper instead of a voice. He stood in front of her, six feet of pure man—broad shoulders, narrow hips, and mouth tight with tension.

"It's your call, Samantha."

She should do something. Move, walk to the window, break their locked gazes.

Just kissing her, his mouth had stirred flames. What would it be like to lie with him, to feel his mouth on her breast, his erection against her naked belly?

Stop it!

He captured her hand and lifted it to his lips. Her heart

slammed into her rib cage as he pressed a light kiss into her palm. She lifted her chin slightly.

"What are we going to do about the bed?"

"I could sleep on the sofa," he said.

"It's a love seat. You'd be crippled by morning."

He grimaced acknowledgment. "Let's have dinner; then we'll tackle the bed."

"Tackle?" She felt laughter bubble at the image of Cal taking a flying tackle at the monstrous king-size bed.

"Badly chosen word," he admitted, and somehow they were laughing together.

She found it easier then to turn away and walk to the window. Outside, the shadows from tall cedar trees blurred the path leading to the ocean.

"We're a hundred feet from the beach," she said. "Let's walk after dinner."

When she turned to face him, the look in his eyes sent uneasiness flooding over her. He would reach for her . . . she would step into his arms and this tension, this hideous tension, would melt away when their lips met.

"Do you want to change for dinner?" he asked abruptly.

She shook her head. She'd been too many years without touch, without sex. This feeling of control slipping away . . . just hormones. A psychologist would probably call it repression, all those years. And now. . . .

The dining room occupied the ocean side of the resort's central building, a few hundred feet along the path from their cabin. Cal walked beside her, not touching, somehow making her more aware than if he had put his hand on her shoulder or her waist.

When she stepped on an uneven piece of ground and stumbled into him, he caught her arm and she gasped.

"All right?" he asked, releasing her abruptly.

"Yes. I just tripped."

"Your shoes?"

"They're fine. I'm fine."

She wasn't fine at all. She was jangling with nerves. She'd said not tonight, hadn't she? And he'd agreed. So why couldn't she relax? She'd walked with him a thousand times, down the corridors of Tremaine's, on sidewalks, in restaurants. Walked side by side without touching. Except for the last few days, since she'd agreed to marry him. Now, when they walked, he often touched her, a hand on her waist, her arm, a touch on her shoulder, as if her consent had conferred the right. And she'd . . . somehow his touch on her had begun to seem right, natural. Taking the baby from her, they often—

The baby. If Kippy were here. . . .

She hadn't realized how nervous she'd feel once they were alone, with no baby to care for, no wedding to plan, no prenuptial clauses or company contracts to discuss. Nothing. No agenda, just Samantha and Cal . . . and a king-size bed.

In the dining room, the hostess seated them at a window table that looked out on the island-studded ocean.

"What's that island?" asked Cal when they'd ordered their drinks.

"Hornby Island. I spent a few summer nights there in my teens, camping."

"I didn't get this far north on my cycling tour."

The waiter delivered two glasses of wine and Cal lifted his to her. "To us."

"To us," she agreed. "To our partnership."

They both ordered—seafood nibbler for Cal, and neptune salad for Samantha. Cal questioned her about the Gulf Island chain that included Gabriola and Hornby islands while the ocean turned from blue to gray and the sky slowly darkened.

"Tell me about your childhood," Samantha asked, a

fork filled with greens and crab halfway to her mouth. "Did you grow up in San Francisco?"

"Denver."

"Cold winters."

"Makes you tough," said Cal. "Addie and I were born in L.A. My parents met when Dad was a medical student, Mom a trauma nurse. They got married two months after they met, had me a year later. Not wise, Mom always said, but they were in love and they got by between his student loans and her nursing salary."

"I thought she was a doctor?"

"Not then." Cal speared a small round ball of something and chewed it with evident pleasure.

"What is that? Scallop?"

"Stuffed with something delicious. Want one?" He speared another and offered it to her.

She parted her lips and he slipped the tasty morsel inside her mouth. She couldn't look away from him, trapped by the intimacy of his casual action.

"It's good," she mumbled, disobeying Dorothy's strictures not to talk with her mouth full. "Delicious. When did your mom become a doctor?"

"After Dad finished his residency. He did his residency in Denver, started a practice there. I was about six when Mom went back to school, fourteen when she finished her internship in Denver. Then she got a chance to do her residency in obstetrics under a doctor she admired in San Francisco, and we moved.

"Your father moved his practice?"

"They supported each other. She got him through medical school; then he got her through. Together they made sure we had what we needed. Love. Consistency. Good role models."

His strong confidence came from his family, his secure childhood . . . and something else, a fire deep inside. She wondered what sort of child he had been, wondered how old he'd been when he started taking charge of his own life.

"What were you like as a boy, Cal?"

"Troublesome," he said with a grin. "Always taking apart the basement for my projects, getting Adrienne involved. Making a spaceship when I was eleven, raising gerbils, then rats when I was thirteen and wanted to make money. Adrienne made an animal hospital out of the basement later, after I left for college."

"You never wanted to be a doctor?"

He pushed his plate aside. "Those genes skipped me. Addie got them all. I wanted to take things apart, build things, make computers stand on their head—once I got into computers." He sipped his wine and she found her gaze caught on the movement of his lips. "What about you, Sam? I've met Wayne, but I know nothing about your parents. I don't even know how you got to be a dual citizen."

She picked up a piece of parsley and rolled its stem between her fingers. "I was born in on Lasquiti Island. Canadian mother, American father."

"Where's Lasquiti Island?"

"Not very far from here. On the other side of Georgia Strait, near the mainland."

"And. . . ."

She dropped the parsley onto her plate and pushed the food aside, her appetite gone. "I grew up, went to college, took a job at Tremaine's."

He reached for her hand, took it between both of his. She stared at their hands. She needed to change the subject. "Did Adrienne—"

"Tell me about your mother."

Her eyes flew wide open, meeting his.

"It's a place to start. You seem to have trouble getting started."

"Started what?"

"Telling me about yourself."

She stared down at their linked hands. "The details are boring."

"Sam, look at me."

She didn't want to, but her gaze seemed pulled back to his eyes, as if he controlled her.

"You don't need to lie to me, Sam."

She shivered and pulled her hand away. "It's complicated."

"We've got time for you to explain."

She told herself to stare out the window, but her eyes seemed locked on his. "I don't remember Lasquiti Island. We left when I was three, Sarah a few months old. We went to New Mexico, Arizona, Montreal, San Francisco."

"Was your dad in construction?"

"My dad. . . ." She searched for the short version. "Gerry, my mother's third husband, was in construction in Montreal. He built houses. Sarah and I used to sit on the sawhorses, pretending they were real horses. I remember when the electrician came. We collected all the round metal plugs from the electrical boxes and pretended they were money." They'd planned what they would do with the money, Samantha remembered with a frown. They'd go to the bus depot and get a ticket to Grandma.

"What happened to Gerry?" asked Cal.

"Well. . . ." She shrugged and tugged at her hand, but he wasn't letting go. "My mother moved around. We left Lasquiti Island after my father died. He was an American who came to Canada to avoid the draft during the Vietnam war. He met my mother on Gabriola, talked her into moving with him to a commune on Lasquiti. New Mexico was a commune, too. I do remember that wedding. I was five . . . strange music, laughter. Later came the fights. I was seven when she left us at the commune on Sarah's fifth birthday."

His hand had tightened on hers. "She left you there?"

"She came back a few months later, collected us and drove us to Montreal. She always came back."

She saw the shock in his eyes. "You spent your whole childhood—"

She pulled her hand free. "My mother couldn't stay in any relationship for more than a couple of years, but she generally picked good men. We were looked after, and when I was thirteen, we got off the roller coaster."

She thought he was going to take her hand again, so she folded her hands together in her lap. "Can we talk about something else?"

He gestured to the waiter and asked for the bill. "Let's go for a walk."

"Yes." She needed to get outside, to walk hard and long. "I'll slip back to the cabin and change my shoes. I'll meet you outside."

He didn't stop her. Somehow, she'd thought he would, maybe because she needed so much to be away from him and wasn't sure she could cope if he touched her now. She half ran to the cabin, stumbling on the path, cursing the shoes that had been so right for the wedding.

She shouldn't have told him anything.

But he had a right to know about her childhood, of course he did. They were married, and it would be ridiculous if he couldn't answer his own family's curiosity. She wished being honest about her upbringing could be done in a couple of sentences. But *we moved around a lot* hadn't worked, and anything more just led to more questions.

In the cabin, she rummaged in her suitcase for jeans. Nicely practical, so he'd know she wasn't angling for a romantic walk. Unfortunately, she hadn't packed anything as basic as a sweatshirt, so she topped the jeans with a silk blouse. The evening was warm. She wouldn't need more.

She pulled on socks and sneakers, yanked out the combs from her hair, and brushed it hard, then tied it back.

She stared at herself in the mirror, decided she looked

too young and too vulnerable with her hair pulled back tight like that. She yanked out the fastener and refreshed her lipstick.

Maybe she should put her hair back up?

Maybe she should tell him she wanted to go to bed now, get it over with.

Was it normal to feel so uncomfortable? She had ridiculously little experience with men. Just Howard, who had romanced her back in college. Love, she'd thought, and she couldn't remember now exactly how it had been before the first time they made love. Had she felt awkward, jumpy? She didn't think so. But then, when Howard kissed her, she'd never lost track of the rest of the world.

She wouldn't with Cal either, not this time.

She stared at herself in the mirror, relieved that her panic didn't show on the outside. Was she actually planning to—well, not *seduce* Cal, but . . . ?

To invite him.

Then, at least, he wouldn't be asking her about her childhood, her mother, and looking shocked as if he pitied her. She was damned if she would tolerate another minute of this horrible tension. She'd been sitting across from him at the dinner table, answering questions as if she had no control of anything. As if she had to answer any question he asked, as if she had no will, no power over what happened.

As if she were thrown back into her childhood.

That would change now.

She left her hair down, locked the cabin, and stepped outside—straight into Cal's arms.

Nine

"Easy," Cal breathed, holding her shoulders in his hands as if to steady her.

"I'm fine." She didn't need steadying, didn't need holding, and wouldn't let this breathless trembling take hold. But there was nowhere to step back except through the door to the cabin. "Let go. I'm fine."

He stepped back, his hands dropping to his sides. "Sorry."

"It's OK." This had to stop, inanities on the edge of the path. "Shall we walk? Or did you want to change, too?"

"No. Let's go."

Was he as uncomfortable as she felt? Probably not, because her nerves felt ready to scream, but he wasn't relaxed either. This weekend away together had been a bad idea, but impossible to avoid when his parents presented the gift.

"We should have brought our computers," she said.

"We'll get by. Here, down this way. There's a path."

When he took her arm, she didn't jerk away, didn't lose track of her breathing. Before, it had been panic, and she'd better stop it. She was thirty-one years old, too old for such silliness.

"Nice," he said. "I always like the water at night. Is that a small freighter out there?"

"I think so. There used to be lots of small freighters along the coast, but not so much now."

"I wonder what he's hauling," said Cal.

When she slipped at the edge of the water, Cal let go of her arm and took her hand instead. Over the water, the moon had risen enough to send streaks of white through the ripples. Her fingers curled, returning his grip. Friends held hands.

So did lovers.

Cal lived right on Washington Lake. She hadn't walked on his beach, but she'd seen it from the windows of his house, moments stolen from being hostess to look out at the water.

"Do you go walking on the beach at your place on Washington Lake?"

"Not often enough. When we get back, when you move in, I'd like to make a habit of it, walking like this."

Her heart took a jagged stumble at the thought of moving everything she owned inside Cal's walls, of living with him.

"I like the sounds," she said desperately. "Water sounds. Listen."

Very soft whispers of water on the sand, through the trees. A bird, crying in the night. A muted chorus of frogs from farther away. Sand shifted under her feet as they walked along the edge of the water. When he released her hand and touched her shoulder, she turned into his arms. His hand brushed her chin, lifted to bring her eyes to his in the moonlight.

"Moonbeam," he said softly.

"Samantha," she corrected. "Moonbeam was my name until I was thirteen. Then I changed it."

She felt his kiss coming, felt her own lips part and knew she would need to hang on tight this time, to give herself without losing control.

"A lot happened the year you were thirteen. You

changed your name. You got off the roller coaster—your mother's roller coaster?"

"Yes."

He lowered his head so slowly that she stopped breathing entirely, and he became only a black shadow blocking out the night sky. When his mouth settled on hers, her breath drained out.

The kiss was too soft, too brief, and left her trembling and hungry. He took her arm and tucked it securely through his, drawing her along the beach again.

"Tell me about it," he commanded gently.

The night had grown more silent, her nerves more ragged. The frogs had stopped their chorus, or she and Cal had walked too far to hear. The water had stilled, the birds silenced.

"Sarah and I were in foster care in San Francisco when my mother married Wayne. That was the second time the system got upset about us; we weren't going to school, and someone must have told. Maybe it was Edward. Her fourth husband."

Cal drew her to a massive log lying on the beach, then wrapped his arms around her and sat down with her. She was on his lap, in his arms.

"I'm glad she didn't come to the wedding," he said, and although his voice was soft, she heard grimness. "If I'd known this, I couldn't have been civil to her."

Samantha shrugged. There had been anger once and hurt many times, but neither had helped. "It's a long time since she controlled my life. Sarah and I were lucky because we had Dorothy. It's Dorothy she hurt most, because I think my grandmother always worried that somehow she'd done something wrong in raising my mother."

"What happened after your mother married Wayne?"

"When she left him and us, he carried on as if we were his. Made sure we got to school, rearranged his work to be home early every night."

Cal slid his hands into the hair at the back of her neck, sending ripples of sensation along her back and scalp. "Then?"

"Then she came back." She was trying to talk steadily, trying not to let the sensations from his caress leak into her voice. " 'Get your things, girls,' she said. 'We're going to New Orleans.' "

The wind had picked up, sending ripples onto the shore. She shivered as cool air brushed her arms.

"Cold?"

"No." She was, which meant she'd lied again. "When Mom said we were going to New Orleans, Sarah started crying. She had friends. I had friends, too, but I'd known it wouldn't last. Neither would New Orleans. But Sarah crying—I told Mother we wouldn't leave with her. Wayne backed me up. She cried, but she didn't know what to do about my refusal. I realized that day that I could stop it, that I could refuse, that I was stronger than she was. She couldn't make us go with her."

"You stayed with Wayne?"

"No, we went to Dorothy. That's what Sarah wanted. She remembered Dorothy from when she was seven, when Mom left us with our grandmother for a few months."

He shifted his arms to shelter her from the wind. "And you changed your name?"

"I hated being teased about being Moonbeam. When I decided nobody would ever have control of my life again, for a while I was pretty busy proving it. If it weren't for Dorothy, Sarah and I might never have learned what it was like to have a real home, a real family."

"I'm glad she was there for you."

"I'd do anything for Dorothy." She shivered. The warmth was gone now, night settling in. "She's my family—and Wayne. Until Wayne, whenever we left a place, we never saw the people again. Life just kept going forward, no looking back. Wayne didn't let us go, though. He had us down for holidays, insisted on helping Dorothy with our education." She shivered again.

He slipped off his jacket and put it around her, then wrapped his arms around her again. "You're still trying to prove you're in control of your own life."

"I am in control."

He slid both hands into her hair. "You're afraid of losing control."

She stared at him, felt his hands in her hair, felt his lips although they hadn't touched her yet. "I won't lose control," she said soberly. "No one will ever control me."

"Some men would take that as a challenge." He drew her head closer, so slowly, so gently she could have broken his hold with one quick motion.

"Are you one of those men?"

She saw his lips curve, felt her own mouth dry in some mysterious chemical reaction.

"Yes, I'm one of those men, Samantha. I've dreamed of you losing control."

"That's sex," she said stiffly. "That's just. . . ."

His mouth touched hers. "Just sex?" he breathed, drawing back and letting his fingers slip away, out of her hair.

She stumbled to her feet, escaping his touch. His jacket fell to the sand, and they both reached for it, their hands colliding. She let go, stood up, and jammed her hands into her pockets.

He was manipulating her step by step, the forced intimacy of their conversation probing her life. Teasing touches, words. Drawing her slowly, steadily toward that bed, controlling every move.

"I've changed my mind," she said abruptly.

"Let me put the jacket around you again. You're—"

"Cal, stop it!"

He settled the jacket around her shoulders, murmured something soothing she couldn't hear over the pounding in her head. She shrugged the jacket off, jerked away as he reached to catch the garment. His hand twisted, and suddenly he was grasping her wrist, imprisoning her.

He pressed his lips to the inside of her wrist. "What is it you *do* want, Sam?"

She felt her pulse beating against his mouth. "I want you to stop—stop this seduction thing. Stop manipulating me. Trying to—"

"Trying to get you to want me? To make love with you?"

Something clenched in response to the image, muscles deep inside her.

"Just do it," she muttered.

"It?"

"Sex." She felt like striking him, tearing her wrist from his fingers and punching him, tearing the amusement from his voice. "Not tonight, I said, but I've changed my mind. But not this way, not . . . just kiss me. Properly."

His mouth moved along her arm, tracing nerves from wrist to elbow. "You want to make love?"

"Sex," she said, her voice strangled. "For God's sake, just kiss me!"

He tangled one hand in her hair and tilted her head back. She swallowed, felt the long line of her throat exposed to his lips, but he didn't touch her with his mouth, and he still held her wrist with his hand.

"If you want a kiss," he growled, "then take it."

He still held her wrist, still imprisoned her head with his in her hair. If she asked him to free her, he would . . . surely he would? She couldn't see his eyes, felt them as he stared down at her.

"Damn you," she hissed. She reached up with her free hand, tangled her fingers in his hair, the curls slippery around her hand as she pulled his head down.

Her lips were closed when his touched, her body trembling with anger. Then she felt his mouth open and she clenched her fingers more tightly in his hair, his arm a solid bar up her back and his fingers moving in her hair, sending shivers over her scalp and down her spine.

He pulled her hand up, between them, placed it on his chest.

"Feel me," he said, his voice harsh. "Feel what you do to me."

His heart hammered against her palm.

"Kiss me," he growled. "You wanted it."

Her hand fisted in his shirt and she pulled his mouth closer. Her lips parted, her own heart shuddering in the beat of his. He took her then, his mouth and hers, the world dizzy and spinning out of control.

When he lifted his head and stared down at her, the moon bright behind his head, she had forgotten how to breathe.

"I don't want to lose control," she whispered.

He lifted her in his arms.

"You can't carry me. . . ."

Her body crushed against his, her arms clinging now around his shoulders, his head, his mouth. . . . He pressed a hard kiss on her mouth, his tongue sliding inside, taking hers. She held on tighter, fought the dizziness.

Then his mouth tore from hers and he said in a low voice, "I am carrying you."

She turned her face into his shoulder, felt the hard play of his muscles as he walked up the gravel path. "Your jacket. Your jacket's on the beach."

"I don't give a damn about my jacket."

He reached the cabin. He wasn't breathing hard, but she could feel his heart as if it were her own, shaking her with each hard beat. His arms holding her. Lying in his arms, she felt uncomfortably vulnerable, unable to speak, to free herself.

He set her down but kept one arm around her while he unlocked the door. Then he pulled her inside and the door slammed, and she heard the lock snap home.

"Are you sure?" he asked. His voice sounded rough, uneven, and harsh. He wasn't touching her now, had stepped back, a threatening shape against the moonlight streaming through the patio doors on the other side of the room.

"What if I'm not sure?"

She'd have to be crazy. This wasn't Cal, the man in a suit, civilized, controlled with the fascination of fire burning inside. This man's fire was dangerously close to the outside, raw, and uncontrollable.

"If you're not sure," he growled, "then I'll go for a walk, see about getting another room."

If they stayed in the same room now, after that kiss, after he'd carried her with his heart hammering and her body trembling. . . .

"What if I am sure?"

"Prove it."

She wished she could see his eyes, wished she could stop her pulse from hammering. She knew there were reasons why this was a bad idea. Earlier, she'd decided it was best to . . . for them to do this now, tonight. That waiting would. . . .

There'd been reasons why, but she knew there were a thousand reasons why not. Because he was dangerous, a thousand times dangerous to her.

She lifted one hand and fumbled with the top button of her blouse.

"Samantha. . . ."

The button finally sprung free. Her fingers were steadier on the next one.

Cal stared at Samantha as she slowly unfastened the buttons of her blouse. She was standing there, staring at him with vulnerable moonlit eyes. He wanted to tell her not to be afraid, that he would protect her, forever.

He couldn't speak, couldn't get a sound past the swelling in his throat.

I don't want to lose control.

But she would. He promised himself she would, that he would show her the joys beyond control, that he would show her everything, here, tonight. Joy . . . fulfillment . . . love.

When her hand dropped away from the buttons, he could see the creamy silk of her flesh between the panels of the open blouse. He wanted to reassure her, to soothe her, but he knew she wouldn't admit her fear, knew he didn't fully understand her unease, could only soothe it with loving.

He stepped closer, cradled her cheek with his hand. Then he bent and slowly, very slowly, his own heart thundering in his veins, he took her lips with his.

She opened for him and he slid inside, tasting the sweetness of her mouth, sliding his tongue along hers and feeling her sigh. He moved his hand to her throat, felt her heart beat against his palm.

When he drew back from the kiss, her lips remained parted. He felt his erection throbbing and prayed for time, for control. She'd said she didn't want to be teased, seduced, and he knew that if he took her hard and fast, she would accept his invasion of her body.

Only sex, and it would be over quickly, leaving her in control.

He slipped her blouse over her shoulders, watched as silk slid away from her, dropping to the floor.

"I couldn't sleep last night," he told her in a low voice. "I couldn't get the feel of you out of my mind. Your mouth hungry under mine, the way your breast felt under my hand. I could feel your nipple through your clothes, erect, hard against my palm."

He saw her tremble, couldn't read her eyes with only moonlight to guide him.

"Are you cold?"

She didn't answer, or couldn't. He touched her face, her throat, and the curve of her breast above her lacy bra. She trembled when he touched but stood passive. *Yes*, she'd said, but this wasn't what he wanted, her body passive, as if submitting.

He took her hand and replaced it on his chest. "I'm not doing this alone. I'm not *taking* you. We do this together, or not at all."

He felt her hand jerk on his chest. "Damn you," she hissed.

"If you think we can do this without you losing control, I won't let it happen. I promise you, Samantha Moonbeam, we're both going to lose control."

"No!"

He feathered his fingers lightly over the curve of her breast, brushed his thumb over the peak, and felt her nipple harden, pressing against his thumb. "I've imagined suckling you so often, your nipple hard in my mouth, drawing you inside. . . ."

Her nipple was rock hard and he felt the shudder tear through her.

"Kiss me, Samantha. Now, with nothing held back."

She shuddered and he drew her closer. Her hands pressed into his chest—to hold him or to push him away? Her mouth parted under his and he felt her fists clench into the fabric of his shirt, but didn't let himself dive into her mouth.

Slowly, he traced her mouth with his tongue. Then he dipped deeper, learning the shape of her lips where they covered her teeth, the dark sweetness of her tongue as it finally tangled with his. But her body was still passive against his and he drew back, pulling his mouth from hers.

She made a sound, half whimper and half protest. Then he felt her arms tangle around his neck. Then she was pressing into him, her curves softly firm, hot under the hungry touch of his hands. He tasted her hot mouth as he swept his hands over her back, her hips, the firm curve of her buttocks. He gathered her in, held her against his throbbing erection, and heard her moan against the aching pleasure of her body against his.

Then she was restless, twisting, her breasts thrusting into his chest and he swept her up and carried her to the bed. He heard her whimper and covered her breast with his hand.

"Like this?" he asked, drawing his thumb over her nipple, his need tightening as she arched in response to his touch. His woman. Now, tonight, she would understand completely that this was meant to be . . . that they were forever.

She was burning, couldn't get her breath. He had to stop touching her like that, had to. . . . Her breasts throbbed and he wouldn't . . . she couldn't . . . his thumbs brushed over her nipples again, too lightly, and she bit back a whimper.

Then he drew away, his hands so light over her flesh, her midriff, and the underside of her breasts. She reached for him, grabbed iron-hard shoulders and pulled him down, down.

"No," he said, his voice low against her ear. He took her earlobe between his teeth and . . . oh, God, he was sucking on her earlobe and she . . . how could it feel so. . . .

She heard herself moan and she turned her head, needing his kiss, his mouth. She caught his mouth with hers, her hands tight against the back of his neck.

"Cal, now . . . just . . . just do it."

His laughter was low, soft as he escaped her mouth and pressed lips to her throat. Then he reached up and took her hands from behind his neck and said gently, "I told you, darling. We're going to lose control, both of us."

He stretched her hands back over her head and held them trapped, his fingers pinning her wrists. She twisted and felt her body arch with the movement, her breasts under the covering of her lacy skin-colored bra thrusting upwards.

"If you want to be free," he said softly, "all you need to do is ask."

Then he bent and placed his mouth on her breast, his breath hot through the fabric of her bra. Sensation ripped through her and she closed her eyes.

Through the bra, he drew her nipple into his mouth, then took it between his teeth. She moaned, a long shudder of sensation. She felt his hand pinning her arms, his fingers around her wrists, felt herself twisting, throbbing under his mouth.

"Cal . . . Cal, please. . . ." She couldn't bear it, couldn't bear the throbbing, the aching, needed. . . .

He took his mouth away from her breast and she moaned.

"Do you want me to let you go?" he asked softly. He took her mouth then, pulling on her lower lip, sliding his tongue along the sensitive nerves inside. She twisted, needing the hard press of his body against hers, needing . . . moaning as another wave of tension throbbed between her legs.

His fingers loosened on her wrists. "Do you want me to let your hands free?"

Before she could answer, he bent and took her in his mouth again, and she needed . . . needed his mouth on her skin. His hand on her wrists felt . . . she fought against his grip and felt her whole body twist against him, felt . . . now, finally, his hard pressure against her thigh, her belly.

"Cal, please. . . ."

He caught her nipple gently between his teeth again and she groaned.

"Tell me," he said against her. "Tell me exactly what you want."

She couldn't talk, couldn't. . . .

"More . . . please . . . I need more."

He released the fastener of her bra in one swift motion. She felt air play over her sensitive nipples, wet from his kisses through the fabric of her bra. She shuddered once before his mouth drew her nipple deep inside and she felt her body convulse.

Then he must have released her hands because her arms were tangled around him and he was driving her mad, beyond madness with his fingers on her throbbing nipples, his mouth plundering hers.

She had to touch him, needed to taste his flesh, his heat, and she fought with the fabric of his shirt until she felt the hot smoothness of his chest and heard the groan ripped from his throat as she grasped his tiny nipple between her fingers and tugged.

She rolled, or they did, and she was sprawled over him, his erection throbbing against the fork of her body, and she bent her mouth to his nipple and suckled, felt a tight band of need pulse harder as she pulled a moan from him.

"God, woman . . . stop or this will be over before it starts." He moved and she was flat on her back on the bed, his thigh pressing against the pulse that beat at the core of her sex.

"Now," she said, her voice husky with need. "I need you inside me now." She could feel it, the pulse tightening her whole body, consuming it with each beat.

He covered her mound with his hand, and even through her jeans the sensation was overwhelming. She heard the zipper, felt him stripping her jeans away. Then she was naked, only trembling flesh and the scrap of lace that was her panties.

She reached for his belt, but her fingers fumbled and he brushed them away.

"If you touch me, this is going to be over too damned soon." He traced her shape through the silky fabric of her panties and sent her head thrashing on the pillow. Then he slid his fingers under the elastic and into her creamy folds and she convulsed around him with a low, keening moan.

He stilled, holding her center with his hand still buried in her as her sex gripped him with spasm after spasm.

His mouth found hers and she felt herself open, felt as if her body lay wide open, his fingers in her, his tongue tangled with hers . . . as if he possessed her completely and she were only shudders of sensation.

"Do you have any idea what this feels like," he whispered to her. "Your climax holding me, tightening?"

The spasms were fainter. She could breathe, almost . . . if it weren't for the sensation of herself enveloping his fingers. She had to . . . needed to move, to turn away . . . hide her face from him.

"Easy," he murmured, sliding out of her. She heard a sound, her sound. Tried to cut it off, couldn't.

He pressed her head against his shoulder and held her, stroked her with long, slow caresses from his hands. She felt the shudders easing, felt her body moving, curving to the motion of his hands.

"Cal, I can't—"

"Hush." He took her mouth with his and she felt something release deep inside, taking the kiss deeper, further into her.

Heaven. His mouth on hers, their tongues stroking in long slow caresses. She felt so completely relaxed, so loose, as if her muscles had simply released everything. She let her hands trace the ripple of muscles across his chest, the hard breadth of his shoulders. Then she put one hand on either side of his face and gave herself up to his kiss.

No one had ever kissed her like this . . . or she'd never kissed like this. As if it would simply go on forever, as if the only pleasure she needed was simply to have his mouth to explore forever.

She shifted to reach his cheek with her mouth, then his ear. Earlier, he'd taken her earlobe in his mouth, and she'd. . . .

She felt the hard pressure of his erection against her hip.

"Cal? You didn't . . . ? I. . . ."

"Easy," he murmured. "Just kiss me again."

She opened her mouth and breathed in his scent. Her hands on his naked chest, his mouth, her breasts throbbing, tingling from the memory of his mouth.

His mouth. . . .

As if he could feel the sensations deep inside her body, he placed his hand over her breast and she felt the air drain out of her lungs in a long sigh.

"Samantha?"

She covered his hand with hers and closed her eyes to hold the sensation tight. "Kiss my breasts again, Cal. I want your mouth on me."

This time, she gave herself entirely to the sensation of his mouth on her nipple.

"What do you want?" he asked against her soft flesh.

"You . . . everything."

Then, somehow, he was on his back, sitting against the end of the bed with Samantha facing him, astride his hips, the pressure of his sex throbbing through her panties.

She wasn't sure when, how, but then they were naked and he was hard against her, little shudders running through her body as he moved. He lifted her breasts and slowly licked the peaks, sending spasms of sensation to her center.

"I can feel you," he breathed against her hot flesh.

"When I'm inside you, I'll feel everything." He licked her nipple again and she moaned and twisted against him.

He took her hips in his hands and her head fell back and she felt him, flesh to flesh, against her entrance. He held her hips and slowly lowered her onto him.

She couldn't breathe . . . couldn't . . . he filled her, pressing hot places inside. She felt Cal, deep inside her, so hot, her thighs gripping as he thrust deeper and her body arched and stretched to accept him.

She held tight, his mouth . . . she could die from the pleasure of his mouth suckling her breast as he thrust deep inside and she tightened to pull him even deeper, pressure building unbearably. She heard words, her voice, begging him, and he thrust deeper, driving her wild and high, higher, until she couldn't bear it . . . couldn't stop . . . would die if he stopped . . . and deep, deep inside, she shattered and screamed, a long driven scream as she convulsed around him.

The waves of sensation went on and on, drowning her, as if they would never stop, clutching her body around his hard, hot sex in waves that tore small sounds from her as she felt him grow, filling her beyond full, harsh breath tearing through his lungs. Her body clenched, and he spilled himself into her with a harsh groan of release.

Afterward, he drew her to his chest and she lay on him, her body drained, her breath coming in uncontrollable shudders. She closed her eyes and felt his heart hammer deep harsh heartbeats that eased only slowly.

It seemed as if their breathing took her away to a place where time ceased and the only reality was their bodies damply clinging together, hearts beating in tune as the air slowly cooled around them.

She took his heartbeat with her into her dreams.

Sometime in the night, she half woke to the sound of his voice gentle in her ear as he moved her. Then she was lying on her side with Cal spooned against her back, his arms wrapped around her and the blankets covering them.

Much later, when she woke again, the moon had left the sky. She lay in his arms, his breath soft on her shoulder, her body naked in his arms. Then his breathing stilled and she knew he too was awake.

His hand slid down, over her hip, and she turned in his arms.

Slower this time, with a deep, aching sweetness that took her up gently until there was only the high cliff and Cal drawing sensation from her body in deep, shattering waves. When he took her, his slow thrusts drove sanity from her. Then faster, harder, more urgently, and he led her past the edge. When she climaxed she felt herself trembling, falling through empty space with only Cal's arms to keep her safe.

She fell asleep with him still inside her, his arms holding her as if he would never let her go, his breath slowing in the aftermath of their loving.

The sun woke her, uncomfortably hot through the blankets.

She turned away from the light, the heat, buried her face in the pillow. She felt stiff, so drowsy she could almost have been drugged. Kippy. She had to get up and see to Kippy. Change her diaper, get a bottle ready.

Cal.

Her eyes flew open.

She lay alone in the bed, the blankets on *his* side tossed back. Where was he? She pushed herself up and the blankets fell away. Her breasts felt sensitive, tingling with the memory of his touch, his mouth.

Deep inside, another memory pulsed. Last night.

She shoved back her hair—it was a wild tangle, as if

she'd spent the night thrashing her head against the pillow.

Where was he? The bathroom? If he walked out and into this room, found her here—

She wasn't ready. She needed . . . time. Time and a shower, maybe a long walk.

Had he gone to get his jacket from the beach?

She needed to get herself together before she saw him. Right now she felt raw, open, vulnerable.

He wasn't in the bathroom. She grabbed jeans and another silk shirt—why hadn't she brought any damned sweatshirts?—and locked herself in the bathroom. She scrubbed her hair with shampoo and rinsed the tangles out, washed her body with soap, trying not to remember how his hands had felt on her.

She damned well wasn't going to stand in this shower, fantasizing him in here with her, his hands caressing her as he slowly washed her with foamy soap. He would smooth the suds over her breasts, stare down at them as the water rinsed the suds away. Then he would soap her midriff, her belly, and his hands would slip inside—

Stop it! Get control of yourself!

She rinsed off roughly and fled the shower, toweled herself half dry and wrapped her hair in a towel. Then she pulled clothes over her damp body, cursing her jeans when they clung. She yanked the towel off her head and raked her fingers through it to release the last of the tangles. Once it was dry, she would come back in here and wrap it securely in a roll at the back of her head.

She left the bathroom and started yanking the bed into order. They'd had sex. That's all it was. Sex, and now it was morning. This was a business marriage, and she wasn't wandering around in a sex-hazed cloud. Last night had been . . . last night Cal had been—

We'll both lose control.

She shuddered. He was a man and probably felt a masculine need to know that she wanted it, too, that she was as carried away as he had been.

That's all. Nothing more, and she. . . .

She'd never felt so undone, so out of control . . . filled with deep hunger that wouldn't be denied. She hadn't known . . . hadn't dreamed she had that inside her.

And she wasn't comfortable with the knowledge now that she did know.

She found his note as she stood in front of the bureau and brushed her hair.

I didn't want to wake you, you were sleeping so peacefully. I'm in the dining room. I'll bring back coffee. Yours, Cal.

She smoothed the note and replaced it on the bureau. She wanted a long walk on the beach alone, but that was a luxury she couldn't count on this weekend. They were together, alone, without computers, in the enforced intimacy of their honeymoon. She was going to have to face him soon, and the dining room seemed a much more controlled atmosphere for their morning-after meeting than . . . well, than the bedroom.

Cal was enjoying his second cup of coffee and allowing himself a pleasurable fantasy of returning to the room to wake Samantha. He would put the coffee beside the bed, on that end table. Then he'd bend down and touch her sleeping lips with his mouth. Her mouth would cling to his before her eyes opened, and under the morning sun awareness would dawn in her eyes as her cheeks flooded with the flush of memory.

The image shattered when Sam walked into the dining room. She wore jeans and a peach-colored blouse, her hair smoothly contained as if she were heading for work. The waitress met her three steps inside the door. Their brief conversation resulted in the waitress leading Sam to Cal's table.

"Good morning, Cal." Her voice was cool, friendly, the greeting he'd heard hundreds of times. First encounter of the morning. Efficient, the controlled woman he'd once thought was her true self.

Last night's Samantha was gone, buried deep inside. This was Sam, businesslike, efficient, wearing a mask.

She sat and the waitress bustled with coffee and a menu. Sam ordered toast and orange juice, picked up her coffee. Black coffee. He wondered if she'd ever taken it with sugar or cream, wondered if it was discipline that dictated it be black and bitter, her need to keep control.

She wasn't looking at him.

"Take your hair down, Sam."

She looked up at him then, eyes cool. "No."

He stared at her until he saw her face stain with the memory of last night, but her expression didn't change, nor her eyes. She'd warned him, last night, that she wouldn't lose control. Then she had, in his arms, but she had it back now.

"Do you intend to leave your hair up forever?" he asked, keeping his own voice steady, hard enough to mask his desire to reach across and shake her until she turned real again.

Her eyes skittered away from his, but he saw her force them back, saw her swallow, the only sign of her discomfort. "I always take my hair down before I go to bed."

The waitress brought toast and orange juice, and Sam busied herself spreading marmalade on a triangular piece of toast.

"Is that how you want it, Sam? Ice in the daylight, fire after dark?"

He saw her hand tremble, but she recovered and spread the yellow preserve evenly over the toast. She put down the knife, but didn't pick up the toast.

"We made a business deal," she said finally.

"And last night was business?"

"No." She shook her head. "It was—"

"Sex?"

"Yes." She couldn't quite manage to keep the coolness in her voice, and her face stained with color.

"There's something you need to know, Samantha."

She met his eyes. Hers were mostly under control now. "I'd rather you called me Sam."

"Sam's okay for business, but it's Samantha I made love to last night."

She shook her head and picked up her coffee.

"I understand you're afraid—"

"I'm not afraid!"

"—of losing control. Have you ever done that before, Samantha? Lost control in a man's arms?"

Her face was deeply flushed, but her voice was steady, husky and low. "No."

"It will happen again," he said, and he wasn't sure if he meant the words as a promise, a threat, or as an affirmation because he was afraid she would get up and walk right out of his life and he'd never hold her again.

"Is that what you wanted me to know? If so, I'd rather we changed the subject. We're not far from the Horne Lake caves. Since we don't have computers, e-mail, business, I thought we could spend some of the day exploring caves."

She had a firm grip on her coffee and if he touched her he figured she might bolt.

He said, "Samantha, I need you to know that I'm in love with you."

She put her cup down with a clatter. He saw coffee flow over the edges of the cup, panic in her eyes. "No, Cal. That's not part of the deal."

"It's not forbidden in our agreement, and it's only fair I warn you that I want more, much more than unwilling fire after dark. I want you, Sam, I want you crazy in love with me, and I'll do whatever it takes to win you."

Her eyes were wide with shock, fixed on his.

Cal had negotiated enough deals to know when to step back. He lifted his cup and forced calm into his voice and his body before he took a long sip. The coffee was cold, faintly bitter because the waitress had refilled it and he hadn't added more sugar.

"Now I'll go change," he said, pushing his chair back. "Exploring caves doesn't sound like the kind of excursion one undertakes in dress slacks and leather shoes. Take your time over breakfast."

Ten

Cal was in love with her. Samantha shivered in the cold air blowing through the entrance of Horne Lake's lower cave. Cal had gone ahead, checking the cave out, she supposed, making sure it was safe or whatever it was primitive man did when he led a woman into a cave.

Her imagination supplied the image. Primitive man . . . Cal standing at the entrance to a dark cave, his hand stretched out to her. She would step forward until she saw him clearly, perspiration glistening on his naked shoulders. Those shoulders, naked, were broader than she'd realized, corded with muscle that didn't show through his clothes. His hand . . . she should have known from his hands, taut and strong. Inside, fire flickering on the walls of the cave.

Fire . . . fire after dark. He drew her into the cave and she went into his arms, eager for his touch, his words of love. . . .

Samantha shook the image away. The cave in front of her, one of two the Horne Lake Provincial Park deemed suitable for self-guided exploration, held no flickering flames. She knew this cave would be mysterious, wet, dank, its walls running with condensation and trickles of streams from the spring runoff.

She'd been here before, though not to this particular cave. She'd been in one of the larger caves, on a guided tour. She was the one with local knowledge, yet she'd let Cal go ahead today, to scout the way.

Impatiently, she stepped inside. The entrance was narrow, tightening even more as she stepped into it. Beside the rock she stood on, a river of water rushed out of the cave. She would have to step across, find her footing on that knob of rock, then squeeze through the crack.

She took one step and the world darkened. No light in here, only damp, cold mysteries, and somewhere ahead, Cal. She reached up and switched on the light on the helmet Cal had rented for her at the park office. They'd stopped at the little building a half mile back, had rented lighted helmets for the dark exploration. Then they'd driven to the parking lot and crossed the swinging suspension bridge. She'd refused to be nervous on the bridge. After all, she'd crossed it before.

It was bright outside; a hot sunny day, her skin tingling with awareness every time Cal glanced at her.

But it was cold in the cave. The man in the park office had said it was only a few degrees above freezing. As if the cold sucked out the light, Samantha's lighted helmet threw only a pale yellow circle on the lumpy rock wall.

"Cal?"

"Right here." His voice came from ahead, on the other side of the narrow fissure. "I'll come guide you."

"No." She reached out her hand and stepped across the racing water, her palm striking the damp rock and clinging. "I don't need help."

The crack was tight enough that she had to twist sideways to get through the narrowest section. She saw Cal's light; then his hand grasped hers as she stepped into the inner cave.

"My hand's filthy," she said, forcing her fingers not to curl around his.

"Neither one of us is going to get out of here without

a certain amount of filth," he said with a laugh. "Come over here."

The cave grew colder with each step. She was wearing Cal's sweater, which he'd insisted she put on before she entered the cave, and he was wearing his windbreaker.

"Are you cold?" she asked.

"No."

"You must be thick-skinned. It's almost freezing—our voices sound strange." She'd expected an echo but it wasn't exactly that. Hollowness, but their words seemed to sink into those damp walls, and the sound of rushing water somehow caressed their voices.

"It's those Denver winters," he said.

"What?"

"My thick skin." He grasped her elbow. "There's more cave up here, to your left, but it's quite a reach. I'll help you."

She turned her head and the light reflected back the sight of rock walls in every direction. "This cave is smaller than the one I was in. Does it end here?"

"No. We go up."

The steep wall on her left had footholds. She pulled away from Cal, climbing on her own. Only a few feet and she could see over the edge, into more empty darkness.

"Spooky." The light showed an expanse ahead, but the fissure led up out of sight. "The water comes from up there."

Cal's hand against her back steadied her. "We'll explore deeper, but I don't think we'll go any farther up."

His decree sent rebellion through her. She'd been here before, during a college Easter vacation with Howard. She'd brought Cal here to the caves today, perhaps deliberately to remind herself of Howard, of the need to maintain control.

But Cal was *taking* control.

He loved her.

It was his nature to take control, and if she made the mistake of letting herself love him in return, she would have no defenses. Her life would slip out of her own control and she'd be trapped, caught in a whirlpool she'd stepped into of her own volition.

She pulled herself up another step, away from Cal's touch. "I think I will climb up here," she said. "It's a tower. The pamphlet said it was climbable."

"The fellow we met in the parking lot said there were bats at the top."

"Bats?" she squeaked. She couldn't see anything moving up there, but she remembered the time a bat flew into Dorothy's house in the summer.

"I don't imagine they'll bother us," Cal said, "if you do want to go up. It's daytime, so I think they'd be sleeping. Whatever it is bats do in the daytime."

"They hide. We had one in the house once." She retreated down the side of the rock face one step, feeling for a foothold. She felt Cal's hand at her back, steadying her. "I woke up in the night and saw it swooping circles over my head. I woke Sarah up to get her out of there. Sarah screamed and the bat flew out into the hall. Dorothy went after it with a broom. Then it disappeared. We couldn't find it for a long time." She shuddered.

"Do you want to leave?"

"No." This wasn't going to help anything, shivering like a maiden afraid of her shadow, cowering in the shelter of Cal's arm. She must have been crazy to bring them here, a place of darkness and mystery. "I'm going up onto this ledge. There's a pool up there, isn't there? The bats won't come down this far."

She scrambled up, felt the damp layer of mud on the rock wall and told herself she'd look like a homeless person who hadn't washed in months by the time she got out of here. Thank heaven she'd put her hair up today. Bats . . . she'd kept shaking her hair that night at

Dorothy's, terrified the bat would fly into it and become tangled.

"What happened to the bat? Where did you find it?" Cal's voice echoed below her now, while she stood on the ledge, which had turned out to be quite broad, although the space wasn't high enough to allow her to stand erect.

Then Cal was beside her, his face macabre in the dim light she wore on her helmet. "The bat?"

"We found it pressed up against the corner between the big beam that runs along the peak of the cathedral ceiling. Just an inconspicuous shadow in a dark corner, way up over our heads."

"That's what, twenty-five feet from the living room floor to the peak of the cathedral ceiling? How did you get it down?"

"We couldn't. Dorothy got up on the ladder, but even with the broom she couldn't reach. So we went back to bed, and we closed out bedroom doors so it couldn't—" She shivered with the memory, managed a laugh. "This is no place to talk about it, especially if there really are bats up there. We kept our bedroom doors closed, and we left the doors to the upstairs balcony open during the daytime for several days, hoping it would fly away to find somewhere darker. I guess it did, because it was still there the next night, but then we never saw it again. I used to dream that it flew into my hair, that I couldn't get it out."

Cal pulled her into his arms. Their helmets bumped together and blanked out their lights. "I'd save you," he said soberly. "I'd free you." He angled his head carefully and drew her into his kiss.

She was breathless when he freed her. "It's just a childhood memory. I'm not afraid of them now. They're night creatures, and they don't want to be tangled up with me any more than I want— I'm glad, though, that I wore my hair up."

He kissed her again and she held him with her hands,

clenched in his jacket. "My hands." Her voice stumbled. "Your jacket—I've been hanging onto those rocks and I can feel the mud."

"Come on, let's get out of here."

She pulled back, wished her breathing weren't so loud in the cave, as if she'd gone spinning when he kissed her. Where was the sound of the rushing water? Could the rock wall they'd climbed mask the sound so effectively from them?

"There's more to the cave, up ahead. I think if we walk along the edge of this pond . . . I'm not afraid of the bats. I'm not some wimpy woman who needs your protection."

"You're afraid," he said in the flat voice she'd heard him use once or twice when he called someone in a tight meeting. Stupid of her to deny it, because of course he could tell. "If I challenged you, I'm sure you'd climb that tower, fight the nausea and fear, and get right up there with the bats. You don't need to prove anything to me, Samantha."

She was behaving like a fool, threatening to climb up there into the bats, if there were bats, because she wouldn't allow herself to be directed by Cal. Ridiculous, because she was being controlled by the desire *not* to be controlled.

This wasn't working at all. Cal had taken what was a straight business deal and twisted it out of her control. She climbed down the rock face like a crab, hands and feet clinging, going down backward. Four steps along the edge of the rock she came to the narrow fissure, saw light marking the way. She turned off her helmet light. With her hand on one wall of the fissure, she turned around to face him.

The sliver of light coming through the fissure wasn't enough to penetrate the darkness. Cal had turned off his light as well, and she saw only a man's shape, broad and threatening, in the blackness.

"You tricked me," she said, and now the rushing water masked her words.

He heard, though. "Did I?"

"You said this was business. You said you wanted me for Tremaine's."

"I do."

She shook her head. "A business marriage. You said you'd help with Kippy if I helped your company. I would never have married you knowing that you—if you'd said anything about loving. You lied to me, Cal."

"I suppose I did."

She tilted her head back, although she couldn't see his face, much less his eyes, in the black of the cave. "I don't want you in love with me."

"We'll see." His voice was cold, and she figured that was good, because she didn't want the controlling tendrils of love. She *would not* want.

"No, we won't see. *I* won't."

"Right." His voice sent shivers along her spine. "We've stated our positions, now let's get on with business. If you're not going to climb up to prove yourself by playing with the bats, turn around and get out of here."

"Cal. . . ."

"Now. Out."

She turned and scrambled through the narrow fissure, stepped over the rushing water. She emerged into glaring sunlight breathless, the urge to keep running clawing in her veins. Up those stairs cut in the hillside, down the path to Cal's car.

Something crawled on her face and she gasped and reached a hand to flip it away. A spider? She slapped at it, panicked, felt it crawl onto the side of her neck. She bent over, slapping at her neck.

Cal gripped her arm from behind and pulled her erect. She struck out at him, and he grabbed her other arm, too. "Easy, it's just your hair. Let me. . . ."

"What?"

"Your hair." He released her and smoothed hair from her face with one hand. "Your hair's come loose. There's nothing on you. Nothing."

She stood, fighting for breath as he carefully tucked strands of hair behind her ear. When he dropped his hand, he just stood there, staring at her. She rubbed the back of her hand over her forehead, tried for a laugh. "I guess that wasn't a very convincing show of fearlessness."

His smile would have relieved her, except that his eyes were cool, darker than usual, as if he'd brought the cave outside with him.

She realized she wanted to step into his arms, so she stepped back instead. She could see every word she'd said inside the cave, and she felt a sick certainty that she'd made a mistake, that she shouldn't have spoken.

"Maybe you want to wash in the stream," he said. "There's mud all over your face."

She realized she'd been holding her breath, and carefully let it out. She crouched beside the stream and rinsed her mud-streaked hands in the icy water. Then she used hands and water to bathe her face as Cal crouched beside her and washed his hands.

"Your face is OK," she said, "but your jacket. . . ." Her muddy handprints marred the smooth beige of his jacket, where she'd clutched him when he kissed her inside the cave.

"It doesn't matter," he said.

She stood and stared down at his sweater. It had been pale blue when he gave it to her, but now it was streaked with mud, and at one spot near the peak of her left breast, she must have snagged the sweater on the rocks.

"I think I've ruined your sweater."

"Forget it," he snapped.

She backed away from the stream and pulled her helmet off. The strap snagged in her hair, and she ripped the clip and pins out and sent hair tumbling down her back. All around her, the trees stretched tall and dark green, the ground under her feet a carpet of last year's cedar droppings. She couldn't remember ever feeling quite so uncomfortable.

Last night she'd been crawling with awkwardness until they made love. Now, after what she'd said to him in the cave, he might never touch her again.

"My jeans are muddy," she said stiffly. "I can't get back into your sports car like this."

"For Christ's sake! Just get moving!"

She turned and started climbing those cedar-lined stairs fast, but the steepness took her breath away and she had to slow. The sun through the overhead blanket of fir and cedar trees warmed her back and her head, and she pulled herself up, grabbing the rail and pulling with each step.

She wasn't going to look back, didn't care if Cal followed. She'd get out of here, up the stairs, then down the steeply sloping path and across the footbridge to the clearing where the car waited. She'd beat the dust out of her jeans, because the mud would be dry from the sun by then, and she'd enjoy the peace, the evergreens, and the birdsong.

Cal could take his time.

He caught up with her at the top of the stairs.

"Take the sweater off," he said, his voice hooking her from behind. "You're too hot."

Because she realized she didn't want to turn around, she turned and faced him. Nothing showed in his face, neither irritation nor affection. Even when he'd said he loved her, in the restaurant this morning, his face had been carefully blank. She'd always liked that about him. The control, despite the passionate emotions she'd sensed underneath from the beginning. Emotions she'd believed safely channeled into his work, his company.

Today his control frightened her, because she understood that he wanted to control her.

"I can figure out when I'm hot and when I'm not," she said grimly. She *was* hot, and she could feel rebellion boiling in her blood, a child's determination to do the opposite of an adult's command.

She dropped the helmet in her hand, ducked her head, and pulled the sweater off, emerging with her hair tumbled around her face. "Your sweater," she said, pulling it right way out and folding it in half lengthwise with the mud tucked inside before she handed it to him. "I don't need it any more."

"Running isn't going to help anything, Sam. We need to talk."

"Talk is the last thing we need." She shoved her hair back from her face and bent to pick up the helmet again. "We need a new contract."

Those were the last words either of them said on the walk back to the car, where Cal put the dirty sweater and helmets in his trunk while she stood on the cedar carpet and beat her jeans, driving the dust out in clouds around her.

"I need a bath," she muttered. "A shower."

He used a towel he fished out of the trunk to beat the dust out of his jeans. This was the first time she'd ever seen him in jeans, and maybe that was part of the problem today. After last night she'd felt off balance enough. Then he'd gone back to the cabin and emerged in jeans tight enough that every time she looked at him, she remembered how he'd felt, rising above her, then thrusting inside in a long slow stroke that had her gripping his tightly muscled buttocks, crying out as her world spun away.

"Your helmet," he said, still standing at the trunk. He'd unzipped his windbreaker and tossed it in, dirt and her palm prints resting on the floor of his sports car's trunk.

She picked up her helmet from the ground and handed it to him.

He slammed the trunk and asked, "How do you expect to negotiate a new contract without talking?"

"I don't want a new contract." She'd just said she did and knew she'd better shut up until her brain started running things again. "I want to break the one we have. You signed it under false pretences. You lied to me."

"What about Kippy? We've got a court appearance this coming Wednesday, to prove we're good parents for your niece."

Kippy. Her anger drained away into a feeling of dread.

He opened the car door on her side. "Get in," he said tonelessly. "We don't need to settle this right now."

She slipped inside the car. How could she have been so selfish as to forget about Kippy? One night alone with Cal, followed by his declaration of love over toast and orange juice, and she'd become so tangled that she'd completely forgotten Kippy, waiting back on Gabriola Island, where Dorothy was only allowed to care for her because she had a medical doctor with her.

"Do up your seat belt." Cal ordered as he slid behind the wheel.

She fumbled with the belt. She'd forgotten about Dorothy, too. How could Samantha be struggling for power with Cal, when Kippy and her grandmother needed her, when she'd promised Dorothy she would look after everything?

She was no better than her mother, promising, then disappearing. Kippy was her responsibility now, and she'd find a way, somehow she would find a way through this minefield with Cal and she *would* make a stable world for Kippy.

They drove back to the resort in silence as the sun slipped lower in the sky. When Cal pulled up outside the cabin, he turned off the engine but didn't undo his seat belt.

She turned her head. She felt cold, empty, needed to stay that way, to clear the emotional turmoil of the last week.

Cal said, "I'll be in court Wednesday, no matter what. I wouldn't harm Kippy."

She managed to swallow the desert dryness in her throat. "Thank you. I—" She swallowed twice, hard. "I'll be back at work after I've got permission to bring her."

The silence grew. She looked away from him. She wanted to release her seat belt, wanted to escape the confines of the car, and wanted him to turn and look at her, to smile.

To smile? Was she insane?

"My mother always fought with her husbands. Not at first, but after a while she'd be screaming at them." Her throat was so dry she couldn't seem to moisten it no matter how much she swallowed. "I didn't know I was like that, too. I'm sorry I shouted at you." He'd said he loved her and she'd said no, and she'd been looking for a fight ever since. "I'm off balance, and this marriage—I thought it was a business deal. I don't know how to cope with anything else."

He turned his head and after a moment, held his hand out. Her hand joined his, and she stared at her fingers lying in his. She hadn't managed to get all of the cave dirt from under her nails. Her fingers twitched, curled, and he tightened his grip.

"Friends?" he asked.

She nodded tightly.

"Let's get cleaned up, then."

She nodded abruptly and escaped the car.

Friends. They'd be friends and after dark . . . lovers after dark. He wasn't Howard, he understood now that she wasn't going to fall in love, that she wasn't going to become soft and malleable, and she'd apologized—sort of—for turning irrational and picking fights all day.

Friends.

Inside the cabin, they shed their shoes and socks at the door. She walked straight into the bathroom and turned on the shower, then turned back to leave the bathroom for fresh clothes before she shut herself in.

Cal stood in the doorway and she stopped abruptly, eighteen inches from him.

"Do friends shower together?" he asked.

She felt her heartbeat in her throat, the moisture again drying from her mouth. If she was going to lose her saliva every time he looked at her, she'd better start carrying lozenges.

He held his hand out to her again. She stared at his hand, couldn't seem to look away. The gold wedding band on his finger, telling the world he belonged to her. Her left hand clenched, felt her own wedding ring tighten with the movement.

Her heart wouldn't stop hammering.

She didn't move the hand closest to his, but her left hand, the one wearing his ring. Their fingers caught, tangled together, and she couldn't look up. She knew it was a bad idea, that letting the loving into the day—no, letting *sex* into the day—would make it harder to separate things in her mind.

She shouldn't have taken her hair down outside the caves, should have kept her bun and her inhibitions and control, at least until dark.

The sun would soon set. Three quarters of an hour more, and she could have hidden her weakness under cover of darkness. He would touch her, his hands sliding into her hair, his mouth seeking hers, and she would hide her response in darkness.

"Have you decided?" he asked gently.

The water pounded into the shower behind her. "Yes," she said soberly.

He unbuttoned her blouse slowly. She stood passive, every nerve stretched for the sensation of his hand brushing her nipples, but he worked the buttons open very carefully without touching her.

When the blouse hung free, he stepped closer and pushed it back. She let it slide down her arms to the floor, then she soberly began unfastening the buttons of his short-sleeved cotton shirt. She had to reach up to push it back, off his shoulders, and her nerves hummed when her breasts brushed his chest through her bra, but he said nothing, although she saw his eyes.

He wanted her. Here, now. In the shower, with evening light bathing the world.

He unfastened the button at the front of her jeans and pulled the zipper down, then smoothed the jeans down over her hips. When he kneeled in front of her, she felt a pulse beating at her center, only inches from his face as he looked up at her.

He placed one of her hands on his shoulder and murmured, "Lift." She lifted first one leg, then the other, as he stripped the jeans from her. Then he smoothed her panties down over her legs, without once touching anywhere near where the pulse was beating so hard and heavy. She should have felt embarrassment, but she stood motionless as he slowly got to his feet, his hands sliding up the outside of her thighs, her hips, settling on her waist.

"Turn around," he commanded quietly.

She turned slowly. Her nerves were screaming from the way his gaze raked over her mostly naked flesh, from the throbbing of her veins. Maybe it wasn't the veins that throbbed and pulsed. Maybe it was the arteries. Maybe—

His fingers slipped under the back of her bra and she felt it spring free. She reached up and slid the straps down off her shoulders and let her bra fall to the floor with her other clothes. He stood behind her now, and every inch of her body was tingling, throbbing, as if he'd stroked, sensitized her with his eyes. She waited for him to touch her, to take her breast or her hips or—anything, to allow her to let this painful tension free, to let her free.

His hands settled on her shoulders, and it wasn't enough. She was strung so tight she dare not move, dare not speak, but he didn't pull her back against him and she almost whimpered.

"In the shower," he said. "I'll join you."

She didn't look back, couldn't because she wanted to beg him to touch her *now,* to thrust inside her so she could scream as her crawling nerves demanded.

She stepped into the stream and let water flow through her hair and down her back. She reached for the soap and turned to face the spray, her eyes closed.

She felt him when he stepped behind her. He took the soap from her, his arms bracketing her with bars of muscle as he worked the soap into froth in his hands and put the bar back on its holder. Then he began to lather her.

Slowly, so slowly she had to stop breathing to feel every sensation. Her shoulders and her back, so slowly. Her breasts were throbbing, and when his hands slid over her buttocks with lather, she jerked and he murmured something she couldn't hear.

He turned her and she was putty in his hands, enduring the slow lathering of her arms and her throat and the flat planes of her chest above her breasts. Then his hand, freshly lathered, slid down the flat between her breasts and she whimpered as he lathered her midriff and her belly. She felt pressure building painfully between her legs, and he crouched down in front of her, his face intent as he slowly lathered her thighs and her calves and her feet.

Then he began again and she pulled the soap from him and started to lather his chest but he kissed her and she felt his erection bump against her hip. She heard a sound, like a plea in her throat, and he started again, slowly lathering every part of her except her breasts and the pulsing curls between her legs.

"Cal, I can't bear it."

He murmured and her voice lost sound, and he turned her and began lathering her back again and she heard herself cry, "Cal, please, now. . . . If you don't touch me, if you don't—"

"Hush." His mouth against her ear, and he pulled her back against him, and she melted and sagged, his chest pressing into her back, his sex hard against her buttocks.

"How long. . . ."

His hands, slippery with suds, slid around to her midriff and she closed her eyes and let her head fall back, the water on her face. If he didn't touch her, if he didn't—she couldn't bear . . . oh. . . .

His fingers slid up the under curve of her breasts and she moaned. Then he began stroking her breasts, milking them with his fingers, his erection hard against her behind, and his hands . . . she shuddered, heard herself whimpering, sobs with each slow stroke.

"I'm going to fall. I can't. . . ." Her legs were failing her . . . his hands . . . how could just his hands be doing this to her?

He turned her in his arms and lifted her, hands on her buttocks.

"Wrap your legs around me," he growled, and she gripped him with her legs and he bent his head, his hair in her face, and sucked so deeply that she cried out.

"Cal, oh, God!"

He gripped her buttocks and thrust up into her and she clenched herself around him and held tight, her arms and her legs and the muscles deep inside that made her feel him hard, filling her, so deep she could only moan, ragged moans with each thrust. Her head . . . she couldn't . . . felt the wall at her back. She let her head fall, gave herself up to the heat clawing inside her, clawing and pulsing, and she sobbed with unbearable ecstasy each time he filled her. She heard his harsh groans tearing the air with hers, and she couldn't . . . she couldn't . . . she would. . . .

The world shattered, exploded inside her and she screamed a long scream that had no end, and in it she heard his release and felt the forceful thrust of his sex spilling inside her.

Air tore through her, gulping breaths. Water streaming over them, Cal's face pressed into her throat. His breath, harsh, ragged.

She closed her eyes and sensations filled her. Inside, the spasms returned, weaker now, draining the last trace of energy from her body. Cal, inside her. She felt . . . she felt. . . .

"Samantha?" His voice was ragged, like his breath.

He tightened his grip on her hips, and she felt him slip out of her. He dragged his mouth from her throat, and she opened her eyes. He was close; his eyes flecked with gold, the water streaming down his head.

"Samantha? Are you OK?"

She thought it was going to be a laugh, but no sound came.

"Sam?"

She looped her arms tighter around his neck and pulled his head close, so she could kiss him. "Cal, I'll never think of showers in the same way again."

She felt his laughter and had to close her eyes again, because the sensation washed through her like water. "Cal?"

"Yeah?" He lowered her, slowly, and her feet found the ground.

She wanted him to do it again. She wanted—heavens, how *could* she want, after that? "Do you think a person can become addicted?"

His grin was wolfish, and she felt a wave of hot weakness

surge through her. "Addicted to making love in the shower?"

She knew she needed to make herself form words to correct him. They'd had *sex,* but the word wouldn't form on her lips.

"I didn't just mean . . . not just the shower." She couldn't hold his gaze and she dropped down and fumbled for the soap, trapped it finally in the corner of the shower.

"It's your turn," she said soberly, and she began to soap his feet.

"Sam. . . ."

She looked up at him. "If you get to make me lose control. . . ." And, heavens, how he'd seduced control from her. "Then I get to do it too."

"Sam," his voice sounded strangled, "after what we just did, it's going to be a while before I can do anything."

She smiled and lathered the soap. "So this shouldn't bother you then," she said softly, and she began to slowly, ever so slowly, turning the soap into lather, covering every inch of his body.

She heard him groan when she did his thighs, a groan of protest, she thought. Later, when she had soaped his chest and shoulders, when she'd stopped to tease his nipples with her tongue, she returned to his belly, smoothing thick lather. By then, he was breathing in harsh explosions, his hands clenched at his sides. She saw his erect sex jerk as she skimmed over his hips, and heard him moan her name. Her chest filled with something too overwhelming to name and she swallowed hard. Then she lathered his clenched hands and murmured, "Such rigid control."

She was kneeling in front of him and she slid her hands up to his buttocks. They were rock hard. His whole body was hard, like steel.

"What would it take for you to lose control?" she asked softly. She wanted to taste him, needed to know what would happen when she did, to feel his body jerk in response.

"If you do what you're thinking of," he growled, "you'll find out."

She'd never done it before, wasn't quite sure how, but she bent her head and took him into her mouth, and when he cried out she felt it through her whole body.

Eleven

She needed to rethink everything. This marriage. The relationship . . . friendship, whatever it was. The whole thing had made sense a couple of days ago, but then they'd gone to Haida Sunset and he'd turned her into some kind of love slave.

Well, to be fair, he hadn't done it all by himself. Her face flamed as she remembered what had happened in the shower. And afterward, in the bed. And the next morning, astride him on the big easy chair by the window, with the cool air-conditioning flowing over her naked shoulders and Cal deep inside her.

She'd never known, never understood . . . never. . . .

Well, she'd just never. This was different, soul-shattering, mind-numbing, hot, overwhelming . . . loving. Not love. Not like *in love*, not like giving control of your world to someone else, but it was just that the word *sex* didn't really cover what happened when he touched her.

He didn't even need to touch her. When he looked at her, telling her his thoughts without words, she felt herself heating, felt moisture. When she sat, like this, in the car, wanting to ask him to stop, to pull off the road before they got back to Gabriola, because she needed him now.

He would pull under the trees on a side road, pull her into his lap, cup her buttocks, and she'd clench inside, hungry . . . ready. Needing.

She didn't. She didn't really. It was . . . cumulative hunger, because this feeling had been waiting for her all these years, and now she'd discovered her own body in Cal's arms . . . his body . . . she couldn't seem to get enough.

They were traveling the new Island Highway, built to take them from city to city. No side roads, nowhere to pull off.

"Cal?"

"Hmm." He didn't turn his head, but he reached out a hand and captured hers to bring it to his side.

Of course she wouldn't ask him to stop. That belonged back at Haida Sunset, with their honeymoon. They had things to do today. Monday, and Cal would be flying back to Seattle for an afternoon meeting. Even now, she could see him thinking of work. He'd be planning, going over the priorities for the Lloyd e-commerce phase. She needed to get back, take over responsibility for Dorothy from Adrienne and look after Kippy. She needed to check her e-mail, too, to make sure nothing had come unraveled over the weekend.

"Did you say something?" Cal asked.

"I was wondering if we'd make the eleven forty-five ferry to Gabriola."

He shot her a smile that sent her pulse hammering. "We'd have made the ten-forty if we hadn't stopped to make love."

"How long will you be gone?" She'd been determined not to ask, determined not to need him so badly she'd beg for him to return, beg him not to go.

"I can't get back tonight." He sounded irritated, and she couldn't stop a stab of satisfaction that he seemed as disappointed as she was. "I'll be back tomorrow night, though it may be late. I'll bring your car, shall I, so we'll have it to drive back to Seattle with Kippy? Do you think there's room in the trunk for Kippy's things?"

"Yes, except the playpen, but we can get one in Seattle."

Yesterday, in the caves, she'd decided she wouldn't live with him, that she would return to Seattle, to her own apartment. A short-lived decision. She'd be alone tonight, but tomorrow night he would love her again, although they'd have to be quiet, not to disturb the baby. Tomorrow, she decided, she would be calmer, tamer. She'd enjoy it . . . oh, heavens, she'd enjoy it, but she was getting used to his touch, wasn't she? And she'd take it more calmly next time.

Right.

They caught the eleven forty-five ferry, though only because it was ten minutes late.

"I'll have to take off right away," said Cal as he drove onto the ferry. He'd arranged to have a local pilot fly the chopper to Dorothy's so it would be waiting for him when they got back.

"Yes," she agreed, unfastening her seat belt as he parked the car in the ferry's center aisle. "I'm going to go up front to watch the water."

He came with her and they stood, staring at Gabriola as it came closer.

"We'll come here a lot," he said.

"You don't take enough time off to go anywhere a lot."

"I will now."

Uneasiness crawled at the back of her mind. She'd lost control this weekend, big time. First in the dark, in bed, then it had spread to the shower, to the daylight, and now she felt sensitized, as if one look could bring her to his bed, no matter where it happened. At work, in a crowded conference, in the car crawling through Seattle's rush hour.

She'd been counting on circumstances being on her side. He'd go back to work and the job would swallow her. They'd touch, love, in the dark, at night, and the rest of her life would return to something approaching normal.

And it would. He might plan to take time off, but Tremaine's would swallow him, because he loved it and couldn't let the reins go. She'd get herself back under control, at least during the daylight hours.

Dorothy was sitting cross-legged on the lawn, some twenty feet from the waiting helicopter, when Cal and Samantha drove up. She got to her feet as Samantha climbed out of the car, lifting the baby into her arms and walking toward them.

"Grandma!" Samantha hurried to Dorothy. "I'll take Kippy. You shouldn't be lifting her."

Dorothy accepted Samantha's kiss and held onto the baby. "She's sleeping. I'm putting her down for her nap. Don't worry about me. Adrienne's watching me like a hawk. When Kippy wakes up, you tell her I'll be back in a few hours. Adrienne and I have an appointment."

"Don't you need to get back to the hospital?"

Dorothy snorted. "That's nonsense, too, and at least Adrienne has the sense to see it. We're off to the university."

"The university?"

"That's right," said Dorothy, and she left Samantha staring after her as she walked slowly to the house, the baby against her shoulder.

"What's she talking about? She's sick. She shouldn't be carrying a baby, shouldn't be tearing around."

Cal said, "We'll get the story from Adrienne."

"You have to leave." She didn't, *wouldn't* let herself need him to get through the day. Bad enough she couldn't imagine a night without him. "You'd better go. I'll look after this."

Cal ignored her words, taking her hand and walking toward the house. Dorothy disappeared inside and Adrienne came through the door to stand on the porch with her hands on her hips, watching Cal and Samantha approach.

"You're looking a little more relaxed, brother," she teased.

Cal grinned. "What have you been up to while we were gone? Dorothy's talking about going back to college."

"Not back," said Samantha. "She's never been."

Adrienne held out her hand to Cal. "Give me your keys. We need to catch the one-twenty ferry. We'll take your car. Dorothy's needs a valve job. You should do something about that, brother."

"What's going on?" demanded Samantha.

Cal's sister smiled at her. "Sorry, I'm so used to teasing Cal, I didn't think—I'm no cardiologist, but I can't make sense of this doctor's diagnosis of Dorothy. She's having spasms, cramps, but no pain in her left arm, and the fever isn't consistent with heart failure. I've called in a couple of favors and taken an extra couple of days off. I'm taking Dorothy over to the university research hospital where a friend of mine has agreed to run a few tests."

Cal frowned. "You're leaving Sam stranded without a vehicle."

"Who's doing the tests?" demanded Samantha.

"Dennis Rachers," said Adrienne. "Head of the cardiology unit."

"Oh."

Cal said to his sister, "I'll get you a rental car."

Samantha shook her head. "Take Cal's. I'll use Dorothy's."

"It's got bad valves," said Cal.

"It's good enough to get around the island."

"We'll be back first thing in the morning," said Adrienne. "The tests are being done tonight, after the place closes." She grinned. "How else did you think I could get her past the waiting lists? We'll stay in a hotel out by the university, and get back on an early ferry tomorrow. There's food in the fridge, diapers, and formula in the pantry."

Cal said, "I don't like leaving Sam with a dodgy car." He was looking at Samantha now, his face stern.

"I'm fine," she said impatiently. "If the car won't go, there's a taxi service on the island. Your sister is getting Dorothy in with a specialist she'd probably have to wait months to see, and she's welcome to my car—to your car, I mean."

He didn't like it. "You'll call a taxi if you need to go somewhere?"

"I won't need—"

"Sam!"

She gritted her teeth. He could be the most infuriating man. "Yes, all right. Now go, get back to Seattle."

"Not yet," he said and pulled her into his arms.

She should have pushed him away, should have closed her lips because she was irritated with him for perpetually trying to run the details of her life. If she let him, he'd be choosing her friends, making her appointments, taking her over.

She knew better, but she met his mouth with hers open and hungry, and they kissed each other breathless in seconds.

"I'll see you tomorrow night," he said when he pulled away from her. "If I'm late, don't wait up. Get some sleep."

She flushed, because neither one of them had got much sleep in the last forty-eight hours. She told herself she wouldn't watch him leave, but she was still staring when the helicopter disappeared over the trees to the south.

Kippy hadn't woken from her nap when Dorothy and Adrienne left to drive to the ferry. Samantha walked back into the house, hoping Adrienne was right and the doctor who'd diagnosed Dorothy's heart condition wrong.

In Kippy's bedroom, she stared down at the baby. She hoped she could be as good a mother as Dorothy, as good as Sarah would have been if she'd lived. Cal would be a good father—he'd promised, and, growing up in a family filled with love and security, he'd learned how.

"Kippers," she whispered. "This scares me. Marriage. Motherhood. I'm not sure I know how to do any of it."

Kippy woke cranky when Samantha was halfway through the flood of e-mail messages that had accumulated since Friday afternoon. Samantha walked her, murmuring soothing sounds that seemed to get Kippy's attention.

She had decisions to make, and Kippy seemed to sense her impatience. Stacey in accounting had just asked for a six-month leave of absence because she and her husband had been called up on an adoption list—babies everywhere! Stacey had recommended her assistant Elaine for the job, but Sam wasn't sure Elaine would be up to it. Tremaine's had more than a hundred employees now, and Cal's plans to promote the company as a major application service provider meant the next six months to a year would be a constant round of recruitment challenges.

Jallison, the developer she'd hired to look after contracting their new premises, had sent a series of five e-mails over the weekend. Problems with delivery of office furniture for the new developers. Problems with the security system. These were exactly the things Samantha had hired Jallison to look after. She needed to have a serious talk with Cal before he signed the agreement with Jallison for the second stage.

She needed to be back in Seattle, now, today.

Kippy wouldn't settle to play on the blanket Samantha spread on the floor, wouldn't sit happily in the high chair, bashing her plastic spoon on the tray. Samantha tried typing a reply to one e-mail while holding the baby in her lap, but Kippy thought bashing on the computer keys was a great idea and Samantha gave up.

Why hadn't she talked with Cal about Jallison over the weekend?

Because I spent most of the weekend in bed. Because whenever he touched me, looked at me, I couldn't think of anything else.

Still couldn't.

"Gaa-gaa," said Kippy.

"You're right." She had a baby to look after, Dorothy to worry about, a court appearance coming up Wednesday, and a few million work details to look after by remote control.

"Gaa," said Kippy.

"Yes, you're right. You come first." She propped Kippy on her hip and went to get the baby pack out of the linen closet. "Things might get more organized after we arrive in Seattle, but meanwhile, let's both take a long walk and clear our heads."

When the baby saw the pack, she gurgled and rammed her fist into her mouth. As Samantha laced Kippy against her breasts, she felt an overwhelming surge of tenderness. Such a miracle, tiny feet and hands, laughing eyes. Alive. She remembered Sarah eight months into her pregnancy, the baby big in her belly. Samantha had placed her hand on Sarah's belly, had felt the strong, living kick of this small human being. She'd asked Sarah what it felt like to have a child growing inside.

"It feels like a miracle."

One day, if she and Cal had a child. . . .

Perhaps even now. They'd practiced birth control, but not that time in the shower.

With Kippy at her breast, her own hands laced over her belly, Samantha felt the memory of an embryonic Kippy kicking against her palm when Sarah invited her to feel the baby in her womb. She couldn't shake the image, couldn't outwalk it, even though she and Kippy walked all the way to Peterson Road and beyond, down the hill to Drumbeg Bay.

"Your mommy loved you so much, Kippy."

Tears kept surging behind her eyes, pressure in her

throat. Fear, joy, hope—she couldn't seem to find her way through the tangle. Cal. . . .

I need you to know that I'm in love with you.

She couldn't be in love with him, could she? Fantasies of Cal's baby, growing inside her. Heaven knew she melted every time he touched her, every time he looked at her in a way that showed desire. Maybe that wasn't love, but it seemed to be a lot more than just sex.

Jessica had been in love a dozen times, maybe more. Over-the-rainbow love that swept everything in her world along . . . especially her children, who were dragged along, always leaping off cliffs with their mother, always leaving people and places behind.

Samantha wasn't Jessica. She didn't have her mother's magnetism, her charm, her fast hot rages, and she certainly didn't have her urge for turning life upside down every eighteen months. Every time Jessica threw one life out the window and leaped for another, the child Samantha had become more careful, more aware that if she didn't look after Sarah, no one would.

Jessica hated responsibility, and that wasn't Samantha by a thousand miles. By the time she'd put time in on a couple of summer jobs, working her way through college, she'd recognized her own desire to create order, stability. Recognized, too, that she was good at it.

"Early training," she told Kippy, who nodded against her chest. Walking like this often put Kippy to sleep, but not today. The baby was wired, full of energy, kept lifting her head and commenting in gurgles and incomprehensible words about their surroundings.

She hadn't talked like this when Samantha first arrived last week, and Dorothy hadn't mentioned it. The talking must be new.

"By the time you're ten, you're going to be running things." That image made Samantha laugh, because, face it, Kippy was running things right now. Wasn't Samantha here, walking a baby instead of sitting down with her e-mail? Between Kippy and Cal, in the space of a week Samantha's life had slipped out of her control.

"That's not true."

The words she spoke echoed off the rock face beside her, and a raven picking at something on the ground paused. Kippy might be running her life, but a baby had a right to. Certainly Jessica hadn't let her children rule her life, which had been part of the problem. Yet Dorothy had willingly accepted responsibility for two young girls at a time when she could reasonably expect to have her home to herself. She'd let her life be torn upside down by her grandchildren, although Samantha had never seen any sign of resentment.

Neither would Kippy. She promised herself that.

Cal was a different matter. She'd stood her ground with him well enough at Tremaine's, but up at Haida Sunset, she'd lost her footing. Their lovemaking had softened something deep inside her, awakening need. It was easy to imagine Cal's power over her growing, spreading. He was always making decisions, telling her what to do, and she'd got to the point now where she reacted to every word he said, she was so aware of the risk.

The bossiness had started when he flew her to Nanaimo last week had extended into almost every part of her life, to the extent that he'd managed to make her promise to call a taxi if she needed to go somewhere, even though Dorothy's old clunker was perfectly safe.

Last week, she'd been a competent woman he respected, but today he didn't trust her to choose her own transportation. He'd used the helicopter and his sports car to take over her transportation. He'd brought in his medical family to take over Dorothy. Right now Adrienne was at the university hospital with Dorothy, when it should be Samantha standing at her grandmother's side.

Cal had taken over Samantha's right to decide where

she worked, and how, by getting her to sign a prenuptial agreement that committed her to eighteen years as Tremaine's second-in-command. Eighteen years as Calin Tremaine's wife.

She stumbled as she stepped off the road and onto Drumbeg Bay's wharf.

He'd already done it, had already taken over every part of her life except this, her care of Kippy. And he meant to take that over, too. He'd be Kippy's father, and as the weeks went on, Samantha would find herself controlled more and more.

Didn't she know the pattern? Hadn't she been here before? She'd been so sure she wouldn't repeat her mother's life, so different from her mother. And she was right, she was different, because there may have been far too many men in her mother's life, but somehow Jessica had always picked good, secure men.

Not that Cal wasn't secure. But he was also a man who needed to control everything he got near. Damn it, she'd known that about him, had recognized it. At work, it had been a challenge, because she knew she was strong, knew she wouldn't knuckle under. She'd done that once, with Howard, and she'd learned her lesson forever.

Maybe it was excusable for a woman to fall in love once, to make one major mistake. After all, control had never really been an issue with the men Jessica chose. As far as Samantha had been able to see from her child's view of Jessica's relationships, it was her mother who ran the men ragged, not the other way around. So she'd had no way of knowing that Howard would be different.

He'd been strong, affectionate, in love with her, and she'd fallen for it. She'd ignored her own warning voice, because Howard was a young man who obviously loved her, wanted to care for her, to shelter her. She didn't need sheltering, she'd learned to stand in the rain, but she was seduced by affection and sex and a dream of enduring partnership. She'd fallen in love.

In January of her senior year, she'd become Howard's lover. In March, she'd accepted his ring of engagement, and they'd planned the wedding for June. A week later, he urged her to move in with him because he couldn't wait, and at the end of March, she did.

Janice and Maggie, her roommates, disappeared from her life. It was only later that she discovered Howard had intercepted messages from her friends, had failed to pass on messages from Sarah, and had opened her mail and held back letters from Dorothy, who wanted her to come visit in May before she took a summer job. She didn't know about his interference with her friends and family at the time, but every day she felt him taking over another piece of her.

At first it thrilled her, proof of his love that he met her for lunch every day, brought her flowers several times a week. Until the morning she told him she was meeting Janice, and he began shouting at her. Stress, he said later, stress over upcoming exams, and he needed her to help him prep for his statistics exam.

When she went to the library to work on her management term paper, he followed because he needed her at home. She barely slept through April, studied in the night when he slept because there never seemed to be time in the day. Having a relationship was work, in ways she hadn't expected. It would be better after exams, because the stress was telling on Howard.

They had their first real fight over her application for graduate school. Looking back, she knew she'd given in on everything else he wanted, until that day. He'd interviewed for a job with Microsoft, and if he got it, she wasn't going to need a graduate degree. Howard Demmer's wife didn't need to work. He'd support her.

She ran away from the shouting, walked the streets and

knew it wasn't going to work, that she was drowning. But when she returned at one in the morning, she met a different Howard. He offered to help her fill out her application for graduate school, and even delivered it for her.

A week later, when one of her professors called to ask if she'd decided not to take postgraduate studies, she discovered that Howard had never delivered the application. She should have known it was over then, but she'd struggled through another two weeks—lost a job that she'd been accepted for when he didn't deliver the message, lost the keys to the old car Wayne had bought for her to drive.

Howard helped her search for the keys, without success, but when she lay in bed that night she couldn't stop the suspicion that filled her. Finally, she slipped out of the covers and walked to the chair where he'd draped his pants. In the left front pocket, she'd found her keys.

She'd moved out the next day, packing her clothes, toiletries, and books while he was writing his last exam, driving to the restaurant where they always met for lunch with everything she owned in the back of her car. She'd told him over a chicken salad sandwich, had taken her apartment key off her ring, and put it on the table between them, adding her engagement ring.

When she'd walked out, he'd followed her, shouting. Someone in the restaurant, a muscular student who looked like he was probably on a football scholarship, had blocked Howard's path and growled, "Leave the lady alone."

The two men had still been arguing as Samantha drove away.

Howard didn't give up easily. He phoned her, parked outside her new apartment, called her friends incessantly. And Samantha learned just how important it was to hold her own in a relationship. She learned that love wasn't worth the risks, not for her. She had her family, Dorothy, Sarah, and Wayne. She didn't need more.

Last year, when Kippy's birth stirred her own maternal

instincts, it hadn't been that hard to persuade herself that being an aunt was far better than getting lost on the turbulent seas of another male-female relationship, the price for having her own child.

Cal had sneaked up on her from behind when she wasn't looking. He'd seduced her with a business deal in a weak moment, when she'd been overwhelmed with the changes Kippy was going to make in her life and uncertain she could handle it all. It had been too tempting to let him take some of the responsibility.

But he'd taken more, much more. He'd taken her, and when she thought of him sitting across the table and telling her he loved her, she was tempted, heavens she was tempted. But she was drowning in alarm bells, too, because she'd heard the words *I'm in love with you* a few hundred times too many. Jessica's words to a procession of men. Howard's intense vows of adoration.

One way or another, the words *I'm in love with you* had always meant trouble for Samantha. With Jessica it meant Samantha and her sister abandoned, sent to foster homes, or acclimating to a new dad. With Howard, it meant losing control of every goal, every dream, and every minute of her life, an inch at a time.

With Cal. . . .

She should stop it now, leave him before it was too late.

She felt the pain of loss as if it were physical, spearing into her chest.

If she *didn't* end it, she needed to walk very carefully. She'd really lost it over the weekend, and she wouldn't do that again. The next time she felt her control slipping, she'd back off, get herself a breather. Cal wasn't Howard. He had his own life, and he didn't have Howard's ridiculous ego, but he did have a massive tendency to take over. She could hold her own, but only if she kept her head.

If she was very careful, if she walked warily and kept

control, could she let herself fall in love with Calin Tremaine?

"Mum," shouted Kippy, and Samantha felt her heart lurch.

"You scared me, Kippers." They were standing at the rail looking down on the boats below. A sailboat, a couple of under-construction workboat-looking vessels, half a dozen speedboats.

Cal would phone tonight.

She covered her belly with one hand, the other on Kippy's rump. It wasn't likely they'd made a baby. The timing was wrong, and besides, it wasn't a good idea. Too soon. Maybe it would always be too soon. She had a career she didn't want to lose, and Kippy needed all her maternal energy right now.

She hadn't been all that sure she actually had maternal instincts, but they seemed to be strong and healthy inside her. Those biological urges, to nest, to breed children, must be undermining her good sense, enhancing the hormonal response she felt to Cal's lovemaking.

"We've got to go back to work, Kippers."

Kippy babbled agreement as Samantha turned and began the walk back toward Peterson, back to Dorothy's home on Crocker Road.

Business, she thought desperately. She needed to focus on business. Tonight, on the phone, she'd talk to Cal about the problems with Jallison. Before he signed the phase-two contract she'd left in his in-basket, they should check out a few options.

"We're going to do a couple of hours work now," she told Kippy as she climbed the hill. "You can play on the blanket and keep me company, or you can go to Diane's for a couple of hours. Your choice."

Kippy chose the blanket and a noisy rattle she threw away every few minutes. Samantha picked it up and tickled Kippy's tummy between e-mail replies.

* * *

Half an hour north of Seattle, Cal realized he'd forgotten the Jallison contract Sam had asked him to bring. She'd been stiff on the phone, worried about Jallison. It would have to wait now. If he encountered a lineup at the border crossing into Canada, he'd never make the eight-fifteen ferry to Vancouver Island. And if he missed it, he wouldn't be in Nanaimo until after midnight, too late for the final ferry onto Gabriola Island.

He should have brought the helicopter, rented a car up in Canada to bring Sam and Kippy home, made some other arrangement to get the helicopter back to Seattle.

"If you don't get the last ferry," Sam had said the night before, "we'll meet you in Nanaimo Wednesday morning before court."

He disliked talking to her on the telephone these days. The conversations always seemed stilted, as if they were both choosing words too carefully. He wanted her to miss him, wanted to hear something in her voice other than efficiency.

He damned well didn't need to hear her tell him that it didn't matter if he got back to her Tuesday or Wednesday or next year. After last weekend at the resort, he'd taken it for granted that things were okay. They'd been together, so close together that he could feel every beat of her heart. Maybe she needed a little time to get used to the words, but he'd seen love in her eyes. She'd been stiff when he left, but that was because of the car. She got prickly when he tried to protect her and he'd been trying to restrain himself, but just looking at that old rattletrap of Dorothy's made him uneasy. He wasn't going to lose either Sam or Kippy to a mechanically unsound car.

A man looked after his own. She'd understand in time that it had nothing to do with control, with power, but that he couldn't bear the thought of her hurt, of losing her.

Why was she so damned stilted on the telephone? After last weekend. . . .

He floored the throttle and sent Sam's Honda roaring past a semitrailer hauling something too heavy to make the hill decently. The Honda didn't have the power of his Porsche, but it wasn't bad. If he could hit the border by seven-thirty, he'd be on that eight-fifteen, and he'd be with Sam tonight. When he saw her eyes, touched her, he'd be able to stop this damned worrying.

From everything Adrienne and his mother told him, this sort of worry about a relationship was women's territory. Women were welcome to it, he thought grumpily. He could do without it, and maybe he was being paranoid imagining that this new coolness meant she'd withdrawn from him again, hiding behind the M.B.A. mask.

He was expecting too damned much. He wanted to tell her how much he missed her on the phone, but the time felt all wrong. She was stressed, looking after the baby with little help from him, because he seemed to be spending most of his time in transit. Of course she felt moody. Maybe he'd been moody, too, driving back from Haida Sunset, his mind occupied with reviewing his plans for the development teams. It was important, crucially important, to do a terrific job developing Lloyd's e-commerce site. Cal had a bank of five servers on order, to handle their Internet presence, not to mention their intranet server. In a few months, once the e-commerce phase was implemented, the place would be crawling with SAP consultants, Seagate consultants, and Lloyd's IT personnel. Maybe he'd been crazy, promising to get both internal and external servers in business within a year, but it was that promise that had got him the ASP contract.

He shoved the throttle down again and left a camper

and trailer in the dust, then passed a couple of dozen cars before the road emptied in front of him.

It would help when Sam got back to Seattle. She was doing a superhuman job of keeping things together by e-mail and phone, but he could feel the difference at Tremaine's. Tension in the people around him. Not the tension of excited urgency over the latest project, but the edge of chaos. It didn't help that the head of accounting had just asked Sam for a leave of absence.

She would look after it. She'd find someone to replace the missing staff member, and she'd probably manage to get her day care established and stream all the new employees into the system while he was overseeing the development of Lloyd's e-commerce.

Sam was damned good at keeping wildfires under control. He smiled, because there was one fire she didn't have under control at all—the fire that raged whenever they came together. One day, when he was deep inside her, she would look up into his eyes—or down into his eyes, depending—and she'd tell him.

I love you, Cal.

One step at a time. First he had to help her get her life back in control, because Sam might be a master of control, but a baby, a flood of new employees, and the expansion of their facilities were a bit much for anyone to handle all at once. No wonder she'd seemed stiff on the phone.

"Adrienne phoned," she'd told him, "and I don't know what's going on. She said Dorothy is still undergoing tests, but I couldn't talk to her. I'm worried about Dorothy, and Adrienne didn't really tell me anything."

"I'll try to reach her," he'd promised, and he'd dialed his sister's cell phone four or five times through the day but didn't get through.

Damn Adrienne! Dorothy was Sam's grandmother, and Sam had a right to know what was going on.

At the Canadian border, Cal got stuck behind a massive

motor home. The line hadn't been that long, about six cars, and it had been moving ahead every minute or so. But now, two vehicles back from the Canadian customs booth, it stopped with the motor home at the booth.

Damn. He should have taken the other line.

If he missed the eight-fifteen, he'd be on the ten forty-five and he'd end up spending the night in Nanaimo, separated from Sam by a harborful of water. Maybe he could find someone to run him across in a speedboat, but he'd be without at car, and he wasn't going to let Sam come for him in that junk heap of Dorothy's.

The motor home rolled forward and into the containment area. Good, let them search the motor home, but if they pulled some sort of border check on Cal, he was going to—

"Citizenship?" demanded the customs officer.

"American."

"Is this your car?"

"It's my wife's." Damn. If they stopped him for some red-tape nonsense—

"What's the purpose of your visit?"

"Pleasure." Tomorrow morning in court wasn't exactly a pleasure trip, but tonight would be all pleasure. "I'm picking up my wife on Gabriola Island. We're coming back tomorrow."

The officer gestured him on, the I5 turned into Canada's Highway 99 and Cal hit the Honda's accelerator with the word *wife* echoing in his mind.

Sam was his wife, all his and he'd have the pleasure of saying it over and over through the years. My wife. He had a daughter, too—or a niece. He needed to get to know her, to learn her smiles and her cries. He'd held her a few times, but when it came down to it, he'd been more or less leaving Kippy to Sam. He'd change that tonight.

He had forty-five minutes to make the ferry at Tsawwassen terminal, and he was going to make it. Thankfully, the ferry terminal was south of the Vancouver traffic crush.

He called Sam on his cell phone ten minutes after the ferry sailed. She told him Dorothy and Adrienne would meet them in Nanaimo Wednesday morning.

"They're not back yet?" he demanded, irritated all over again with Adrienne.

"Not yet."

He could hear Kippy crying in the background. "I just left Tsawwassen. I think I'll be there about eleven-thirty. I'll get up for the baby tonight so you can get some sleep."

"There's no need for you to do that."

Damn, she *was* in M.B.A. mode. "We'll talk about it when I get there." When the baby was in bed and they were alone, he'd get past the executive to the woman.

He spent the rest of the two-hour ferry trip checking all the team assignments for the developers. He was having doubts about Gary Neville, so ten minutes before the ferry docked he shuffled Gary's team with Hank's and put the new guy from Boulder under Gary. If Gary didn't make the grade, Cal would replace him before the end of May. By then he'd know if the new kid was up to leading a team under supervision.

He arrived at the Gabriola ferry terminal with fifteen minutes to spare. He spent the wait and the short twenty minute ride to Gabriola reviewing the e-commerce specifications for probably the fiftieth time, looking for anything in the specs that he'd omitted to allocate to a team.

It was past eleven-thirty when he got to Gabriola Island, almost twelve when he turned Sam's Honda into Dorothy's bumpy driveway. Would Dorothy ever live here again? It seemed unlikely, but she wasn't enthusiastic about coming to Seattle to live with them. She didn't want to go into the nursing home either, although her doctor had got her a bed in record time and she was supposed to have gone in yesterday.

Adrienne, he assumed, had managed some sort of extension or leave. He knew she meant well but felt irritation at the way she'd simply taken Dorothy off and left Sam in the dark.

The house was quiet. He rolled up the drive and parked Sam's Honda beside Dorothy's rattletrap. Had Sam been driving this thing? She'd promised him she would call a taxi if she went out.

She must have gone to bed. He closed the car door quietly, left his computer and bag in the car, and stepped up onto the porch. He saw a light through the window, the television playing in the living room. He could see Sam now, watching television. She hadn't heard the car.

He crossed the veranda and lifted his hand to knock, but something about her pose stopped him. She was asleep.

He turned the knob and the door swung open. He shed his shoes and jacket, walked into the silence on stocking feet. On the television, Michael Douglas was dancing with Annette Bening at a formal White House dinner. Sam had muted the television, perhaps for a commercial. Or maybe she'd been sitting in the easy chair, watching their lips move without sounds.

Did she like to watch movies with the sound off? He'd always found it amusing to speculate on the dialogue spoken by actors on a muted TV. He wanted to wake her, to ask if she shared his weird habit.

He slipped into the baby's bedroom and found Kippy lying on her back, snoring softly, an angelic smile on her face. Last night, Sam had told him Kippy had been talking all afternoon and evening, a whole new vocabulary of baby talk. Then she'd changed the subject abruptly and began talking about problems with Tremaine's developer.

He felt a breeze blowing in through the window and quietly moved to adjust it so the breeze wouldn't fall directly on the baby. Then he slipped out of the bedroom.

He was going to carry Sam to bed very carefully, and with luck she wouldn't even wake. She needed her sleep, and he had no intention of waking her.

She did wake, though, halfway up the stairs. He heard her gasp and looked down into her open eyes.

"Cal, what are you doing?" She looked started and confused, pulled from sleep.

"Go back to sleep, sweetheart. I'm just putting you to bed."

"Put me down."

"You're not heavy." Women were always worrying about their weight, but Sam had no cause. She was perfect, with real curves and her own slender beauty. "You're tired."

"Cal!"

It dawned on him that she was really upset and he finished climbing the stairs and stepped into her room, shut the door to keep their words from disturbing the baby's sleep downstairs. Then he set her on her feet and she immediately stepped back from him.

"What are you doing?" She sounded panicked now, not sleepy.

"You were sleeping. I was carrying you to bed."

She shoved her hair back, but it had become tangled in her sleep and it promptly spilled back over her cheeks and shoulders.

"I . . . you startled me."

"I gathered."

"I think I'll—I need to get to sleep."

He could see the energy sparking in her eyes. Nerves. Unease. She wasn't sleepy. Not now. They could have been back on the beach on their wedding night, with Sam jumpy and him not knowing how the hell to soothe her.

Everything should have changed. She'd walked naked in front of him, for heaven's sake, had seen his reaction and strutted, deliberately teasing him. She'd kneeled at his feet in the shower and made love to him with love flowing over in her eyes.

"Yeah," he said. "You'd better get some sleep."

"I . . . are you—I don't . . . I'm tired tonight."

"I've got some work to do. I'll be up for a couple more hours."

He saw relief in her eyes and inside him, something snapped.

"Good night, then." She stood, waiting for him to leave. She was wearing the now-familiar jeans, but topped with a sweatshirt he hadn't seen before. He saw her bra lying on the top of the dresser behind her and knew she was naked under the shirt.

He could see forced coolness in her eyes and wariness. While he'd been gone, she'd been rebuilding her mask. Now, standing here, just staring at her, he could feel her slipping away from him.

"One thing," he said. His own voice wasn't working right.

She was his lover, his wife. What had happened to the intimacy they'd shared? Were they to be strangers every time they met fully clothed? What would it take before Sam would cease needing to restore the barriers every time they separated for even a few moments?

She shoved at her hair again, didn't seem to know what to do with her hands. He wanted to hold her, to feel her nestle trustingly against him as she closed her eyes and drifted to sleep. Maybe she wanted the same, but he couldn't see anything of the other Sam—of Samantha.

"What one thing?"

"A good-night kiss."

"What?"

"You're my wife. I'd like a good-night kiss before you go to bed." He needed her to look at him, to admit that she cared, that she ached for him as he ached for her. He needed her to be his lover, not just in passion but in life, and hadn't he seen that kind of love in her eyes, deep down, hidden behind the mask worn by the woman facing him?

"Cal, tonight I . . . you don't mean us to make love?"

"I want to kiss you good night," he said and admitted to himself that he intended to use that kiss to find the way through this mask she wore.

She stepped a few inches closer, offered her closed lips to him, her eyelashes dropped, concealing her eyes from him. Not quite trusting him. Did she think she would cool his desire by waving a challenge like that in his face? Passive lips, lowered eyes.

He took his time, sliding his hands into her hair first. She'd made a mistake, lowering her eyes, because he could study her freely. As he let her hair slide through his hands he saw the muscle jump in her throat.

"Sam?"

Her eyes fluttered open and he stared down at her confused.

"Samantha," he said softly. His fingers stroked the curve of her cheek where the hair kept tumbling back. "You looked very beautiful sleeping in the living room." He smoothed the hair back and curved his fingers to the sweet contour of her cheek, her jaw.

He felt her swallow. Nervousness? Desire?

He intended to find out.

He covered her mouth with his, lips closed, and brushed her lower lip softly. His lips paused against the tiny dip at the corner of her mouth. Surely that was a tremble he felt go through her?

He angled her face just enough to allow him to seek the curve of her cheek, then the trembling fragility of her eyelids with his mouth.

Her eyes fluttered, closed, opened. He pressed the softest touch to close them again and returned to her mouth.

"Cal?" Her voice sounded thin, fragile. "We . . . you said we weren't. . . ."

He soothed her with kisses to her eyelids. "Hush, sweetheart."

She whimpered but didn't pull away.

He didn't take her mouth, which had relaxed enough that it might have given permission for him to slip his tongue into her. Instead he gentled her with his mouth on her throat, her earlobe. He felt her tremble again and he stroked her face, her throat, the slender curve of her shoulders through the sweatshirt, ran his hands down the outsides of her arms and linked his fingers with hers.

Then he angled his head and returned to her lips, but despite the slow hammering of his pulse, he forced gentleness, soothing lightly, refusing to slide into the temptation of her parted lips when she let out a long breath and her hands clenched in his.

He returned to her eyes, smoothed his hands up her arms. Her breath hitched.

"Should I stop, Samantha?"

She made a sound. It wasn't a word, more like one of the sounds she said Kippy had been making today. He stroked her with his voice. "I wouldn't want to keep you up when you're eager to go to bed."

When his hands slid down to her wrists this time, he felt her pulse hammering. She might hide her response from his eyes, but her heartbeat gave her away. He covered her lips with his and lifted her into his arms, lowered her gently onto the spread of her single bed.

"Good night, Samantha," he murmured, his lips against her throat where her pulse throbbed. Her hands clenched in his shirt and he knew he had to leave, now, before this went too far. She'd told him, trusted him when he said it wasn't lovemaking on his mind. But he'd needed. . . .

This was wrong. She'd trusted him.

Then she opened her eyes and he was lost, because it was there. Open and fragile, vulnerable.

"I want to love you," he said, his voice hoarse.

Her fingers clenched tighter in his shirt. He unfastened them and kissed the tension from them; then he lowered them to her sides and began slowly stroking her through the big sweatshirt. Her shoulders, her arms, the soft trembling of her midriff.

When her hands moved to him, he stopped her. "Hush," he murmured. "Let me do this for you."

He held his throbbing need harshly under control, forced his hands and his mouth to slow, slow gentleness. When she moaned under his touch he slowly drew the clothes from her, kissing her hands when they grew restless.

"Let me," he urged softly, and something happened to the hard knot of need within him. It eased, soothed by the soft touch of her skin, arrested by the pleasure of stroking her so softly he could almost hear her pulse.

He rolled her over and slowly massaged her shoulders, her back, and the curves of her buttocks. He heard her breath grow soft, relaxed, then ragged, and each time she moved, to touch, to grasp, to ease her own growing passion, he soothed her with his voice and his mouth.

When she was a soft bundle of ragged breathing and flushed skin, he gently rolled her onto her back again and stroked her feet, her calves, and her thighs. When she was moaning, her head rocking on the spread, he gently opened her thighs.

She opened to him, moist and trembling.

He covered her with his mouth, and she swallowed a scream, convulsing under his kiss. He felt his own breath tearing, as if he'd come with her, and he gentled her with soft kisses to her thighs, his fingers stroking hips and buttocks.

Then he took her up again. This time, her climax sent shudders echoing through her whole body and she spoke to him in soft moans, and when he stroked her she opened to him again and he kissed her mouth and felt her arms cling, holding him, needing.

Her mouth against his, he slipped his fingers into her creamy folds and felt her groan in his throat.

"I can't. . . ." And she shuddered, deeply, and opened further to him. "Please . . . inside me . . . please. . . ."

He entered her, thrust deep into her and felt her body tighten on him in strong spasms as she screamed into his mouth, her passage milking him, her tears spilling onto their faces.

His tears, too.

Afterward, he managed to get the blankets over them, and she nestled against his chest, her body trembling. He smoothed the hair back from her face, gently dried her tears with a corner of the spread.

"Samantha?"

Her eyes opened slowly, and he felt a shaft of pain at the vulnerability he saw there. *Tell me you love me,* he wanted say, because if ever she would love him, surely it would be now. But her eyes stopped him.

"Sam? I need to know—"

"We'll talk about it tomorrow," she said, her voice husky.

He held her as she slept, but he'd seen her eyes and he couldn't fool himself that he'd won any battles tonight. He might just have lost the war.

Twelve

Had she actually taken a walk with Kippy yesterday and told herself she would keep her head? That she'd talk business with Cal, discuss Jallison when he arrived Tuesday night, keep a bit of distance until she could handle intimacy without losing control?

Deluded! She'd been deluded, simpleminded.

Maybe she'd have done better if he hadn't caught her sleeping, if she hadn't woken in his arms, fighting the need to reach up and pull his head down to her, to tell him how desperately she needed him to be here, to be close, never to leave again.

Never to leave again.

She was in trouble. Big trouble, and she was lucky she'd woken in the bed alone, because if he'd been here, she would have curled right into him, would have melted, would have . . . might have started crying again, as she had last night. Crying when he made love to her.

I'm in love with you, he'd said, but she hadn't understood. Last night . . . it was his tenderness that had undone her so completely last night. Loving her . . . so . . . so *lovingly,* as if he would stroke and soothe her forever, as if her needs overwhelmed his.

Love. Cal's love.

She stared at her eyes in the bathroom mirror as she brushed her teeth. She didn't know how to face him, how to look at him after last night. She wanted to find him, to run into his arms, to cling. She didn't know if she could do that, if she could *make* herself do that. And even if she did, how was she going to face the moment when she needed to pull back and meet his eyes?

I love you.

No. No, she didn't. At least—maybe she loved him, but she wasn't *in love.*

"Fool," she muttered at the woman in the mirror, a woman with big, vulnerable eyes, flushed face, and tangled hair. She couldn't handle *in love.* She really couldn't— she'd cling to him, needy, as her mother had clung to so many men. Then time would shift everything, and she'd be screaming, demanding, out of control.

She *wouldn't!* She wasn't like that, wasn't her mother. She was Samantha Moonbeam Jones, and she knew moonbeams were allocated to fantasy, not reality. She'd always known. She had to know, had to keep control. She *would not* be her mother.

She stepped into the shower, soaped herself hard, as if she could scrub away need and vulnerability and spinning out of control in the daytime as well as the evening.

Where was Kippy?

She'd woken, had got up, gone into the upstairs bathroom, brushed her teeth, and showered without even a thought for Kippy. Why hadn't the baby's early morning cry woken her?

She rinsed off and hurriedly toweled herself.

When she stepped out of the bathroom, she heard the baby's gurgle from downstairs.

"Right, open up." Cal's voice. "Cereal and fruit, just what you wanted."

Kippy's gurgle turned bubbly, as if she'd accepted a mouthful of food and was blowing bubbles with it now.

Samantha stepped back.

She felt herself tremble deep inside.

Grow up, woman. He's your husband. He made love to you—spectacular, earth-shattering love. You're going to be facing him for a lot of years—eighteen years, at least. So grow up and face him.

Clause eleven in the contract. Eighteen years, to bring Kippy through childhood. Eighteen years wouldn't be enough. She wanted more. She wanted forever.

Oh, no. She really couldn't. . . .

Her fingers trembled as she dressed. Not jeans, because today was the day she and Cal would stand together in court and tell the judge they were a couple, a real couple, and exactly what Kippy needed, a real mother and father.

She'd thought it a lie, but it was the truth. Deep truth.

She put on the suit she'd worn the day Cal flew her to Nanaimo to rescue Kippy. How astounding that he should do that—leave Tremaine's in the midst of important changes and take hours, days, to make sure she got where she needed. To help her with Kippy, to care.

He'd wanted to be sure she didn't leave Tremaine's.

No, it was more than that. Even then, he must have cared, loved her.

Pantyhose, bra, blouse, skirt. The jacket over it all. In the mirror, she looked like a child in grownup's clothes, the business suit's effect softened by the long, unruly hair streaming over her shoulders.

Better put her hair up. Didn't want the judge to think she was too immature to be a mother.

When she went downstairs, she would walk over to Cal and she'd kiss him. Then she'd tell him—there, in front of Kippy, with Cal's black eyes staring questions at her, she'd tell him.

I'm in love with you.

She caught her hair back and brushed its length to smoothness, then twisted it up in the familiar roll. She wondered if she could say the words. It would be easier in his arms, in the night.

No. She'd say it now, this morning. With daylight flooding in the windows and Kippy as her witness. She'd kiss him first, and that would help. Then she'd say the words.

She tucked a stray strand of hair into the bun, and she could see her nervousness in the mirror. All right, so she was nervous. She'd been nervous before, hadn't she? When she'd done her first solo consulting job for Mirimar, she'd been terrified she'd mess up. She'd survived that, hadn't she?

She'd be fine. Cal loved her, so it wasn't as if anything could really go wrong.

She dropped her arms, took a deep breath, and walked to the stairs.

Downstairs, Cal was sitting in front of the high chair, a spoon of baby cereal in one hand, a damp cloth in the other. She froze when she saw him. He was her husband. *Hers.* The thought dried her throat.

Kippy had spread cereal everywhere. Spatters on Cal's chin, his shirt, his hands.

"One more," he said, his voice rumbling with the vibration she remembered from last night, so gentle, so soft, his touch so achingly loving. "Come on, kiddo. Open up and take one more; then we'll quit."

He slid the spoon in Kippy's open mouth before he saw Samantha. She saw him freeze, and she told herself to smile, to walk to him, and take the spoon, then cover his mouth with hers, wish him good morning.

This morning was the real beginning of their life together. They'd exchanged civil vows last weekend, but today was the first time she understood that she and Cal were meant to be together, that this man was her only lover, partner, husband.

"Cal. . . ." She shouldn't be frightened, didn't need to be frightened after last night. "You've got Kippy's breakfast all over you."

He drew the spoon out of Kippy's mouth. "Yeah, I do."

This was where she crossed the empty space between them and kissed him, but his eyes weren't inviting. They were cold.

"I can take her," she offered. "I'll clean her up."

"You're not dressed for it." His voice was cool, too.

"Cal, I need to talk to you."

He put the spoon in Kippy's bowl and placed both out of the baby's reach, wiped Kippy's hands and face with the cloth.

"About last night?" he asked.

"Sort of." She didn't know what was in his eyes.

"Gaa-gaa!" shouted Kippy and bashed both fists on the high chair tray.

Samantha needed to close the distance between them, to kiss Cal before she lost her nerve.

"Last night should never have happened," Cal said.

Kippy bashed the high chair tray again and Samantha reached for her, but Cal beat her to it, lifting the baby out of the high chair.

"What? Cal, what do you mean?"

Cal grabbed the cloth and gave another swipe over Kippy's face, where a new lump of cereal seemed to have emerged.

"I made a mistake, Sam."

"A mistake?" She didn't know what to do with her eyes, her arms. She folded them across her midriff. "What do you mean? What mistake?"

"I think that's obvious," he said grimly.

"What's obvious?" She sounded like a windup toy, repeating everything he said. Last night shouldn't have happened. A mistake. Obvious.

He shifted the baby to his shoulder and rubbed her back. Kippy squirmed.

"I should have left you sleeping in the living room." He jerked his head. "Can you step aside? I need to take her into the bathroom, to clean both of us up."

She stepped back, right into the log archway. When his eyes met hers, passing her, she saw nothing but ice. She didn't watch him go, but she heard water running in the bathroom.

"Why don't you go out and start your car," he called through the bathroom door. "Didn't you say those morning ferries sometimes have an overload? We don't want to waste any time."

She hugged herself tighter. "Yes, I'll do that."

He didn't answer.

She could shout *I love you* through the bathroom door, but if last night was a mistake, then she'd made a mistake too. She'd believed it was real. Two hearts, two souls.

He'd said he was in love with her. He *had*. But last night was a mistake.

"I'll pack Kippy's diaper bag!" she called.

He didn't answer.

She packed the diaper bag. Five diapers, more than enough. A rattle and the big plastic baby spoon she liked to chew on. A bottle of formula from the fridge. Fill up the little travel container of baby wipes. She heard Kippy babble through the bathroom door, but not a word from Cal.

Tonight they'd be in Seattle. They'd talk. Maybe, by then, she'd understand, or at least figure out how a woman handled this sort of situation. Right now, she'd better get the baby carrier and put it into her car.

She wouldn't cry. She *wouldn't*.

At her car, she placed the diaper bag in the back seat and discovered a brand-new baby car seat fastened right where she'd be able to turn her head and check on Kippy if she was driving.

He must have bought it in Seattle. He'd taken the time to look after her and Kippy, despite what had to be a very hectic day at Tremaine's. And he'd come here, late last night. He'd wanted to see her, or he'd simply have slept over in Nanaimo.

She slid into the front and started the engine. She couldn't reach the pedals, and her mirrors were out of adjustment. Everything set for Cal's height and length.

Maybe he'd like to drive?

Maybe he would, but she needed the wheel between her hands, needed something to do. Kippy would be belted into her car seat, so Samantha couldn't shield behind the baby.

This wasn't right, feeling so awkward, so tense. She had to stop it, had to find a way to be natural with him, to get past the fear and the panic. He'd been abrupt this morning, and she'd reacted, giving it meaning it might not have. After all, he'd had to get up with Kippy, because she must have slept through the crying. Maybe he—

Last night was a mistake.

All right. If it was a mistake, she'd bury it, push it down where she'd never think of it and never remember. They'd signed a contract, and the clauses were clear enough. Business. For heaven's sake, she at least knew how to be businesslike.

She had the car running, mirrors and seat adjusted, herself behind the wheel, and the passenger door and rear door open for Cal and Kippy when they came out.

"I need your key to lock the house," he called from the porch.

"Dorothy never locks it!" she shouted back.

He put Kippy in the baby seat, slid into the passenger seat beside her.

"I think you should lock it. This is an island, but there's no guarantee every resident is honest."

She shook her head. She wasn't going to get out of the car and walk to the house, lock the door under Cal's orders. Not with him watching. Not when he said last night was a mistake. She pulled the shift lever into drive.

"Did you bring the developer's contract?" she asked.

"No. Tomorrow is soon enough."

She concentrated on her driving. When they got to the ferry, the lineup was almost to the overload point. Samantha parked, said, "Did you bring my baby pack?"

"No."

They were doing great, talking up a storm.

"The ferry won't load for a while," she said stiffly. "I'm taking Kippy for a walk."

She walked to the top of the hill, by which time her arms were aching with Kippy's weight. Kippy didn't want to be carried up against her shoulder, so she had to carry her propped in the cradle of her arms in front, and her arms ached.

"Samantha!" called someone from one of the cars.

She turned and saw an old school friend waving from one of the cars in the lineup. "Hi, Barbara."

She walked over to the car and Barbara got out to see Kippy. "Is she yours? I didn't know—"

"She's Sarah's."

"I didn't know Sarah had a baby— Oh, Samantha, I'm so sorry about the plane crash. I couldn't believe our Sarah—I sent you a card, but what can you say in a sympathy card. I didn't know what else to say, what would help."

"Thanks, Barbara. It was rough for Dorothy and me. Kippy helped."

"She's a doll. Do you have her, or does your grandmother?"

"Dorothy's had her here on Gabriola, but I'll be taking her now, to Seattle."

"Come in the car," invited Barbara. "The ferry's fifteen minutes late. What's new? We can talk, catch up on gossip."

Samantha got into Barbara's car and didn't return until

she saw the cars unloading from the ferry when it came in.

"I'd better get back to my car," she said, lifting Kippy, who had been sitting propped between the two women, babbling at a plastic cup Barbara gave her to play with.

"You're married!" Barbara exclaimed. "I didn't see the ring! Why didn't you tell me? Who is he?"

"From Seattle." Samantha backed out of the car, Kippy in her arms. When she grasped the cup to give it back to Barbara, Kippy howled.

"Sorry about the fuss, Barbara. Here's your cup."

"She can keep it. We've got a dozen of those plastic mugs. When did you get married?"

"I'd better run. The ferry."

She hurried back along the lineup, Kippy hiccuping in her arms.

"Sorry, Kippers, but it's not our cup."

Kippy gave one last sob, then tried to launch herself out of Samantha's arms when she spotted the car.

Cal was inside, a computer open in his lap.

They spent the ferry journey with Cal clicking keys on his computer, Kippy dozing in the car seat, and Samantha sitting behind the wheel, staring through the front window.

What the devil had she done to get Cal so angry with her? It had taken her a while to recognize the signs, because Cal didn't usually fume. If he had something to say, he usually said it. If he thought she'd done something wrong, he didn't waste time on tact.

Last night was a mistake.

Why? Why was it a mistake?

Dorothy and Adrienne were waiting for Samantha and Cal in the lawyer's waiting room.

"Dorothy, you look radiant!" Samantha hugged her,

then stepped back to study her. "I was afraid the trip would tire you."

"Everybody's been treating me like some kind of invalid," said Dorothy. "Stop it, now."

"Your doctor—"

"I'm getting a new doctor. Adrienne's friend gave me a name, a recommendation. And Dexter's drawing up new papers."

Kippy gurgled and Dorothy turned to lift the baby out of Cal's arms.

"I don't understand," said Samantha.

Adrienne said, "Your grandmother's fine."

"But she had spasms, her heart—"

"Two top cardiologists went over her, and they've determined that last week's episode was due to pericarditis."

"Peri—what's that?" asked Sam.

"Talk English," said Cal.

"Pericarditis, an inflammation of the sack that surrounds the heart—an infection of the heart cavity. There's been no damage to the heart. Her symptoms were similar to congestive heart failure, but her fever was the biggest clue, that and the fact that she had no pain in her left arm. It's much better now. She's on heavy-duty antibiotics to clear the last of the infection up and she'll be fine. There's nothing wrong with Dorothy's heart, Sam. She's as healthy as you or I."

"No nursing home," said Dorothy. "I told him all along that I didn't need a nursing home."

Samantha felt Cal's hand at her waist. She wanted to reach back and grip his hand, but she remembered the look on his face as he'd opened the lawyer's door for her.

Dorothy turned and Samantha saw that Kippy had a fistful of gray hair clenched in her hand.

"Moonbeam, honey, this means I'm perfectly capable of looking after Kippy. It means the Ministry has no reason to take Kippy from me, and you and your husband can adjust to your marriage the way God meant, just the two of you."

"Grandma. . . ." She stepped away from Cal's touch. If anyone touched her at all, she thought she might break down in tears, and she mustn't.

"I'm not a fool," said Dorothy. "I'll be seventy this year. I expect to be healthy for another twenty years—my mother lived to ninety-five. But I won't risk Kippy like this again. I've been talking to Dexter. He tells me the medical reports Adrienne brought will squelch the problem. I'll be able to get Kippy back, but I won't get any younger. We need to set up formal joint custody, you and I, so this custody problem won't happen again."

Kippy reached out for Samantha. As the baby settled into her arms, Samantha fought tears. In every way that counted, Dorothy was Kippy's mother. Samantha had been a stand-in, just a substitute.

"I'm so glad you're not sick, Grandma. But are you sure you don't need me to stay? To help."

"I'll be fine. I'll get Diana to baby-sit a few hours each day until I stop needing an afternoon nap. The specialist says that shouldn't be more than a week. Honey." Dorothy patted her cheek. "I know you love Kippy. You can visit her. She can visit you and Cal."

Samantha kissed Dorothy's cheek. She wouldn't cry. She *wouldn't.* "I know she belongs with you. I'll visit more often, and if you and Kippy ever need me, I'll be here."

She lost the battle with her tears, but thankfully Dorothy didn't see because Dexter came out just then.

"Got the new documents ready," he said to Dorothy and Samantha. "Let's go. We're due in court in twenty minutes."

Cal touched her shoulder and her tears threatened to get out of control. She pulled away and hugged the baby closer. "I'm fine," she said.

Behind her, Adrienne said, "So, brother, I suppose you want your wheels back."

He must have taken his keys from Adrienne, because when they drove to the courthouse, Cal and Adrienne went in his Porsche, leaving Samantha, Dorothy and Kippy to take Samantha's car.

Dorothy placed her hand on Samantha's arm in the car. "Honey, are you OK with this?"

She turned and looked at Dorothy. "I'm sorry about the tears. I started feeling like her mother." She turned her hand and clasped Dorothy's. "She's lucky to have you. Sarah and I were lucky. She'll have me, too, from now on. I'll be more than a monthly visitor. I promise."

Dorothy studied her. "You and Cal will have your own children."

"I'm OK, Grandma. Don't worry about me."

Cal was waiting for her at the courthouse. He took her arm when they were called into family court. When they sat down, she eased away from him. Last night, she'd thought she needed him, that he was part of her. Maybe that's why he'd said last night was a mistake. She'd clung too much, been too needy.

The truth was, the man-woman thing didn't work for her. First she'd picked Howard, who turned into a major manipulater. Then Cal, who was so exactly perfect, except it wasn't working.

The judge reviewed Dorothy's medical certificates, Dexter's presentation. He questioned Dorothy, Samantha, and Brenda, then expressed himself satisfied that Dorothy and Samantha should share joint custody.

Samantha walked out of the courtroom numbly. It was over. Kippy would go home with Dorothy. Cal would—she didn't know what Cal would do, but she supposed she'd be expected to turn up at Tremaine's for work within a couple of days.

"I need to talk to you." Cal's voice, his hand on her arm as she left the courtroom. The others had flooded out of the building, the baby in Dorothy's arms. Cal walked her through the crowded outer waiting room to the un-occupied alcove that led outside.

Samantha turned and faced him. He wasn't smiling, and she wondered if they'd ever figure out how to smile at each other again.

"What is it you want, Sam?"

This morning, she could have told him her needs, but now she could only shake her head. She saw a muscle jerk in his jaw and he said, "I can't do this any longer."

She'd thought she felt love, but it couldn't be, because she stared at him and felt nothing. He crammed his hands in the pockets of his jacket. He must have changed his shirt after feeding Kippy this morning, because there were no traces of baby cereal on the collar.

"I was in love with you. I thought I could wait, believed that if I proved to you that I love you, that you'd learn to trust me, to trust us. I was wrong."

"Cal, I want—"

"I'm not willing to wait any longer, Sam. I can't wake up one more morning after having you in my arms, all fire and love, only to find myself picking my way through the ice in your eyes."

He loved her. He did. Why didn't she feel joy?

I was *in love with you.* That's what he'd said. Was, past tense.

"I'm not sure I'll ever be free of you, but I can't take any more of this. You're a coward, Sam, a twenty-four carat, gold-plated coward."

"Cal, I—I suppose I am."

His face seemed to harden with her words. "You're afraid of me, of love, of giving up control. What the hell do you think is going to happen? What happened last night? Do you think I'm going to swallow you whole?" He laughed harshly. "When you took me in the shower, I thought I'd never breathe again. You cracked me so wide open—and it wasn't the damned *sex!* It was you, on your knees, looking up at me with your eyes filled with love."

She felt tears coming. How could she feel so frozen when tears pressed against her eyes?

"It's fake, isn't it, Sam? Because when it comes to the crux, you're gone. Just like your damned mother. You don't walk out, but you leave just the same. You leave your body and your eyes behind, and you hide yourself from me."

Her eyes were burning and she couldn't talk for the lump growing in her throat, but she wouldn't cry. If she kept blinking, she wouldn't cry.

"If this is a battle for control—let's call it a war—then you take the gold medal, Sam. You're brave enough when it comes to bats and battles of will. But you're so afraid of losing control, you're too much of a coward to let yourself love. Because you know damned well that you can't love without being vulnerable, and you'd rather live your cold life, alone, trapped in the past with your miserable childhood."

"Cal, please—" She wasn't supposed to feel pain, but it was shafting inside her with every word.

"You've kept control, Sam, kept yourself safe from love. But you're out of control regardless, and that's a hell of a situation, because you're the lady that can't stand to give up control. You're so damned trapped in your own cage that you don't even know it's a cage."

The door to the outside world opened and a woman walked in. She crossed the hall with a clatter of high heels and disappeared through the door. Cal and Samantha stared at each other in silence, and she knew that if she managed to walk out of this building, she wouldn't be able to face him again.

She managed to say, "I think we should dissolve our contract."

"If that's what you choose. What about the marriage?"

"The marriage, too," she whispered. "I'd better leave Tremaine's. I'll find you someone to replace me."

He angled his head. "Get someone else at Mirimar to look after it."

"I'll have to tidy up some, get things ready in the office for someone else to look after."

There was nothing in his face, and his eyes were coldly impenetrable as he said, "I'll be in New York for a few days."

She reached out her hand, couldn't seem to stop the gesture.

Cal turned away and she stood rooted in the family court corridor, watching him walk out of the building, out of her life, her hand stretched out to grip empty air.

Cal got his portable computer from Sam's car and fished Dorothy's bag from the trunk. He stopped in front of Dorothy, who was holding Kippy.

"Can I say good-bye to her?"

Dorothy handed the baby to him, and Kippy settled in his arms and started babbling. Dorothy demanded, "What's wrong with you and my granddaughter?"

He lifted the baby and said softly, "Have a good life, kid."

Kippy gurgled in return, and he handed her back to Dorothy. Behind her, Samantha climbed into the driver's seat of the Honda, her face stiff.

"What have you two fools done?" demanded Dorothy.

Cal couldn't think of anything to say. He shrugged and said, "I've talked to the service shop on Gabriola. They're going to be fixing your car tomorrow. They'll give you a loaner."

Behind him, Sam started the engine.

"You're not coming back to Gabriola with Sam?" demanded Dorothy.

"No."

Dorothy glowered. "You're walking out on her?"

"I guess that's true."

"What is it? Five days? I thought you were a fighter, not a quitter."

"I thought so, too." He hadn't imagined how hard it would be, every time he got to Sam, every time he thought he'd won her, facing that coldness in her eyes afterward.

"Take care of yourself, Dorothy."

Dorothy glared at him. "You're a fool, young man."

When he got in the Porsche, Adrienne said much the same. "I thought you were driving back to Seattle with Samantha?"

"No. With you."

"You've had a fight? That's it? You've had a fight?"

He started the car and shoved it into first. The Porsche took the road with a snarl.

"Why aren't you back there with her, fixing it?"

He shoved into second gear and laid rubber turning onto Commercial Street. "You can't fight with someone who's not there."

"You damned fool!" Adrienne settled herself in the passenger seat, arms crossed and face filled with impatience. "You're the one who hasn't been there. Ever since you walked into the lawyer's office, your face has been as rigid as one of those guys guarding Buckingham Palace in London. How the hell's a woman to talk to you when you look like that?"

He made an illegal left turn on Commercial Street.

"You're a fool," she said. "You're in love with her, and you're throwing it away."

"I didn't do the throwing," he growled, but he wasn't sure it was true. Last night had been the real mistake. She needed her defenses, needed careful wooing to learn to trust him, to trust herself to let go, to allow love to take control. But last night he'd deliberately stripped every defense from her. He'd made her cry, and he'd seen her eyes afterward.

If that weren't enough, he'd made a mess of the scene outside the courtroom. He'd meant to suggest they go back a few steps and take it slow. But she'd looked at him and he'd felt the overwhelming need to strip away the stiffness, the distrust. And he'd known that if he promised to go very slowly, very carefully, he wasn't all that sure he'd be able to pull it off. Look at last night! He'd meant to find a crack in her mask, but he'd gone way too far.

No wonder she couldn't trust him. He'd told her she could safely kiss him, that they weren't going to make love. Then he'd deliberately used her sleepy vulnerability to get under her skin.

If he hadn't done irreparable damage last night, that scene in the law courts entrance must have finished it. He'd said things that might be true, or half true, but he should never have done it that way. A woman who grew up being dragged around by an out-of-control mother had every reason to have some control issues. Any man who loved her owed it to her to understand, to make allowances.

Not to attack her and call her a coward.

"You're a fool," muttered Adrienne again.

Yeah, he was. Not only had he proved to the woman he loved that she couldn't trust him, he'd topped it off by ranting on like an out-of-control kid about all the things that were wrong with her, when the blame lay right here, in Cal Tremaine. He should have waited, kept his hands off her last night the way she'd asked; should have suggested they take a lot of time, that they go back to Seattle and date, take it one slow step at a time.

Instead, he'd attacked her, and he'd lost her completely.

Thirteen

"I want you to go to Paris next week," said Tim Mirimar.

Samantha looked up from her computer. "I'm still working on the Brooks file."

Tim dropped his lanky body into the client's chair on the far side of her desk. "I've got a midsize software company just outside Paris about to make the jump. Staffing problems, facilities problems, and fulfillment problems. The company president wants *you*. He's heard about your work with Tremaine's."

Her fingers jerked at the word *Tremaine's*. Where was Cal now? She'd heard Tim's secretary mention last week that Cal couldn't make a meeting because he'd had to fly to San Francisco. Had he returned? Was he at his house on the lake, or still at Tremaine's, working late?

"Sam? About Paris? Next week?"

"Sorry." She shook herself and dragged her mind away from Cal. "I'm spending the long weekend up in Canada with my niece. I could fly out Wednesday."

"Do you want to fly out of Vancouver? Spend a few extra hours with your family? I can courier the file up to you there."

"I'll think about it. I'll call the agent tomorrow to book my flight." Tim was at the door before she asked, "Have you found someone to fill my old job yet?"

He turned and leaned against the door, considering her.

"Cal has picked faults with every candidate. I don't think it matters who I give him, he'd find reasons to turn it down."

"But he needs—there were problems with the developer, and the accountant was off for a leave of absence. Have you—"

"You said you didn't want to talk about Tremaine's unless I needed specific information."

Forbidding the subject hadn't stopped her thinking of Cal, missing him, hadn't stopped her searching for his name in industry news reports or thinking of him constantly. If he would hire someone to take her place, maybe that would help.

"What about Trace Olsen?" she asked.

"I can't headhunt a key man from one of my clients to look after another client."

She flushed. "No, of course you can't. I shouldn't— It's hard for me to keep my hands off it after being there so long." Hard to forget Cal, to go back to being Samantha Jones, consultant and free agent.

"You could go back. He doesn't want anyone else. He wants you."

Her hand froze on the keyboard. "He didn't say that?"

"Not in so many words."

If he had, would it change anything? *I'd better leave Tremaine's,* she'd said.

He hadn't tried to stop her.

"I'm thrilled to have you back, Sam, but from where I sit, your leaving Tremaine's doesn't make a lot of sense. I've seen your contract. Six months and you'd have had a major block of stock, a seat on the board."

She closed down her computer and stood. "You're a good friend, Tim. Don't ask."

"Hmm. You're driving to Canada tonight?"

"In the morning. I'm too late to make the ferry connections tonight. I'll call the travel agent from my cell phone." She slipped on the jacket she'd shed a few hours ago and reached for her purse.

"There's a rumor at Tremaine's that you and Cal were getting married."

She shook her head. "Tim, leave it alone."

"Over the weekend, why don't you ask yourself why you left Cal Tremaine's?"

Because he told me he'd had enough. Because he looked at me as if he hated me.

Samantha's apartment on Magnolia Bluff overlooked the harbor, and after she'd let herself in, she stood on the balcony staring out over the ocean.

Why wouldn't Cal hire someone else? She'd arranged for Tim to consult, had drafted a job description and a list of possible people Tim might try headhunting for the position. Cal couldn't sit there without anyone at the administrative helm for long, not with Tremaine's rate of expansion. Last week, she'd heard that he'd closed a new ASP deal with a major telecommunications company in California. The administrative fallout would be massive. She'd have to—

It wasn't hers any more. Cal wasn't hers any more. She felt the too-familiar wave of tears rising and let them come. Fighting the tears didn't help. They only waited for her, sabotaging her when she felt weakest.

She drew the chain she now wore around her neck from under her blouse, found her wedding ring, and held it as the tears flowed. If only she'd been different, able to love easily, to be what Cal wanted. If she hadn't been so militant, so damned determined to keep control of everything including her own feelings for him, she might have kept his love, might have earned the right to keep it.

If she had a chance to do it all again. . . .

She wiped her tears with the sleeve of her jacket. She

was such a wimp, standing on the balcony, *pining* for a man who'd told her he'd had enough.

She thought of the men her mother had left. Samantha had managed to witness a wide variety of men dealing with Jessica's abandonment. Most of them had been angry. Pete had gotten drunk for a week. Wayne had locked himself in his room for three days, emerging hollow-eyed and grim. They'd all managed to look pretty normal after a couple of weeks.

Maybe that's why she'd thought she'd be over the pain of Cal in a matter of weeks, but it wasn't going to be that easy. Two months now and she had her life working, but without Cal everything seemed flat, empty.

Maybe Paris would help. It was too easy to pick up gossip and news about Cal in Seattle. If Paris worked, if it helped, then maybe she should consider a move. She'd move to Vancouver, where she'd be only a fifteen-minute seaplane ride from Gabriola. She'd spend all her weekends with Kippy and Dorothy, fill her life with her niece and her grandmother, and look up some of her old school friends.

Leaving wouldn't be fair to Tim, but he seemed to know she wasn't content and he'd been urging her to go back to Tremaine's, so he must be prepared to lose her. It had been a mistake staying this close to Cal, but she'd underestimated the power, the endurance of her feelings for him.

She turned and stared through the open patio doors into her apartment. She'd have no trouble subleasing, and with her dual citizenship there'd be no work-permit problems. Vancouver had a booming software industry where she could put her consulting talents to good use. She had contacts up there, had done a couple of jobs for Tim that took her into Canada.

Maybe she'd start her own firm in Vancouver. The challenge might wake her up again, make her stop spending every night yearning for Cal's arms, every morning devastated that she hadn't woken beside him.

This is bad, Jones. You can't live this way.

She jerked when the telephone rang. Dorothy. Of course it would be Dorothy, calling to confirm that she'd decided to stay the night in Seattle.

She grabbed the remote from an end table and pushed the TALK button.

"Moonbeam? Darling, I've been calling all day! You're finally home!"

"Mother?" Jessica sounded close, as if she were next door. "Where are you?"

Jessica laughed the heated, overexcited laugh Samantha had heard so often. "Moonbeam, darling, I'm in the airport. In transit, would you believe, and I'm with the most wonderful man. Darling, wait until you meet your new father!"

Samantha sighed. "Mother, when your daughter is thirty-one, marrying a man doesn't make him her father. What happened to Frank? You told me Frank was your forever man. You said you loved him as you'd never loved another man."

"Oh, Moonbeam! Frank was such hard work. All that self-analysis, and he made such a scene when I quit therapy. He said I had a *borderline personality!* Can you believe it! A man who spends his life listening to crazy people!"

"Oh, Mom—" What was the point of saying anything to Jessica? She'd always been this way, wouldn't change. "I hope you'll be happy," she said, and it was true, although the odds were against this husband lasting any longer than the others.

"You'll love him, Moonbeam! We're flying to Spain to visit his family—he has the sweetest granddaughter."

"You have a granddaughter, too. Kippy's eight months now, and you've never seen her."

"In good time, darling. We'll come to you after Spain. We'll discuss it all then. Good-bye, Moonbeam darling!"

"Mother, I'm—" Samantha heard a click and the line went dead. "I'm going to Paris," she muttered. "I'm probably moving to Vancouver, and where the devil are you?" No phone number, no address. How typically Jessica. Another marriage, because Frank had become such hard work. Jessica never lasted past the honeymoon in any relationship.

. . . When it comes to the crux, you're gone. Just like your damned mother. You don't walk out, but you leave just the same. You leave your body and your eyes behind, and you hide. . . .

Samantha dropped the phone on the chair and backed away from it.

It hadn't been like that. She'd woken up intending to tell him she loved him. He was the one who didn't want her any more. He was the one who'd given up.

You didn't tell him you loved him, didn't have the courage because he looked up and frowned at you.

Just a frown, and she'd wimped out. She'd made a promise to Cal; she'd exchanged vows. Not in a church, but civil vows. She'd signed the contract, too, promising him eighteen years, but she'd only given him five days.

The night before the wedding, she'd had doubts, and Wayne had assured her that she could do it by pointing out her promise to be there for Kippy. *If the going gets tough, if that promise means you have to rearrange your own life, it doesn't change the promise, does it?*

Frank was such hard work.

Cal had been hard work. He'd stirred her every time he touched her, made her nervous every time he tried to do something for her. He'd accused her of putting on a mask, shoving business between them when she felt control slipping, and he was right. She'd done that, deliberately.

He'd sat across the table from her at the resort and told her he loved her, and she'd said *no*, she didn't want it. He hadn't given up then, but in the end he'd lost faith in her. And he'd told her it was over.

Once she got to Paris, it would be easier.

Running again. Always running. Paris. Vancouver. God help her, she was playing some backward version of her mother's craziness. She couldn't forget Cal, so she was running. How far would she have to go? Would she escape Cal in Paris?

You're a coward, Sam, a twenty-four carat, gold-plated coward.

She hadn't even tried to change his mind. She'd gone to court to fight for Kippy, to get her out of foster care and back to her family, but she hadn't said one word to stop Cal leaving her. She pulled in a jagged breath and pushed back a strand of hair that had escaped the fastener. Next week, she'd contact him. She'd drop him a note, ask him to lunch. Then she'd. . . .

She'd be in Paris next week.

A note wasn't exactly the height of courage.

Tonight. She'd call him tonight and ask. . . .

She stared at the phone. Ask what? If she could see him? Wasn't she enough of a businesswoman to know better than to make it easy for the other party to say *no*? The phone wouldn't do, and forget e-mail and faxes. This had to be face to face, without giving him time to decide he'd rather not have to deal with her again.

She'd drive over to Tremaine's. She'd go up the elevator and face him across his desk in his office. She'd tell him—

It was after hours. What if he wasn't there?

What if he was and wouldn't let her in?

She'd go to Tremaine's first, find out. If Cal was in the building, she was pretty sure she could talk the security guard into letting her in. He'd recognize her, and she didn't think Cal would have given orders to forbid her entrance.

If he wasn't at work, she'd drive out to Washington Lake

and pound on his door. Surely he'd let her in, and if he wouldn't—

He would. She'd treated him badly during the few days of their marriage—at least, during some of the daylight hours, she'd treated him badly, but he'd been unfailingly patient until the last day, in the courthouse.

She'd better wash her face, put on some lipstick.

In the bathroom, she stared at her face. Lipstick wasn't enough. She ran cold water and soaked her swollen eyes with a cold cloth. What if Cal wasn't in Seattle at all? What if—

So she'd waste an hour driving out to Washington Lake and back? What else was she going to do with the evening?

What if he wouldn't listen to her?

With the cool cloth and a bit of makeup, she looked fairly normal, pretty much as she did every day in the office. The first time Cal saw her with her hair down, he'd stared at it as if he'd never seen long hair before. Afterward, he'd touched it. She closed her eyes and she could feel his hands in her hair. So gentle. He'd been so careful with her.

Next time, if there was a next time, she'd drive him beyond gentleness. She'd show him exactly how much she ached for him.

She reached up and tugged the clasp out, then she brushed her hair to dark glistening smoothness. Maybe he would remember.

A business suit wasn't exactly the best choice to tempt a man. She stumbled into the bedroom and impatiently rummaged through her closet. She didn't have anything that seemed right. Business suits. Summer shorts and brief tops for hot summer evenings when she escaped to the lake for a swim after work. Jeans . . . she'd worn jeans all through their honeymoon weekend. Would he remember?

She pulled on a pair of jeans. Her hands were shaking. She had to keep control of this shaking, had to be prepared for him to frown and look uncomfortable when she told him she loved him. He'd had enough, sent her away.

A blouse.

She pulled out one of the silk blouses from her honeymoon, then put it back. In its place, she chose a lacy black camisole and hurriedly changed into it. Then the jeans and the shell Dorothy had crocheted for her last birthday.

Grandma, I could be thrown in jail for wearing that.

Honey, that's a man catcher. When you find a man you want, put on one of those lacy camisoles, and wear this over it.

The shell was almost sleeveless, a fine network of beige crochet work that hugged her breasts and showed the lace beneath. She'd never worn it, because it was the kind of garment that made a statement.

I want you.

Telling him she loved him was going to be hard enough, uncomfortable enough. What difference was it going to make what she wore? Maybe it would help her say the words she needed to say. And if he sent her away afterward—well, maybe he'd remember how much he'd once wanted her to be his wife.

She picked up her purse and left the apartment before she could change her mind and her clothes. In the car, she dialed the number for security in the Tremaine building. Two months since she'd used it, but it was there, at her fingertips when she dialed.

"Is that Jerry? Good, this is Samantha Jones. Is Mr. Tremaine still in the building. . . . He did? Thanks, Jerry."

He'd left more than an hour ago.

She headed across the Ballard Bridge and toward Cal's place on Washington Lake. By the time she turned onto his road, her heart was pounding as loudly as the music on the stereo. What if he wasn't there? What if he was out with another woman?

What if he was *home* with another woman?

She turned into his drive. The lights seemed to be mostly

out, but Cal's Porsche was standing a few feet from the front steps. She stopped her car behind it.

If he wanted another woman, he'd do something about the marriage. Two months, and she hadn't heard a word from his lawyer. They were still married, and Cal wasn't the sort of man to get involved with one woman when he was legally married to another.

She gulped and undid the chain from around her neck. She dropped the ring trying to get it off the chain, had to rummage on the floor in the dark. When she found it and put it on her finger, she stumbled out of the car.

She had to get control of her breath, of herself.

Light, shining through Cal's front door.

Cal, standing in the open doorway.

She wasn't ready. She needed time, courage. If she tried to talk now, her voice would be jagged. She might even cry. If she didn't get hold of herself first, she might even beg him.

She mustn't beg.

You're a coward, Sam, a twenty-four carat, gold-plated coward.

There wasn't much doubt about that, she decided raggedly. She slammed her car door and walked unsteadily toward the house and Cal. She couldn't see him properly with the light shining from behind him, couldn't see his face or his eyes, couldn't tell—

Coward.

She put her foot on the first step, then the second. She didn't stop until she was on a level with him, but she still couldn't see his face.

"I need to talk to you, Cal. Could I—" Her voice broke and she gulped. "Can I come in? Or I can say it here, outside."

He turned his back and disappeared into the house. He didn't close the door, and maybe it wasn't an invitation, but on the other hand it wasn't like Cal to turn his back on someone who was talking to him, so maybe it *was* an invitation.

Coward.

She followed him inside. He'd gone into the sprawling room that was his study, had crossed the room to the big bay windows.

"Do you want a drink, Samantha?"

She could see his eyes now, and they were so cool she didn't think there could be even the smallest feeling left.

"No, thanks." Alcohol wouldn't help her say this without making a mess of it. Nothing would.

"What is it you want?"

He'd asked her that before, in the courthouse, and other times.

She wanted to run, but if she ran, he'd remain in her heart, right beside the knowledge that she'd been too much a coward to fight for the man she loved.

"I do want a drink, please."

"Wine?"

She shook her head. "Scotch."

He raised his brows and turned to the sidebar to pour it for her.

"I came because I'm in love with you." She said it fast, while he was turned away. "Because I want to—I want us to try again."

He put the glass down and turned to face her.

"Don't say anything, Cal. Not—let me finish." She shoved her hair back from her face with both hands and tried to organize her words, but everything was a jumble. "You have to listen. I'm really bad at this. You were right about everything."

"Samantha—"

"I am a coward, and I—it frightened me, falling in love with you. I couldn't control anything. My thoughts, my needs, and I wanted—I always seemed to— I was terrified I'd lose control and somehow never get it back. Afraid I'd love you, really love you, really need you, and you'd leave me. I didn't—wasn't—"

"Sam—"

"Please, I have to say this. Even if it's too late. I didn't know how much I feared you leaving me until you said you didn't—wouldn't wait for me any longer. You said I was a coward, and it's true."

"You're not." He took her hands, wove his fingers through hers. "You're not a coward. I said a lot of things I didn't mean."

"You were right." She stared at their hands, not daring to hope his touch meant what she needed it to mean, but her fingers curled tightly with his. "Every time you did anything for me, I accused you of trying to manipulate me. I was afraid to love you, and the more I did, the more frightened—I was going to tell you that morning, when you were feeding Kippy, but when I saw you I chickened out."

His hands had tightened to the edge of pain. "You were wearing your business suit, your hair up, your M.B.A. armor. I knew I'd screwed things up royally the night before. You were right when you said I was trying to manipulate you. When I first saw you with Kippy, with your hair down, it was as if you came into focus for the first time. I knew then that I had to have you. I should have—I wasn't honest with you. I wanted you for the company, but the marriage was never about business. I wanted *you,* and I thought I could make you fall in love with me. Manipulate you. You had every right to be suspicious."

She could see into his eyes now. They were troubled, and more. She tilted her head back. "You loved me all along," she said. She could feel tears filling her eyes again, but what did it matter? "Cal, I couldn't resist you from the first time you kissed me, but I told myself it was just sex, that it was separate from our business together, something we could keep separate and I wouldn't have to be vulnerable. That way I couldn't get hurt. Then, the night you came to Dorothy's and carried my into my bedroom . . ."

"Samantha, that night," he said raggedly, "that night I could feel myself losing you. You were half asleep, and even then you were trying to put distance between us, to shut yourself off. I was wrong, Sam. I manipulated you, tricked you into letting me kiss you, telling you it was only a good-night kiss, that I wasn't going to try to make love with you—"

"You didn't actually say that."

"I let you believe it," he growled, "and then I very deliberately set out to make you want me."

She freed her hands and touched his face. She felt a muscle jerk in his cheek. "I wanted you," she whispered. "That night, when you loved me so selflessly, so tenderly, I knew, really knew deep inside, what you meant when you said you loved me. You didn't mean my mother's kind of love, just for her. You *treasured* me, and I'll never forget how that felt. I couldn't talk afterward. I was so filled with you, with loving."

"I made you cry."

"Oh, Cal! You made me feel. You made me love. I know I really messed it up, but I do love you. I was stupid enough to think it would go away, but it's not an episode or a—it's me and you, and I—" She'd gotten this far, surely she could go the rest of the way. "Cal, I need to know. Could you—do you still love me?"

She felt a shudder go through him. "Samantha Moonbeam Jones, I love you with all my heart."

But he hadn't kissed her, wasn't moving to kiss her even now.

Maybe it was her turn.

She stretched her arms up and looped them around his neck. "I'm going to kiss you," she said softly. "And I should warn you. . . ."

She saw his lips twitch in a half smile and felt her heart lurch. He loved her. It wasn't too late.

"Warn me of what?"

"I might try to seduce you into something more." She covered his lips with hers, then softly drew them away to kiss his cheek, the tangy smell of aftershave below his ear.

He pulled her tight and took her mouth with harsh hunger. "Sam . . . darling. . . ."

She kissed him back and initiated her own hungry kiss. "I was afraid you'd send me away tonight. I was afraid you wouldn't listen, more afraid it was too late, that you wouldn't care."

He held her away from him, his eyes raking over her face, her shoulders, and her breasts. "What is this you're wearing?" he demanded. "You almost gave me heart failure when I opened the door and saw you get out of your car. I was terrified to go near you. How the hell was I supposed to keep my hands off you, when I can see your breasts move with every breath you take? When I can't stop remembering . . . I needed you to be here because you couldn't stay away. I prayed for that, feared it was something else until I saw you were wearing my ring. Sam, if you keep breathing like that, in that thing you're wearing, we're not going to get as far as the bedroom."

She felt a smile grow. "There isn't really any way to wear a bra under this. My grandmother made it for me."

"Dorothy? You're kidding?"

"She said it was a man catcher. I've never worn it before, but I have some very pleasurable memories of times when you didn't keep your hands off me, and I was hoping I could tempt you to do it again." She tilted her head and studied him. "Is it important for us to get as far as the bedroom?"

"You'd tempt a monk." He slid his hand over her breast and she pressed against him, taking his erection against the softness of her belly. She felt his response and saw his eyes darken.

"I want you to make love to me, Cal." She said it very clearly, deliberately, and felt a thrill of sensation when she saw his eyes heat and felt his body's response. "But first, there's one more thing I need to say."

His hands slid to her hips, then slid slowly over the lacy shell, forming her back. She leaned into him and let herself enjoy his touch. She'd missed this so much, missed him so much.

"Enough talking," he murmured, bending to place his mouth over the lace covered mound of her breast.

He was seducing her again. She moaned and let his hands on her back take her weight. How could she have waited? How could she have let her fears make them both miserable for two whole months?

"I can't think when you—I need to say this, Cal."

"Say it," he growled.

"I'll be here tomorrow. I mean afterward, in the morning. I'm nervous about it, so if I— What would you do if when I woke up tomorrow and you were already up, and I came out and you were in here, working on the computer . . . and I climbed into your lap and kissed you good morning?"

"Tomorrow?"

She nodded soberly.

"I'd probably pick you up in my arms and carry you back to bed. But I'm not going to be working on my computer tomorrow; I'm going to be right there, in bed, holding you when you wake up. But in a few weeks, or a few months—I'm not sure it's ever going to happen, but if we get to the point where we can share a kiss without both of us going off like rockets, then I'll kiss you back and make sure you know that I want you here, every morning, forever."

She wondered exactly what it was she'd been afraid of.

"Could you put some music on?" she asked.

He walked to the stereo and she heard soft music. She felt muscles quiver deep inside. Anticipation. She hadn' had a lot of experience, but Calin Tremaine was an in credible lover and her body was already singing.

Deliberately, she waited for him to turn back toward her before she slipped off her sandals, then reached to unfas ten her jeans. She slid them off her hips, then slowly down her legs. She felt a flush of embarrassment on her cheeks as she moved to the music.

"Samantha. . . ." His voice sounded choked.

She stepped out of her jeans.

He was frozen, watching as she danced closer to him. She remembered the last time he had loved her, so slowly so tenderly, soft seduction, not touching her sexually until she was throbbing with sensation, quivering with need.

"Stay there," she said and very slowly drew the shell over her head.

"Darling, are you trying to drive me mad?"

She dropped the shell onto a chair and danced closer to him. Not close enough for him to touch, not yet. Just close enough to tease.

"Yes, Calin Tremaine, I want very much to drive you mad." She smoothed her palm over the satin of her cami- sole, "Is it working?"

"Oh, yeah." And he was enjoying it, she could tell.

She danced closer, brushed against him, stopped him when his hands lifted to touch. "Not yet," she murmured. "You must admit, it's my turn."

"You've got thirty seconds," he said harshly. "I've been aching for you for two months, and it may be your turn, but—" He caught her hand and pulled her into him, ran his hands over her in long sweeping caresses that left her shuddering.

"You said I had thirty seconds." She slid her hands up under his shirt and smoothed a caress over his chest.

"It's been at least an hour," he said, lifting her into his arms. "We're going to the bedroom. I promised myself that if I ever got you back, I'd take you to bed for a week."

She pressed her mouth to the pulse in his throat and felt his heartbeat. "We've got the weekend. Dorothy and Kippy will understand if you let me up long enough to phone them."

"There's a phone by the bed."

She laughed and let her head fall back. "Do you have any idea how much I want this? I've dreamed of you every night. Do you think you could come to Paris? I have to go to Paris next week. I told Tim I would, but I don't want to leave you, not for about seventy years or so."

"Ah, Sam—" He lowered her to the bed. "I'd better confess. Paris is a setup."

"What do you mean?"

He sat beside her and took her hand with his. She pulled it to her breast.

"The job in Paris is a friend of mine. I thought if I could get you to Paris, if you walked in and it was me, not some stranger who'd sent for a miracle worker—I gave you two months, Sam. I told myself I'd wait three, but it was too damned long."

She placed his hand where he could feel her heart beating. "I should have known. I've watched you for a year and a half. When you want something, you don't give up. I'm going to have my hands full with you, aren't I?"

"Probably." He slid his hand under the edge of her camisole; brushed her breast with a touch so light she couldn't stop herself arching to him for more. "But you know how to handle me."

"Yes, I do," she agreed, "but I want more than the eighteen years we signed for. I want our children and I want—"

"Everything," he promised. "We'll tear up that contract, get married again in a church, the way it should have been, until death do us part. We'll have children together, and Kippy, if Dorothy needs us."

She held him tight and stopped trying to hold the tears back. "Please," she said. "Yes, please."

"Darling, do you have any idea how glad I am that you came tonight? Have I told you how much I love you?"

"Oh, Cal, I love you so. It fills me, and I—please, darling, stop talking and start loving me. I've ached for you inside me."

"You'll have me," he promised. "Forever."

Then he covered her lips with his, and together they loved.

BOOK YOUR PLACE ON OUR WEBSITE
AND MAKE THE
READING CONNECTION!

We've created a customized website just for our very special readers, where you can get the inside scoop on everything that's going on with Zebra, Pinnacle and Kensington books.

When you come online, you'll have the exciting opportunity to:

- View covers of upcoming books
- Read sample chapters
- Learn about our future publishing schedule (listed by publication month *and author*)
- Find out when your favorite authors will be visiting a city near you
- Search for and order backlist books from our online catalog
- Check out author bios and background information
- Send e-mail to your favorite authors
- Meet the Kensington staff online
- Join us in weekly chats with authors, readers and other guests
- Get writing guidelines
- AND MUCH MORE!

Visit our website at
http://www.zebrabooks.com